HEART OF THORNS

S. MASSERY
S.J. SYLVIS

A NOTE FROM THE AUTHORS

Dear reader,

We hope you enjoy Heart of Thorns. This reverse grumpy/sunshine, fake dating book is the equivalent of a warm cup of tea that may bite you if you move too fast (that's Briar… we're trying to get her under control, really).

Content warnings include arson, attempted murder, and possessive heroes. Well, just one hero.

Happy reading!

xoxo,
    Sara & S.J.

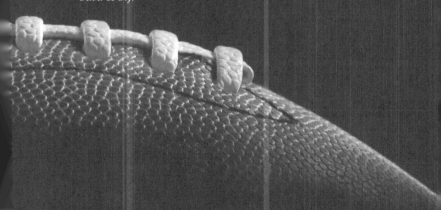

BRIAR

MY HAND FALLS to my hip as I chew on the end of my wooden paintbrush. At some point, I had to take a step back from my work, but now I'm just nitpicking the fine details.

The apexes of each mountain hit at different heights, and the colors blend so well that I find myself questioning if they're real or simply painted onto the wall.

"Damn," I whisper. "I'm good."

The building I'm working in is completely empty. The sound of scratching draws my attention to the ceiling. Rationally, I know the sound is probably from some critter that has taken advantage of the abandoned building and made a home. Irrationally? It's clearly a murderer who has come to strangle me with the paint-spattered drop cloth beneath my feet.

I roll my eyes at my thoughts and begin cleaning up my painting supplies.

Three more murals to go.

The owner, a friend of my art professor, is some fancy investor who decided to purchase an abandoned and semi-dilapidated building three streets down from Shadow Valley

U. He has plans for turning it into a new apartment complex for college students.

Makes sense from a financial standpoint, and who am I to complain when I'm being paid to paint the murals inside? Professor Garcia knows I need a creative outlet. Hockey is my one true love, but sometimes I need quiet to... *breathe.*

Plus, what college student doesn't need extra money? Women's hockey is the runt of the litter. Our gear isn't supplied for us like it is for the men. Not all of it anyway. Fancy scholarships aren't offered. I need every dime I can get.

I snap a photo of the mural and send it to Professor Garcia for her approval. I stare at it for a few more seconds before she texts back and tells me how much she loves it followed by a reprimand for working after dark. I peek over to the window and shrug at the glare from the moon.

ME

The moon has plenty of light. And I have my headlamp.

I'm sure I look ridiculous. I'd probably scare the raccoon —or rat?—that's making a home in one of the air ducts on the fourth floor, but the evening is my only free time. Between classes, hockey practice, and conditioning, I hardly have time to study, let alone paint murals. Even if I am being paid.

I'm in the middle of hammering the paint lids back on when the scratching from the building's pet starts again. I take back what I said earlier. It isn't a raccoon or a rat. It's a fucking bear.

My hand rests on top of the paint lid.

What the fuck is that?

Abandoning my mural and supplies, I make my way to the doorway and angle my ear for a better listen. The longer I stand there, the faster my heart beats. There's another crash, and a second later, I detect a faint scent in the air.

"What is that?" I whisper.

The building is supposed to be empty—and yet, something is clearly going on above me. The hairs on the back of my neck stand, but I can't ignore it.

Like a dog after a bone, I follow the smell farther and farther. I creep up the steps until I'm at the top of the stairwell. I shove open the door, and a rush of smoke whooshes past me.

My eyes water, and a cough works its way up my throat. Then I register the reason for the smoke and freeze.

Fire.

It's a fucking a fire.

I run down the steps, taking two at a time, and race toward the exit. The smoke is traveling faster than me, blanketing the building in a haze. Vivid streams of red and orange catch my eye when my foot hits to the bottom floor.

How is it moving so quickly?

Get out, Briar.

I finally catch sight of the open door, and my fear lessens. I'm so close—I'm going to be okay.

I'm going to make it out.

Suddenly, a ball of fire whizzes through the air from the opening and explodes mere yards away from me. The heat sears my skin, and I fall to my knees. The used furniture clustered in the back of the room bursts in flames. Fire licks at the old wood, crawling up the walls and disappearing into thick smoke.

It's getting harder to breathe. I need to move. I scramble to stand, and that's when I see him. Her. *Someone.* They head for the door I need to reach.

He. Definitely a he.

He seems unbothered by the smoke and fire raging around us.

I cough a few more times and tug the collar of my shirt up over my nose and mouth.

"Help me," I rasp. I stagger after him, my hand stretching out toward him. Toward the door. Toward safety.

The guy seems to pause with his hand on the door. I stare at the woven bracelet he's wearing—it's the one all the football players wore last year to show respect for their fallen player who was diagnosed with cancer.

Thank God. I stumble, but I keep moving toward him. My lungs are screaming, and my head swims. I'm so close.

Just when I think he's going to reach out and pull me to safety, the door is slammed in my face.

Smoke fills my lungs.

I panic.

I fall onto the door, yanking on the handle. It doesn't budge. And it *hurts*. The knob is too hot. I release it fast and spin around frantically. I need a window or another door. There isn't time to think about anything other than getting out alive.

My lack of curiosity about this building bites me in the ass.

The fire seems to chase me. The first floor is completely engulfed in flames, and my only option is to return to the stairwell. I bump into the wall a few times. My vision playing tricks on me.

I run back into the room with my mountainscape. There's a little more room to breathe in here, so I suck in air greedily. I can barely inhale without it triggering a cough.

The more pressing issue is *escape*. I'm educated enough to know that soon, the fire is going to cause a collapse. The roof, the foundation… This building wasn't exactly the picture of sturdy before the fire, and now, it's definitely not.

If I don't get out right this second, I'm going to die here.

My attention clings to the huge windows.

I'm on the second floor, but I have no choice.

I grab my stepladder stool and throw it at the window. It

shatters, the bits of glass and the ladder crash to the ground below.

No time to waste. I vault myself over the edge.

Next thing I know, I'm free falling.

CHAPTER 1
BRIAR

FOUR MONTHS LATER

"DAMN IT!"

Lydia winces when I curse. She does that a lot, and from her position on the couch, I've got a direct line to her expression. Wrinkled nose, flattened lips, closed eyes.

You know what else she does a lot? Scans the internet for a new place to live.

Scoring a roommate at the last second was probably a relief to her. Except, instead of getting a built-in bestie like most of the college girls who share an apartment, she got *me*.

Briar Hart.

The girl with a heart of thorns.

I used to be the girl everyone wanted to be around. Now, even *I* don't want to be around me.

Lydia leans forward, closing her laptop. "Do you want hel—"

"No," I snap.

I rest my forehead against the living room doorway, a hiss escaping my lips. My bag is slung over one shoulder, and I'm ready to walk out the door. Crawling back into bed sounds *so* much better, but if I don't physically force myself to get out of the apartment, I'll stay here forever.

"I'm fine." I soften my tone a little.

Lydia has been nothing but kind to me. She continues to offer help and does things around the apartment that she probably thinks I don't notice.

Like when she rearranged the furniture to give me more space to move around, or how she *always* empties the trash, knowing I struggle with it. She turns the thermostat to near arctic temperatures without complaining because she knows I'd sweat to death before I choose to wear shorts or anything that shows off my leg.

She sighs. Setting aside the laptop, she grabs her hockey gear from the floor next to the table. "*Fine.* I'll see you after practice?"

I nod, hiding my resentment with a neutral expression, and scoot out of her way.

There's a twisted part of me that wants to hate her so bad, but it's not her fault that I'm unable to play hockey this season.

After my surgery, I was told I'd walk with a limp for the rest of my life. The metal in my leg will cause arthritis and discomfort for years to come. The doctors told me there may even be a time when I opt for another surgery to accommodate my healing.

But they were wrong about the limp. I only limp when I'm extra sore. With weeks of intensive physical therapy—the sanctioned kind and the tips I found on the internet—I'm heading in the right direction.

They could be wrong about me never playing hockey, too, which is why I'm holding out hope for next season.

After half dragging my sore leg toward the table, I swoop up the remainder of my books and phone. I have a text from my friend, Marley.

MARLEY

Want a ride today?

Do I want a ride? Yes.

Should I get a ride? No.

Walking the two blocks to the arts building will hurt, but moving is the best way to stretch my leg. I need my agility and stamina back, especially now that school is in session. If I snag a ride with Marley to my art history class, it'll be like taking the easy way out, and I refuse to do that.

ME

> I need to walk today. I'm stiff. I'll see you soon.

MARLEY

> I'm stiff, too. For you. 😉

I huff under my breath, which is practically a laugh. It's the closest I come to humor nowadays.

Outside, I inhale the cool air and start down the sidewalk. It only takes one minute before I'm shouting at some jock for narrowly missing me on his run. He's wearing a backward baseball cap that has SVU embroidered on the front. I'd bet my life that he is a baseball player.

Not because of the hat he's wearing.

No—his bag is half open, and baseballs fall out every few seconds.

What the fuck is this? An obstacle?

Four months ago, I was weaving in between my opponents on thin ice, scoring goals and rushing the arena with my team. At the moment, I can barely navigate baseballs rolling down the sidewalk.

Dodging errant baseballs, I opt to walk in the street. If I step off the sidewalk, it'll hurt. It's the height difference... I wince and shut my eyes for a brief second. But instead of my toes touching asphalt, I'm jerked backward.

My eyes shoot back open, and I land with a thud on the

sidewalk. My books break my fall as sudden hot rage bursts through me.

"What the fuck?" I practically shout.

And this is why I need hockey. I'm so prickly, all the time.

"My bad."

I swear to God, if it's the baseball jock, I'm throwing one of those balls at his head.

A large hand appears in front of my face, and I smack it away without even hesitating.

"Uh... okay?"

Not the baseball player.

But a jock nonetheless.

I can tell by the width of his shoulders and good looks.

Dark, chestnut-colored hair that's tousled in this perfectly messy kind of way. Angular jaw that's sharper than a knife. Tall but lean with defined muscles that tense when he reaches for me again.

I try to scramble to my feet, but that simply isn't happening.

Damn it.

It's really hard to act like this fierce, independent woman when I'm actually very fragile and in need of his sturdy hand that he's shoving in my face again.

"I don't need your help," I grit between my teeth. I blow a piece of loose hair out of my face and attempt to haul myself to my feet. It's awkward and slower than I'd care to admit, but at least I do it on my own.

He chuckles, but not in an arrogant way. More so in a *yeah... okay* kind of way.

Instead of helping me, he picks up my scattered items on the sidewalk and gathers them swiftly before handing them over to me. My Meloxicam rattles against the plastic pill bottle, and his eyebrows furrow.

He reads the label, because clearly he doesn't care about privacy.

"Meloxicam?"

"Yeah, so?" My cheeks redden with embarrassment. So what if I take Meloxicam? It's for joint inflammation. Lots of people probably take it.

Sure, they may be in their seventies with arthritis, but whatever.

"Make sure you take it for at least a week. It needs to get in your system for it to work."

I snatch the bottle out of his hand and scowl. "Thanks for the unsolicited advice."

He snorts and quickly moves out of my way so I don't steamroll him.

Not that I'd make a dent. He's much taller than me and stronger. Plus, with an ego that big? Nothing could harm him.

"No thank you?" he shouts from behind.

I refuse to look back. Instead, I flip him the middle finger and keep heading in the direction of class.

CHAPTER 2
THORNE

THE GIRL across the table from me is probably forty percent plastic. If she's ever had an original thought in her whole life, I'd be shocked. As it is, she keeps circling the same three topics: social media trends, what her future plans are, and football.

I kind of glazed over the social media aspect. Every girl recently seems to be doing the latest dance video or *ask my boyfriend*. But she describes them in detail, then pauses. As if I might volunteer to make a shitty video with her? No, thanks.

I'd rather be raked over hot coals.

Her future was fascinatingly dull. She wants kids—two or eight, I have no idea—but I'm pretty sure a girl with two brain cells to rub together shouldn't be procreating. She isn't the type to poke holes in the condom, but she probably doesn't believe in birth control.

My attention keeps snagging on the blinged-out cross in the center of her chest. It's so glittery, her cleavage can't even compete.

Why is it always the religious ones?

But hey, she hasn't mentioned God—

She leans forward and touches my hand. "I just have to thank the Lord every day…"

And there it is.

I twist my wrist slightly, catching the time on my heavy watch. We've only been here twenty minutes, and I am ready to bolt. However, I plan on sticking to my obligatory hour and a half, if only to appease my parents.

Instead of shifting my weight, or otherwise conveying my boredom, I focus on her forehead. Her brows haven't moved this whole time.

Where on earth did my parents find this chick?

I can guess the answer. They run in elitist, blue-blood circles. So she's probably the daughter of one of Dad's golf buddies. If I had to guess… a parent owns a Fortune 500 company, she's got a trust fund to match mine, and she's floating her way through school to emerge with a fancy, useless degree and a husband.

I can tell you one thing: it isn't going to be me.

These dates mollify my parents. Their desperation is thinly veiled, and I wouldn't dare accuse them with the word. But that's what they are. *Desperate.* For me to find a wife to protect my image.

I wrinkle my nose.

"Oh, is everything okay?" The girl reaches for me.

I manage to dodge her fingers by wrapping mine around my glass, then I lie through my teeth. "Just thinking about the week ahead."

She smiles. Her *cheeks* don't even move. "I'm so excited for Friday! Daddy got me tickets to your game. You know, there's just something magical about football."

My eyes glaze over as she continues.

Don't get me wrong—I fucking *love* football. But it's physically painful listening to her go on and on about it. She probably went to all the games in high school. On the cheerleading squad, dating the star player. And for whatever reason, she dumped him and came to Shadow Valley.

Shoot.

I don't actually know if she even attends this school.

She keeps prattling on about the SVU Knights, how this week is going to be *terrific*.

A faint throbbing starts up behind my left eye.

When I check my watch next, I've dutifully sat here for an hour. Our meals are mostly consumed. The waitress has kept both of our drinks replenished.

"Excuse me for a second." I toss my napkin on the table next to my silverware and make a beeline to the bathroom. This place has single-user ones, which means when I lock the door behind me, I'm alone for the first time in...

Sixty-three minutes.

I take a breath and pull out my phone.

RHYS

You survive?

Leave it to my best friend and teammate, Rhys Anderson, to make me smile when I feel like screaming.

ME

It's questionable if I'll make it to the end 💀

RHYS

This whole thing is dumb.

He doesn't have to tell me twice.

RHYS

You need a gf on your terms.

I snort. A girlfriend on my terms... yeah, *sure*. I can barely spare the ninety minutes per week on these ridiculous dates. Outside of football, I focus on school. And outside of that, I sleep.

That's it.

Okay, occasionally I blow off steam by doing fun or stupid shit, like get drunk at parties with my teammates, but those days seem few and far between.

If you asked me what I thought college would be like, it definitely wouldn't be *this*.

Perception is everything. A quarterback who's failing English Lit would be the laughingstock of the school. Or, at the very least, his team. I make it a point to have straight A's.

I am an exceptional leader on the field and off.

And no fucking girlfriends.

Yet, when I run out of excuses to remain in the bathroom, I find myself seriously doubting my own philosophy. There's got to be something better than this, right?

The girl perks up when I return. Her tan looks even more fake now that I've been gone for a few minutes. She sweeps her bleached hair behind an ear and tilts her head.

"I ordered us dessert," she tells me. "They had a coconut key lime pie that sounded *ah-mazing*."

I grimace.

"What?"

"Only heathens like coconut." I ball my napkin in my fist. "*Coconut*? It's such a divisive food. Why didn't you pick something normal? Like…"

I snatch the dessert menu and scan the items.

"Flourless chocolate torte." I scowl. "Even the ice cream would've been palatable."

Her laugh grates on my last nerves. "Oh, Thorne. You're so funny!"

I am not funny.

I do not want to be funny.

Unfortunately, the waitress returns with the pie. I lean back in my chair, trying to put distance between me and the table. And the godforsaken smell of coconut.

She eats two bites and then frowns, seeming to debate it further.

There's a slight chance of me fucking her anyway, despite her coconut breath. The thought of kissing gives me hives, so that's off the table. Years of watching my parents avoid physical affection will do that to you, I guess?

Kissing is for teenagers—which I am definitely not anymore.

You know what? Touch in general sucks. My teammates learned early on that if they want a happy captain, they need to throw themselves in the path of oncoming fan girls. The only *touch* I like is getting my cock wet. There's some stuff that's unavoidable if I want to get laid, but it's kind of transactional.

Like, I pay for this meal, she doesn't complain when I'm not all touchy-feely.

Literally the only plus side of this arrangement my parents have set up…

Although, I have a feeling her boobs would be rock-hard. They're standing up straight, nipples pointed in my direction like a pair of headlights switched to high beam, and they contribute to at least twenty percent of her plastic look.

"Maybe we should head out." She slides the plate into the center of the table. "We could go back to your place…?"

My place.

Right.

She puts her hand on my arm, and I freeze.

Earlier today, I crashed into someone. A girl. It wasn't on purpose, but I reached to help her up, and she *snarled* at me. I willingly offered my hand out to her, only for that offer to be rejected.

And it was such a fucking relief, even if my stomach twisted with how slowly she climbed back to her feet. And the way her stuff went everywhere… there were pills. Serious painkillers that I've been on. I injured my knee a year and a half ago and did some intense physical therapy to get back on the field. We still wrap it for practice and games, and I regularly do ice baths, but it barely twinges anymore.

So what happened to her?

My date's fingers dig into my forearm.

I shake off the memory, and the image of her slowly walking away from me, and focus on the plastic bitch. Any thought of fucking her goes out the window, and irritation takes its place.

I slowly extricate my arm from her grip. "I've got plans. Maybe next time."

Her expression flickers through a few emotions—disappointment, shame, anger. Maybe she's heard rumors about what an easy fucking lay I am, and she's questioning herself.

She should. This was a painful dinner.

She dabs at the corner of her mouth with the napkin, then tosses it on the table. "If this isn't going to continue, then I'll just... I'll see you around, Thorne. At the game. Perhaps you'll be in a better mood."

I watch her ass sway as she leaves, and my brows furrow.

Did I want that to happen?

I shake my head, then grab my phone.

ME

Please tell me there's a party somewhere.

RHYS

Need to drown out that date?

Exactly. And find someone who feels more real than a Barbie doll.

I've got just the place.

CHAPTER 3
BRIAR

"CAN you at least act like you're having a good time?"

I glance at Marley, and something that resembles a growl leaves my mouth. She huffs in response, blowing a piece of her wavy hair out of her face.

"Fine," I say.

A forceful smile curves onto my cheeks, and she blanches.

"You look like you're in pain."

That's because I am.

Both literally and figuratively.

My back hurts from my earlier tumble in the street just as much as my ego. The idiot football player probably hasn't given me a second thought, but the way he watched my careful movements with pity hasn't left my mind.

Marley shoves a beer in my hand. "Drink this. Maybe it'll help that thing on your face."

I touch my cheek. "What thing?"

She holds back a laugh. "That thing you call a smile."

A laugh tries to creep up from my throat, and I can't help the way my lips actually shape into a crescent.

Marley gasps. "Oh my God! There it is! A smile, everybody!"

My face warms when people chuckle and clap. I quickly close my mouth and shoot her a glare.

She laughs and drags me farther into the party, over to some of the girls I used to hang out with.

That was *before*, though.

There's a before and an after.

The Briar they know died in that fire, and I'm not sure anyone knows what to do with the new version of me.

"Hey, Briar!" Brianna, who we referred to as Breezy on the ice, comes bouncing over.

We.

There is no longer a we, even if my teammates still treat me as if I'm on the team.

"I can't believe you're actually here!" She wraps me in a quick hug, then grips my upper arms. She squeezes, and there's a glimmer of sadness in her green eyes.

Ugh. Stop looking at me like that.

"Yeah, well." I shrug, glancing around the party at all the jocks. This is *clearly* an athlete-heavy party. Hockey players with their wide shoulders and arrogant personalities fill the living room. Almost all of them have a girl on their lap. Most of my old teammates are loitering about, rolling their eyes at the puck bunnies or jersey chasers.

In the midst of searching for the baseball player who scattered his balls all over the sidewalk earlier—I'd like to give him some advice, like on how to keep his balls intact—Brianna nudges me with her shoulder.

"How are you feeling?" she whispers.

I hate this question.

"I'm doing good," I lie. "Stronger every day."

It's bullshit. Absolute bullshit.

She eyes me closely, her expression conveying her suspicion. All she has to do is watch me walk for more than ten seconds and she'll see how much my knee is still bothering me.

The party is becoming crowded, and it makes me antsy. My gaze moves around every few seconds. I eye the windows in close proximity and mentally count how many steps it would take for me to get to them if a fire started.

I turn toward the stairs, knowing I could always climb them if the exits were blocked, whether by accident or on purpose by some lunatic who's obsessed with fire and trapping college girls in burning buildings, like last time.

A chill flies down my spine.

I place the beer bottle on a nearby table and slip through the crowd. The bodies press in on me, and the room seems to be growing hotter by the second.

Bri calls my name, but I don't look back. Every bone in my body urges me to escape. But before I can, Marley steps into my line of sight. She raises her perfectly shaped eyebrows at me, probably picking up on my internal panic.

"I've got to go," I mutter.

"Are you okay?" Concern takes over her features.

I nod. "I'm fine. Professor Garcia texted, and she lined up a project for me to do tomorrow. I need to get my supplies together."

It's not a lie. Professor Garcia *did* line up a project for me. She's been scheduling them here and there since the accident. Only, it's not the real reason I'm leaving.

My heart beats harder when I turn away from Marley's questionable gaze.

I need air.

Cool air.

I head toward the entryway. When the open front door comes into view, I relax.

But it only lasts a second.

A tall, overpowering presence steps out from the shadows. The hood of his black sweatshirt is pulled up over his head, and if it wasn't for the glimpse of his warm, golden eyes, I'd feel threatened by his height.

I put the brakes on so I don't stumble into him, and a rush of pain travels down my leg all the way to the floor.

"*Fuck me*," I say under my breath. *Ow*.

"What was that?"

My attention snaps to his mouth. He's grinning.

I recognize him right away. Unfortunately.

Him? Again? The one who stared at me on the sidewalk after the baseball incident, a not-so-silent witness to my humiliation. He picked up my meds, too. Said the name of the painkiller like... I don't know what.

I don't *want* to know.

"Move," I hiss through clenched teeth.

"Yo, Thorne!" someone calls from the kitchen.

Thorne. I know that name.

The guy in question—*Thorne*—jerks his chin in their direction, but he keeps me pinned with a curious stare. His expression is open, *bright*. I don't understand it, or why he's looking at me like that.

My chest tightens, and my heart thumps against my ribcage. A reminder of my growing need to escape.

"Move?" he repeats.

I raise my eyebrows. *Yeah, move*.

Sure, I'm being rude. But I'm seconds from a fucking panic attack and I'm beginning to sweat. The party is in full-force, and the more people who pile into this frat house, the harder it'll be to get out if something happens.

God, I'm a fucking basketcase.

Thorne crosses his arms, and there's a hint of humor on his chiseled face. "I'll move..." he says, dragging the words out. "When you ask me nicely."

I'm not asking him nicely.

We've had a total of two conversations, and I already know he's an arrogant jock like the rest of the guys at this party.

I glance to the thin opening on his right.

I'm small. I can squeeze right past him, dragging my bum leg along with me.

As soon as I take a step, he does the same.

We look like we're dancing, and my irritation grows by the second. My pulse skyrockets, and my heart is like thunder claps.

I growl. "Get out of my way."

Thorne smiles wider. Does he think I'm flirting with him? Before I became a fearful little mouse, I probably would have. Jocks are all I used to date, and fine, he's *hot*. He's got this sexy yet golden-boy vibe to him. Edgy features, tight muscles, panty-dropping smile, and warm, golden-brown eyes, but I'm in no mood to flirt with a guy like him. His hair must be a paid actor, the way a slightly curled lock falls perfectly in the middle of his forehead.

"Seriously?" I stress. "Get out of my way."

I don't give him time to dodge me. I plow forward, desperate to get out of the stuffy party and crowded room.

He steps backward, and I shoulder check him by accident —though he probably thinks it's on purpose.

"Oof," I cringe with the sudden jerk.

Pain rushes my knee, and suddenly, Thorne's arm is wrapped around my waist, holding me in place. His palm slips under my shirt, and we're skin on skin.

I silently gasp. He freezes.

The contact shocks my system, and when I meet his gaze, his eyes are as wide as mine.

He lets me go a second later, and the cool night air coats my flushed skin.

My shoes spin on the creaky porch, and I face him. He's standing inside the threshold of the party, staring at me like this entire interaction was my fault or something. If he would have obliged, this wouldn't have happened.

His eyes narrow. "You're *welcome…*"

I stand outside, no longer surrounded by the heat of

mingling bodies. My confidence grows. I cross my arms and pop a hip, ignoring the dull ache in my leg. "Excuse me?"

There it is again.

That stupid smirk.

He stares at me for too long. My pulse races, and I'm jittery.

"You're an angry little thing, aren't you? How curious."

His grin deepens, and my stomach flips.

It shocks me so much that by the time I let my anger take over, Thorne's back is to me and he's wrapping his arm around some blonde's tiny waist.

My jaw aches from clenching my teeth, and at the last second, I flip him off *again*, even though he can't see me.

I'm not sure if I'm more angry because I gave in to my anxiety and left the party in a haste, or if because for the first time since the accident, I felt something that resembled the old Briar who had a zest for life and a craving for something *more*.

Either way, the old Briar is dead. And she's not coming back.

CHAPTER 4
THORNE

I CAN'T STOP THINKING about that girl. The snarky one. She just—she stared at me with *vitriol*, and it was a rush I wasn't expecting. I was going to apologize for earlier, on the sidewalk, but then she practically bit my head off.

Is there something wrong with me that I found it refreshing? In a school full of people who would love to bend over backward for me and my last name, she clearly has no desire to do so.

I want her to do that again.

But she left before I could so much as call out to her. I don't know her name or anything about her. So, in a rather interesting turn of events, I've kept my eye out for her.

Parties are not my priority, but the other night... well, how could I let the opportunity of another sparring match with her pass me by?

Tonight is the same story, different day.

Another party, but the same people.

Except *she* isn't here. And I don't really know why I thought she would be. I spent all day getting distracted, fucking up in class, nearly falling on my face in practice. I'm only here because I need a distraction...

Okay, no, that's a lie.

If she was at that party last night, then maybe she'll be at this one.

Right?

I'm not crazy. I'm curious—there's a difference.

Someone calls my name, and I head deeper inside. Rhys has yet to show himself, even though he promised he was here. There are some of my other teammates scattered around the house, along with an even mix of hockey players and lacrosse assholes.

The person trying to get my attention waves, and I change course slightly for the couches in the living room.

"Hey." I look down at my cornerback, a guy whose height and weight belie how fast he is. Opposing receivers never stand a chance against Stephen McDowell.

He's got two girls on him, one under each arm, and doesn't seem bothered by their seeming competition. In fact, I'd guess he was encouraging it.

"Was wondering if you were gonna show." He frees an arm and slaps my hand. "Good to see you, Thorne."

The girls perk up at my name, and I bite back my sigh.

"You see Rhys?" I ask.

I flex my other hand. The one that touched *her* skin the other night.

Stephen chuckles. "Either the kitchen or in a room upstairs."

Great.

"And that, uh, that girl who scowls a lot? Have you seen her?" That really makes it clear I have *nothing* else to go on. Besides the fact that her hair is pretty and seems soft, and her lips are plump even when she's flattening them in annoyance, and her eyes are…

Well, maybe I shouldn't think about her eyes.

One of the girls wrinkles her nose. "The burned-out hockey player? She was at the party last night?"

I pause. "What?"

The other one giggles and pushes at her. "Don't."

"She *literally* burned—"

McDowell covers her mouth, shaking his head. "We haven't seen her around, dude."

But she's a hockey player? Or was. Burned, though? What the fuck does that mean?

I say goodbye and check the kitchen, then sigh and scope out the upstairs for Rhys.

Nothing, except closed bedroom doors. And while I've got no problem checking them, I'm not sure I want to see my best friend in that position. So I shoot him a text that says I'm out of here, then make a beeline for the exit.

Kind of like how *she* did yesterday.

Why was she running? Did something happen?

I lick my lips and replay her walking away, both times. The first earlier yesterday morning, then away from the house. Both times, there was a slight hitch to her step.

It's a mystery I'll solve another time. Those girls with McDowell sure knew, though. So it's gossip. Shit I try not to pay attention to...

Or I'm missing something obvious.

My thoughts revolve around the girl. The fact that I don't know who she is is driving me nuts. Isn't that sad?

Okay, maybe not *sad*. I could've probably found out her name if I pushed harder. Or asked the right people.

What I need to do is... forget about her. And since going home would paint me as the biggest loser on campus, I head to the football team locker room to grab my tennis shoes. Nothing some exercise can't fix...

The walk in the cool night air wakes me up. I take deep breaths, and the crispness is invigorating.

I tap my ID at one of the doors to the stadium. The tiny light on the scanner turns green, and there's a *click* as the door unlocks.

This place has always been my safe haven. The dark halls are familiar, and I navigate the shadows easily. When I enter the locker room, I pause.

The lights are on—not necessarily unusual if an equipment manager was staying late for some reason, or the janitor was cleaning.

I don't see either guy, though.

What I *smell* is paint.

I scowl and follow my nose. If Crown Point football jerks snuck down here and spray-painted our lockers—

Nope.

A girl stands on a ladder. Her brown hair is in a bun on top of her head, exposing her slender neck. She's wearing a paint-spattered long-sleeved shirt and similarly distressed jeans.

And even from the back, I recognize her as the girl who keeps *snapping* at me.

I smile before I can stop myself.

She's painting something, but I can't make out what it is around the shape of her body. There is a lot of red, which isn't too surprising. It's the school's primary color. Still…

"Didn't think I'd see you again."

I anticipate her startled movement. Her knee seems to give out, and she pitches off the ladder. But I'm already there, grabbing her waist. My fingers brush her bare skin, and my mind short-circuits.

Touch is not my thing.

But this…?

Why do I want more of it? I could slide my hands higher under her shirt, put my palms on her back. Her skin is cool, and I'm suddenly on fire.

She rights herself and jerks out of my hold. She stares at my shoulder, and a grimace of pain flashes across her lips. Then she snorts.

"I'm not sorry."

I tilt my head. "About?"

She points with the paintbrush still in her hand.

There's a spatter of paint across my shirt. It kind of looks like blood, and I cough to cover my sudden laughter. She got me pretty good.

"Stop laughing," she orders.

"You can laugh, too, you know." I catch the paint on my finger and reach out, fast as a whip. I drag it across her cheek.

Her eyes widen. "You asshole."

I shrug and step away before she can get back at me. "I didn't go for your tits. I think that makes me a gentleman. And why are you—?"

My focus swings to the wall.

Where my face has been painted, along with half my jersey. The outline of my number—thirteen—is visible on my chest.

I open and close my mouth.

Did I totally misread this chick?

Is she actually a stalker?

"It's not what you think." She sets down the brush and crosses her arms. "I was commissioned—"

"Please save the lame excuses." I pinch the bridge of my nose. "I thought you were normal, mystery girl. But breaking in and painting my face is a weird way to get my attention."

I feel... oddly let down.

I take a step back, then another.

At the last second, I remember my tennis shoes and go straight for my cubby. Her gaze burns into my back, but I can't do it. Short of her coming at me with a knife and *literally* stabbing me, I can't be bothered.

Ridiculous.

I locate the shoes and leave the locker room without a backward glance.

So much for trying something new.

CHAPTER 5
BRIAR

MY HANDS ACHE.

I wiggle my fingers a few times and crack my neck. Standing on the ladder for hours last night and again tonight has my body tight in all the wrong spots. My knee is so swollen I could hardly pull my jeans on this morning. There's no going back now, though.

Typically, if I was on a commissioned job, I'd wear a shirt and loose pants that were already covered with paint. But going home and trying to get this denim off will do nothing but exhaust me.

I end my short break and stand from the bench, then spin around the locker room to stare at the rest of the empty spaces I still have to fill in. I have plenty of time to finish the job, but after another run-in with the football king himself, I'm more inclined to finish fast so I don't have to see him again.

Anger zips to my fingertips as I stare at Thorne's perfectly arched jawline. I worked so hard on it last night. I was proud and I still am, but *God*. My blood boils. The disgust on his face after he *assumed* I was another obsessed jersey chaser pisses me off.

Talk about being full of yourself.

He thought I was doing this to get his attention? If I wanted his attention, all I'd have to do is lift my pant leg up and show him my scars. That'd surely get a second look.

I exhale and pull my pencil out from behind my ear.

Arrogant asshole.

I begin sketching the team's co-captain right beside the painting of Thorne. Nothing but my slow breathing fills the locker room. Where I used to have soft music playing in my earbuds while I worked, now I have nothing. There are times where I'm painting or sketching and I get so lost in the act that I can't hear much except my own thoughts, but now I make sure I know my surroundings.

PTSD will do that to you, I suppose.

That's why I was so frustrated when Thorne startled me.

What was he even doing here so late at night?

Maybe *he* was stalking *me.* Not the other way around.

My hand shakes. I glance around the locker room for a third time.

Chill, Briar.

My parents forced me into taking PTSD classes after my incident. Not many people know that someone trapped me inside the building that night. Except, of course, the arsonist and the police.

The last thing I wanted was for the university to put out a statement that not only did their female star hockey player jump from a burning building on campus, destroying her chances at ever playing hockey again, but that someone actively trapped her in said building and tried to kill her.

I was all for the attention I got when I was their highest-scoring hockey player, but having attention because someone tried to kill me?

Thanks, but no thanks.

Pencil strokes fill the quietness of the locker room the harder I push, and by the end of my mini panic attack, the lead is practically nonexistent.

I slowly lower myself to the floor with a wince and stare up at Jerkface One and Jerkface Two.

It's a job well done.

I move to the other side of the wall and sketch Shadow Valley's mascot—a knight, dressed in silver armor with red accents. It's the same one I drew in the girl's locker room, the one I spent my entire freshman and sophomore year in.

My pencil falls to the floor, and I hiss between my teeth.

After hobbling down from the ladder again, I search for my pencil.

"Come on," I sigh. "Where are you?"

If I have to get down on my hands and knees for this fucking pencil, I'm done for the night.

I'm sore, tired, and irritated with Thorne's stupidly attractive face staring at me.

I walk throughout the locker room on quiet feet, searching for my pencil. By the time I find it, I've already called it quits in my head. I swoop down, snatch it up, and then the realization hits me.

The weight room.

It's honestly unfair that the football team, and even the men's hockey team, both have top-of-the-line locker rooms with well-equipped machines for conditioning, training, and physical therapy. The women's? It's a joke.

We can't even get them to stock quality tampons for us.

That must be what Thorne was doing here so late last night. Not the tampon part—the weight room.

As much as I want to punch him in the face, it's clear he's a dedicated athlete. It takes one to know one, and before my incident, I was the same. His name is consistently in the media. The other day, a video went viral on social media of him walking along campus with some of our peers kneeling along the sidewalk and bowing while he walked by.

I roll my eyes. *What a cocky son of a bitch.*

I mean, fine… he *did* seem agitated by the attention

through his half-smirk. But it doesn't matter. I'm bitter none-theless.

Even more so as I stare into the men's weight room with machines I know would help strengthen my leg.

My parents think I'm in denial because I refuse to accept that I'll never play hockey again—they weren't a fan of the sport to begin with. But I like to think of myself as determined.

I spin in an angry huff, ready to leave for the night, only to run right into a hard chest.

"Shit!" I stumble backward.

Two hands grip my arms, and the first thing that rushes through my veins is fear, only to be replaced by something else much more potent when I peer into *his* eyes.

Of course he's back.

"This is getting old," I snap. "Stop stalking me."

Thorne's brow furrows, his immediate annoyance clear. I mimic his face just to spite him.

"I was here first," I add, beating him to the punch.

I rip my arms out from his grip. I *hate* that the touch alone gave me butterflies. I don't get the feeling twisted, though. I know it's because I haven't been with anyone for months.

Thorne sighs. He's still too close, but his minty breath puts me under a spell. I stare into his eyes and memorize the warm, golden flecks scattered throughout so I can add them to his portrait later.

"This is the men's locker room, jersey chaser. You shouldn't even be in here."

"Jersey chaser? Really?" I roll my eyes and brush past him. My lip bleeds with how hard I bite into the flesh to ignore the pain of my leg.

Thorne grips my bicep, stopping me from getting too far. "Listen. I'm not into girls like you, so stop following me around. It'll just be easier on both of us that way."

Slowly, I drag my attention from his strong grip on my arm to his stern face.

I laugh. "Excuse me?"

He scowls. "I don't know what you think this is, but running into me again, after painting my face on the wall, isn't a good look. It means you're desperate and I'm just not into desperate girls."

He finally drops my arm, like that's going to help. He was the one keeping me close just a second ago.

"Tell me you're an arrogant asshole without saying it." A sarcastic laugh follows my insult.

Stalking him?

Get a fucking grip, Thorne.

I turn the corner and head for my things. I hope he follows me so he can see that I didn't just paint him but that I painted his co-captain and the logo as well. He'll see it soon enough and hopefully he'll feel like a complete idiot and knock his ego down a few sizes.

Loud music blares from the weight room, rattling the lockers around me. My jealousy and irritation kick up a few notches the more I peer up at his face on the wall.

Part of my rage isn't even directed toward him, but I simmer in it anyway.

I pull the ladder over to his portrait and grin.

If realizing that I'm not stalking him, nor that I'm obsessed with him, by learning that I was actually commissioned to paint their locker room doesn't put a dent into his confidence, then surely *this* will.

CHAPTER 6
THORNE

I COLLECT stares when I walk in the locker room two days later.

That's not really unusual—my teammates see me as a leader on the field and off of it. Even though I'm only a junior now, it doesn't matter. My parents raised me to take charge in every situation. It takes guts to command a football team, to get them to trust and follow my orders. I recognize that, I accept it.

But these looks are weird.

Verging on… are they laughing at me?

"What?" I snap at one of them.

He just shakes his head and points.

I turn to the wall.

The wall.

An unbidden image of that girl balanced on her ladder, paint on her clothes and skin, working in dim lighting, rises to the forefront of my mind.

I blink and I'm back in the present, staring at the portrait of me—but not.

My face is too recognizable to deny, but my eyes are red, and twisting horns protrude from my forehead. My nose, too, is twice as big as it should be. A proportion she had right the other night.

The locker room erupts into laughter, and I shake it off fast. I push at Stephen McDowell, forcing a smile to my lips.

"What did you do, Thorne? Piss someone off?"

They don't even know who painted it.

"Hope your daddy didn't pay for that art," another defenseman calls.

I roll my eyes. "You think my head is so big that some devil horns will throw me off?"

It won't.

Football is every-fucking-thing to me, and some girl getting in my head…

Okay, maybe this is a sign that I was an asshole.

Was I, though?

I need to figure out her name.

Speaking of my *daddy*, though, I had a message from him that I need to check.

I toss my bag down at my cubby and get changed. I sit and scan my phone, my stomach twisting at the text.

FATHER

> Cynthia Keenland is coming to your game tomorrow with her father. I told them you'd make time after. Take her onto the field, give her a taste of it.

Give her a taste of *what*? Me? My life?

I don't recognize the name Cynthia until I scroll farther up in my conversations with him. She's the one I went on the date with just the other day.

The plastic girl.

Freaking hell. She said she was coming to the game on Friday, and I had wholly disregarded it.

How do I get out of meeting up with her *and* her father after it?

ME

Okay.

He replies immediately.

FATHER

Bill Keenland is an investor.

Do you understand?

I, unfortunately, do.

It means don't fuck up.

Don't mistreat his daughter, don't make an ass of myself, don't blow them off.

The suddenness of my claustrophobia takes me by surprise. I make a quick exit, waving off Rhys's concerned expression. My skin prickles, and I catch myself on the wall outside.

Deep breaths.

It doesn't really fucking help with the mental struggle, but eventually, the knot loosens enough for me to stand straight. I swipe at the layer of sweat that accumulated at my temples and step back into the locker room.

My gaze snags on the devil horns and my own cutting glare.

I don't look like that, truly, do I?

It's not meant to plague me. For all my talk about football, what I *really* want is to have a break from constantly pleasing my parents. I want to just exist for a fucking minute.

But not like that.

If that's how she saw me… that's how I must be.

The devil.

A monster.

I'm mid-spiral, silent and back at my bag, when my physical therapist comes in and grabs me.

There's no more time to think about it.

I am *great* at compartmentalizing, so I shove down my worries and focus on Jeremy's back. My physical therapist makes small talk that I let wash over me. My knee is definitely better, but we still do regular maintenance while the team does other drills.

Down the hall, into his room. It's a combination of weight room and his work space, with padded tables for the guys who need wraps or tape. The room is bright and airy, not unlike the locker room, but it doesn't smell of sweat. I'm not sure what kind of magic voodoo he holds in this room to make it smell *clean*.

We do some familiar exercises, and there's only an occasional twinge of pain that I put out of my mind. Nothing an over-the-counter painkiller later won't solve. Or, my personal favorite, an ice bath. What's better than hot water? Freezing cold water, obviously.

Just kidding.

He pats my leg and sends me out to join the team.

I stop by our coach on the sideline, and when there's a pause, he sends me onto the field. I catch the football, my fingers flexing on the pigskin. Everything about the ball is familiar and comfortable. More than going to school or driving a car, or even writing my own name.

Inhale.

Exhale.

Throw.

Perfect spiral, a thing of beauty.

Of course, practice isn't *easy*. It's hard and sweaty, and I'm cursing our coaching staff by the time they release us. At the door, my physical therapist awaits.

"Let me guess," I say, holding up my hand. "Ice bath for…?"

"Five minutes today." He slaps my back. "Nothing you can't handle."

I wrinkle my nose and follow him back to his room, and a thought occurs to me.

"You know who's painting the mural?" I ask him. "You know a lot of people and what goes on around here."

Jeremy graduated from SVU five or six years ago. He got a post-grad degree and returned here, and he seems content. But he's the sort of guy who's friendly with everyone. He's a *talker*.

I need one of those right now.

He eyes me. "I saw what she did to your portrait."

I groan. "Who is she?"

He whistles under his breath and gestures to the tub in the corner of the room. Already prepped for me.

Knowing he won't talk until I'm in it, I strip out of my practice gear and down to my black briefs. I put my good leg in first, wincing.

Even having done this a million times, it doesn't quite get easier.

Of course, he doesn't know that I'll go home and do the same thing tonight, with bags of ice bought from the local gas station, in hopes of stretching out the pain-free moments a little farther.

Again—I have nothing to truly complain about.

I'm *fine*. And I will be fine.

It's an annoyance.

A slight grievance.

It's no worse than entertaining Cynthia fucking Keenland and her father for a night. We'll have a drink, he'll tell me how he hopes his daughter and I get married and have eight kids, and we'll inherit our parents' money or companies—or both—and the generational wealth will just continue on and on.

It makes me sick.

A football career is going to one day be a tagline on my

résumé. A selling point for dedication and perseverance and leadership.

The trophy wife will be the second, silent tagline. Unspoken but so, so seen.

"Fuck." That would be the second leg going in, my hands gripping the edges and slowly lowering myself down. The water goes over my knees, then my upper thighs.

My balls have their normal reaction of sucking up practically into my asshole—*not fun*—and I swear again. And again when the icy water rushes over my navel.

Then I'm dropping the rest of the way in, and it hits me mid-chest.

I clench the sides of the tub and glare at Jeremy.

It's no easier when I do it on my own. I have no one to blame but myself. This is necessary. *That* is punishment.

"Name," I demand, refusing to be distracted.

"Tell me how you fucked up without even knowing her name." He drags a stool over, a stopwatch in hand, and shows me that he hasn't even started it yet.

It takes effort to talk without stammering. "Insulted her a few times."

"A *few* times—?"

"Jeremy."

He starts the timer. "So? How did you insult her? Merely for my own curiosity."

Asshole.

"Called her a s-stalker." I breathe out. This water seems worse than usual. "And a jersey chaser. I think."

He rolls his eyes. "You're an idiot. Her name is Briar."

"Last name?"

"The big nose would've probably sufficed," he muses. "If that's all you did. She was on the hockey team, so I'm familiar with her. She hasn't had the easiest year, Thorne. I'm telling you that as someone who cares about you, too. If you mess with her…"

"I just want to apologize."

That's the truth. I want to apologize for my overreaction—clearly she wasn't vandalizing the locker room. If she had, it wouldn't have lasted that long. Someone would've painted over it, or… well, there was more than just me.

Right?

I saw that, although I didn't register it. There were other players, and a scene of the football stadium from the fifty-yard line, the sky dark and the lights shining down on the field.

What's worse is that she's actually a good painter.

Devil horns and all.

"Briar Hart," he finally says.

I nod carefully, then refocus on my breathing. Control, relaxation. It's the same here as on the field, and it's the same on those stupid dates my parents plan.

It's when I lose control that bad things happen.

"Hockey player," I muse. "Someone else said that, too. But you said 'was'—?"

"I did." He clicks the stopwatch. "That's all for today. I'll wrap your leg for the game tomorrow. Same as usual."

"Same as usual," I echo.

Briar Hart.

What I didn't tell Jeremy—and what I don't plan on telling *anyone*, thank you very much—is that my fascination with her goes beyond the devil horns. I mean, yes, clearly I got something wrong there. The stalking bit, I'd guess.

But there's more.

Like the fact her bare skin doesn't make mine crawl, and my heart skipped a beat or two, and I just want to talk to her. I want her to use her claws on me.

Briar… like Sleeping Beauty.

I used to like that fairy tale. The cursed spindle, sleeping for a really fucking long time. The prince who wakes her up—with a kiss, of course.

Somehow, though, I think Briar is more the prickly brambles keeping the prince out of the castle than the sleeping princess within.

Either way—I'll make it right.

And figure out why she's different from every other girl shoved in front of me.

CHAPTER 7
BRIAR

I SIGH after reading Professor Garcia's text, but a little smile plays on my lips when I think back to what I'd done to Thorne's portrait.

ME

I'll fix it.

PROFESSOR GARCIA

What made you do it in the first place?

I'm sure the truth would suffice. Thorne is a complete asshole who is full of himself—everyone knows it. But telling Professor Garcia that he offended me by saying I was a jersey chaser feels... immature. So instead, I give her a truth that will quiet her.

I'm jealous and angry. It was wrong of me. I'll fix it as soon as possible.

I didn't lie.
It's the truth.
It just isn't the entire truth.

PROFESSOR GARCIA

> Fix it now. They have a game this evening, and it needs to be fixed by then or Coach is going to bring it up to Dean Winters.

I snort in the middle of class. The head football coach threatening to tattle on me to the dean doesn't worry me. Dean Winters would give up his left testicle to please me and my parents. As long as we stay quiet about the psychopath who trapped me inside a burning building, he'll bend over backward for us. He's already made that clear.

The university wouldn't want word to get out that there's a student on campus who likes to play with fire. Not to mention, the police have no leads, which would make the rest of the student population fearful.

Never mind me.

Professor Miller dismisses class with a *Go Knights* parting, and I gather my things so I can rush to the locker room to fix my impulsive behavior. Marley asks if I need a ride home, and I shake my head while we wait for everyone to exit the room. It's something I started after my accident—never wanting anyone to wait impatiently behind me while I limp out of the room.

"Why were you snickering under your breath during class?" Marley asks.

I smile because I can't help it. I pull my phone out of my bag and hold it close to my chest. "I kind of... did something."

Her eyebrows rise. "Did something? You look awfully naughty. Please tell."

I roll my lips together and show her the before and after of Thorne's portrait. Her jaw falls, and she covers her mouth with her hand. A laugh escapes in between her fingers, and a breathy laugh leaves me.

"You didn't." Marley snatches my phone and gapes at the

photos again. She laughs even harder. Her blue eyes are as wide as saucers when she stares at me. "Why?"

I shrug. "He pissed me off."

It isn't until we're outside that she hands the phone back and raises an eyebrow at me.

"He thought I was a stalker," I admit. "Called me a jersey chaser. He walked in on me painting his face, and I don't know—" I shrug. "It just irked me."

Everything does.

"You're such a boss," Marley says in between a laugh. She grabs her phone and scrolls while we walk.

"Yeah, well, now I have to go fix it before their game, so joke's on me." I roll my eyes.

"No." Marley laughs. "Joke's on him."

It takes a second for my eyes to adjust when she shows me the screen of her phone. My cheeks grow warm. Apparently the portrait has taken over social media, and there are endless comments and shares of the university's favorite quarterback and his *devilish* face.

"Oh God," I mutter.

At the time, painting him as a devil felt cathartic. I didn't think it'd get *this* much traction. I'd only done it to get back at him, but leave it to the real jersey chasers to inflate his ego even more by sharing the locker room photo all over the internet and adding an emoji drool face beside it.

I read one conversation and can't hold back the utter embarrassment for some of the girls.

@Cynthia_Thorne: Daddy always said to stay away from the devil, but I don't think he'd keep me away from you, baby. @therealthorne

@Rhys: Jeez @Cynthia_Thorne, Did you really change your name to Cynthia Thorne?

. . .

@Cynthia_Thorne: So? None of your business, @Rhys

@Rhys: @Cynthia_Thorne, Should have changed it to Can't Take No For An Answer.

I push Marley's phone away. "Of course he's still on a pedestal. Even with devil horns."

"Do you want help fixing it?" she asks, sending me a pitiful smile.

I shake my head. "It won't take me long. I'll be in and out within an hour."

"Okay, well, call me when you're done. I'll pick you up."

She steps away with a half-smile on her face, and it takes me a second to register what she said.

"Pick me up? For what?

"For the game. You're coming with." She winks and then spins away.

"Says who?" I shout after her. "I'm not going."

"See you in a few!" she calls over her shoulder.

I huff and turn toward the locker room. The entire walk there, I argue with myself over whether or not I want to put my foot down and refuse to go. But I'm getting a hunch that Marley's goal for this year is to soften my hardened, thorny exterior—one I entirely blame on my secret arsonist.

———

The clock is ticking, and although I'm practically finished, I quickly add the last golden flecks to Thorne's eyes before any of the guys show up for the game. If they're anything like me, they'll be here at least an hour before they need to be to get in the right mindset.

I lean back on the ladder, ignoring the burning pain in my knee, and make sure everything is proportionate on Thorne's face. It should be concerning that I don't have to pull up his photo on my phone to make sure I got everything correct. He's the type of attractive that stays in your head after just one glimpse.

"My jaw needs to be more defined."

I gasp and twist.

My paintbrush slips from my hand, and I grip the side of the ladder as my life flashes before me. A rush of heat whooshes down my spine, followed by tingly fear.

"Jeez." Thorne settles the wobbly ladder.

Although I sort of hate him, I'm thankful. Falling off a ladder is the very last thing I need.

"You good?" He stares at me with those stupid warm eyes.

I bristle at his feigned kindness. "I'm fine."

"Let me help you." He reaches for my hand, and I stare at his palm in disgust.

After a few awkward stares from some of his teammates walking into the locker room, he slowly drops his arm. He chuckles. "You act like my palm is going to burst into flames if you touch it."

My lips part.

Did he really just say that?

"You're an even bigger asshole than I thought," I say through clenched teeth.

His brow furrows. "What?"

My throat tightens. Ignoring the throbbing of my knee, I stomp down the ladder and shoulder check his hard stomach after gathering my supplies. I leave my fallen paintbrush on the floor because there is no fucking way I'm kneeling below him.

On my way out of the locker room, ignoring the stares I'm getting from his teammates, Stephen McDowell's chuckle snags my attention.

"That was cold, dude."

"That was a big yikes," someone else adds.

"What did I do?" he asks, pretending not to know.

Thorne's voice fades the closer I get to the door, but I can see right through his dense act.

"Bro—" I shut the door so I can't hear the football team talking about my *accident* and head straight to Marley's car.

Once I'm in the passenger seat, she does a double take.

"What's wrong?" she asks. "Whose jaw do I need to break?"

I massage my leg and sit back farther into the seat to plot. "Do you remember when Jax broke it off with you and we wore the other team's colors to the game to irritate him?"

She smiles. "How could I forget?"

"I think we should do that again."

Only this time, it's to irritate Thorne.

CHAPTER 8
THORNE

@B_Hart: @therealthorne's true face may be gone from the locker room but never from our memories. [IMAGE]

I SHAKE MY HEAD, trying to hold back a laugh. I should be pissed, but I'm not.

This girl is *relentless*. She even tagged me!

Who does that?

Rhys slaps me on the arm, and I quickly shield the screen from him. I grab a towel from my locker and wipe the sweat from my forehead and the back of my neck.

The *fixed* portrait of me glares down at us. There are other guys, sure, but it seems like they're all a little less defined. And maybe it's because she had to fix the details she added to make me into the devil. But it seems like she *saw* me. My eyes are… well, it's kind of flattering, in a creepy way. She got all the details right, down to the golden flecks.

Is she actually a stalker? Or did I insult her?

I'm leaning toward the latter.

Let's not forget that I offered my hand to her. She nearly tumbled off the ladder.

I snicker. I don't know if I've ever seen a more clumsy

person. The details of her injury—the slight limp I spotted, the snide comments that girl made at one of the parties— elude me. Mainly because I can't fucking ask anyone about it without showing my hand.

All I know is that she's a hockey player.

Was.

Was a hockey player.

Briar Hart.

I turn her name over in my mind, unfortunately liking the sound of it. And the way she snaps at me. Brambles, indeed. She's thornier than me—and that's fucking saying something.

My phone buzzes again, and I check it.

UNKNOWN

> So excited to see you again, Thorne!!! Daddy and I are in the stands. You're doing so good!!!!

Holy fucking exclamation points.

My stomach cramps, and I put my phone away without replying. No doubt it's Cynthia Keenland, the name conveniently supplied by my father again a few hours ago. To make sure I give a swoon-worthy performance *after* the game, both to her and her father. The investor.

The day my parents stop using me to further their one-percent, billionaire, blue-blood society friends, will be the day I drop dead of a heart attack.

Coach comes in and gives us a spiel about not slacking in the fourth quarter. I drain half my water bottle and use the restroom, and then we're back on the field.

Thoughts of Cynthia and her dad fade, but Briar's face remains.

Our opponents kick, and we get possession. I put on my helmet and hop up and down, resisting the urge to scan the crowd. That's the kind of shit that gets me in trouble.

And yet...

Maybe she just sticks out in a crowd.

Or maybe it's the blue-and-white jersey she's wearing in a sea of red.

Briar Hart.

"Come on!" Rhys tugs at my arm.

I rip my gaze away from her and follow him onto the field. She's wearing the other team's jersey. Her and another beside her...

Why?

She goes to Shadow Valley U—does she not have any fucking respect for the school?

"The play?" Rhys elbows me hard.

I jerk and look around at my teammates, then call out a familiar play. One that will get the ball down the field. I point at Rhys, and he just nods.

All business.

We get our first down, and I call another play. Line up. *Snap.* The football feels warm in my hands, and I dance in the pocket for a moment, then another. Waiting, waiting... *there.*

I throw. It's a beautiful spiral that just seems to go and go—

Oof.

I'm hit hard from the side. The guy drives me into the ground, his shoulder pad digging into my neck. And for a second, I can't seem to get air in my lungs.

The body is yanked off me. I'm lifted to my feet by teammates, and it still takes another second to drag in a ragged breath.

"That fucker," my center seethes. "You threw the ball already—where the fuck is the flag?"

"Don't worry about it." I clap him on the arm and cast a quick, innocuous glance toward the stands.

Fuck me, does she seem worried?

My helmet obscures my face, so she probably doesn't know I've clocked her. Her hair is up in a messy bun on top of her head, but she's wearing a bright-red lipstick that's totally at odds with the blue jersey.

The image of backing her against a wall and lifting the fabric off her comes unbidden.

Shit.

Before I know it, we're in formation again. My head swims, and I shake out my limbs. My body goes on autopilot, and we're fifteen yards away from the goal line by the time the defense manages to halt our forward progress.

I switch out for our kicker and take a seat. It's only then that I notice the twinge of pain in my knee. My physical therapist, always on hand during games to wrap joints or simply be here during emergencies, appears in front of me.

"How does it feel?"

"Fine."

"You were limping for the last two plays."

"No, I wasn't." I scowl at him. "It's fine."

He just stares at me.

The kicker does his job, sending the ball through the posts. It puts us up ten points, with four minutes left on the clock.

They send the ball down for the other team, and I hop up to pace.

"I just need to walk it off," I tell him over my shoulder.

But with every step, it just aches worse. I grab a cup of water and gulp it down, then another to pour over my head.

The visitors barely make it to the fifty-yard line when they throw an interception.

We're back in.

Ignore the pain, ignore everything.

One minute and fifteen seconds.

Just a few plays left. And, in the blink of an eye, it's over. The home crowd goes nuts as the time counts down. The field suddenly fills with people—the rest of my team jumping around me and Rhys, who puts his hands on my shoulders and shouts something unintelligible.

The excitement is palpable, and I force myself to be just as *in* it as they are.

"There you are! Thorne!" a feminine voice calls.

I turn.

The girl I took on a date a few days ago appears, a man in a suit right behind her. "Oh my gosh, Thorne, you were *incredible*!" She bounces forward and kisses my cheek.

I should've kept my helmet on.

"Thanks," I tell her. Because being cordial is what's expected. My attention swings to her father. "Sir."

"Good game, son."

If there's one thing I loathe, it's being called *son*.

But... it seems like this guy really does want me to be his son. In-law.

Abso-fucking-lutely not.

He continues on about the game, even commenting on things he thinks I could improve. When he reaches that stage, I tune him out. My polite agreements seem to mollify him, but I'm just searching for a hint of blue in the crowd.

"...eager for you to join the Keenland family."

I refocus on him. "Sorry, what?"

He narrows his eyes. "Your father assures me you're serious in finding a wife."

"I..." am not. But the words stick in my throat.

"I love my daughter," he continues. "Do you understand?"

It's like everything he's saying suddenly presses in on me at once.

Wife. His daughter. *Do you understand?* It's a phrase my father often employs when he wants to get his way. When he dictates my life with an iron fist.

I can't breathe with the pressure of it all, and my gaze flicks around for an escape route.

Blue jersey.

An absolutely insane idea strikes me.

"Sir, I think there's been a misunderstanding. I'm in a serious relationship." The words are out before I can stop them.

His eyebrows hike. "You took my Cynthia out on a date while in a relationship?"

"My father set it up, sir. I had no idea she would see it as a date, and I apologize for that."

He stares at me a beat. A flush crawls up his neck, but he doesn't act on his emotions. If anything, all of that seems to drain away. He clears his throat and shakes his head, muttering something.

About a waste of time?

Mine's been wasted, too. Over and over again.

"Well. Give my best to your parents." He motions for his daughter, and they disappear into the crowd.

Okay. Okay, that's fine.

Now I need to convince the girl with the heart of thorns to pretend to date me.

CHAPTER 9
BRIAR

HOCKEY IS FASTER THAN FOOTBALL, but the game is still exhilarating. The crowd rushes the field after the win, a tidal wave of red flocking to the end zone. Marley tugs me to follow. I glance around, suddenly feeling guilty for wearing the other team's colors, but I *swear* Thorne saw me from the field and bristled.

I could be making that part up. But he's the entire reason I did the stupid stunt to begin with—as if he'd even care if I was rooting against him.

The chants are so loud on the field, I can't hear myself think. I glance around after Marley's hand slips from mine. I search for blonde hair in between my peers but I come up empty-handed. My leg slows me down, and before I know it, I'm trapped. Shoulders rub against me from both sides. I move forward and trip into someone's hard back, hitting my forehead on their spine.

I pop up quickly with loose strands of hair falling from my bun. Air leaves my lungs. There's no way out. I spin three times before dizzying myself.

"Move," I grit, bumping into an auburn-haired girl with a big red bow in her hair.

She shoots me a dirty look before brushing me off. I curse under my breath and turn to the left.

My eyes spark to life when I see the small opening between football players.

Go.

I rush over, ignoring the dead weight of my leg and squeeze in between their pads. They're unforgiving. I hardly make it through without falling to my knees.

"For fuck's sake," I mutter.

A gasp escapes when pressure falls to my hips. Hands squeeze me, and I'm hoisted to my feet quickly. I turn and peer at whoever pulled me upright.

"I got ya," he says.

"Thank y—"

My gratitude falls short when I eye the guy standing beside my rescuer. Both of them are football players, but the one who picked me up is wearing the visiting team colors. He eyes me curiously when the words die on the end of my tongue.

"You're welcome?"

I blink a few times.

The one who helped me smirks. "Are you starstruck?"

What?

Ignoring him, I swing my gaze to his friend. He has suddenly disappeared. My attention latches on to his backside as he quickly storms away from us. His last name and number are obscured by a towel.

Dread digs into my lower stomach, and my heart is like sludge. It slips to the ground and leaves me feeling empty. I blink through the memory of the night of the fire fighting to get to the forefront of my brain.

"Wh—who is that?" I ask, nodding to my rescuer's fleeing friend.

The dark-eyed guy peers over his shoulder and shrugs. "Not sure. He plays for Shadow Valley."

My nose scrunches with confusion.

"I've never seen you on campus before. Are you a freshman? What are you doing at an away game?"

The realization hits me. *I'm wearing the other team's colors.*

The crowd thins, so instead of making small talk and explaining myself, I head in the same direction as the other guy. Hesitation creeps into the back of my mind but instead of listening to the warning, I continue moving forward. It's as if there's a rope pulling me toward danger and the tattered threads are woven with fear and curiosity.

What if it was him?

Ever since I was purposefully trapped in that burning building, there's been a black cloud following me around. Whoever it was is faceless in my head. I never got a glimpse of his face, and I'm pretty sure the dean suspects I've made the entire thing up—as if I'd trap myself in a burning building and fling out of a window for funsies.

I follow the broad-shouldered guy, weaving in and out of the crowd and pausing every few seconds to rest my knee without ever losing sight. The emptiness in my stomach goes deeper with every step in his direction.

If I could just get close to him and get a feel for his height and presence, then maybe I'd be able to give myself some self-assurance that I'm wrong.

I was in a panic.

Maybe I'm just attaching any sort of panic to the night of the fire.

Pressing against the side of the bleachers, I do a quick sweep of the fans exiting the field. I dip inside the tunnel when no one is watching.

It's quiet and dark, which does nothing but unsettle me even more.

Choppy breaths fill the air, and I move in the direction of the weight room. The team is loud, following after me.

They're hollering and clapping, bustling with excitement from their win.

It's a little nostalgic. The girls and I did the same thing after a tough game on the ice.

I recognize Thorne's voice and I'm instantly irritated that it settles me. He's going on about how well they did, and I'd never admit it, but he's definitely captain-like. Very motivating and encouraging, while also touching on a few areas of improvement.

I roll my eyes and stay pressed against the side of the hallway until some guys chatting about the party they're going to head to seem to get closer. I panic and slip into the weight room. The lights are off so it's hard to see me, but I can see them perfectly.

If only Thorne could see me now—he'd absolutely think I was a stalker.

And I sort of am, except I'm not stalking *him*.

I'm stalking a potential arsonist.

Several of the players, most of whom I recognize, walk down the hall with their bags slung over their shoulders. Their hair is damp, and I can smell their manly body wash through the door as they head to a campus party.

By the time my heart rate slows, it picks right back up when a tall-framed guy walks down the hallway with a few players I don't recognize. They must be freshmen or sophomores. I stare at the quiet one to the left with his hood pulled up over his head and a lump forms in my throat.

My eyes shut on their own.

Goosebumps rush to my skin.

The sound of broken glass is far enough away in my memories that I know it's not real, but I cover my ears anyway and try to hide from the debilitating fear that comes with the sound.

I sink to my butt and wrap my arms around my knees.

Quick breaths rush into the empty weight room from behind my lips.

"You're fine, Briar," I whisper. "You're being ridiculous."

I've convinced myself before that my head is playing tricks on me or that my eyes are being deceitful. All it takes is one little reminder and I'm back in that building. One sense of familiarity with some stranger, and I find myself wondering if *they're* my arsonist.

The feeling in my stomach, though? That's new.

Deep breaths work in and out of my lungs for so long, my ribs ache. I wince when I stretch my legs out in front of me, pressing into the hard wall. My eyes stay shut; I'm too afraid to open them and find myself in a panic again.

I don't have a choice, though.

The door opens, and the overhead lights flick on.

My teeth sink into my lower lip when I spring to my feet. The grinding of my knee is loud enough to draw attention.

I take off in the opposite direction. I have nowhere to go and I'm terrified to look backward. *What if it's him?*

The PTSD counseling is nowhere to be found as panic shocks me to the core.

I spin and latch on to the door.

Shit. I backed myself up into a corner.

"Briar?"

A rush of relief cools my clammy skin.

Thorne.

I recognize his voice, and just like earlier, it calms me.

There is no rhyme or reason to it, but it's there.

His soothing, smooth authoritative voice stops me in my tracks. I gaze into his eyes from across the weight room, and then... everything goes black.

CHAPTER 10
THORNE

THE LAST PERSON I expect to see in the weight room is Briar Hart.

And her reaction to me?

Fear—until she realizes who I am. Then, her expression shifts into something more at ease.

But then, her eyes roll back, and she collapses.

I have excellent reflexes… but unfortunately for her, I'm across the room. She just seems to fold in on herself, though, and luckily doesn't smash her head into anything on the way down.

What *is it* with this girl?

I rush to her and drop to my knees, rolling her onto her back. I pick up her legs, my fingers digging into the flesh around her ankles. Elevating them should…

Ah, here she is.

Her eyes flutter, and she comes around rather quickly.

"Why am I on the floor?" Her voice croaks.

"You fainted." I crack a smile. "I'd like to think it's because you saw my gorgeous face and swooned a little too close to the sun."

She scowls.

"Briar," I try out.

"Put my legs down."

"You should just lie still for a minute." I pat her calf. "Just, uh, let the blood flow back to your brain."

This is actually good timing, seeing as how she's just who I had in mind for being in a fake serious relationship with—I just need to convince her that it's a good idea, too.

But she's still wearing that stupid blue jersey.

"Are you wearing anything under that?" I blurt out.

Her eyes narrow... and then she smirks.

Smirks.

She pushes up onto her elbows and slowly shakes her head. "Just a sports bra."

I make a face. And I'm probably going to regret this, but I can't seem to stop myself. I set down her legs and grab her wrists, pulling her into a seated position. She smells nice. Like flowers.

I bite the inside of my cheek and shuck my shirt off.

"Whoa—"

I toss it on her lap.

Her eyes widen. The cool air pricks at my skin, which is suddenly hot. But I ignore it when she balls up my shirt in her hand.

"I'm not propositioning you," I inform her. "And I'm not doing this to see your tits."

Before she can voice a protest, I grab the bottom of the jersey and yank it up. Her arms lift automatically, and I tug it free.

She gapes at me, and I smile.

"Give that back," she demands.

"No."

"Thorne."

"Put the shirt on, Briar." I motion to it.

Her breasts are kind of fucking perfect, though. Sports bra... more like some lacy contraption meant to lure guys into her bed. Her cleavage is killer, and the light-blue fabric barely hides her nipples.

She scoots away from me and yanks it over her head. Her bun comes loose, her hair falling in her face.

But once she's covered by the thin white cotton, the block letters of *Shadow Valley University* across the chest, I blow out a breath.

"Was that so hard?" I demand.

"You—"

"I thought you had school spirit," I continue. "I heard you were on the hockey team—"

Her expression turns mutinous. "Asking about me, Thorne?"

"You're intriguing." I shake my head and stand. "And…"

She rises, too. I resist the urge to reach out and touch her again. My skin didn't crawl, and I don't want to jinx it. What if it's just a fluke? That sort of contact has *always* made me feel like there were spiders creeping up my back.

But not her.

I could be delusional.

But I told my father's investor I was in a serious relationship… There's got to be a way to leverage this in her mind. Something she needs?

"What were you doing in here anyway?" I ask.

She scowls. Seems to be her default expression. "Nothing."

"Nothing," I repeat, skeptical. "No need to lie, Briar."

She wraps her arms around her stomach but doesn't go for the jersey I tossed away. She doesn't try to get her hair back into a picture-perfect bun or any other sort of style. She didn't flinch away from me seeing her shirtless…

Who *is* this girl?

"You heard I was on the hockey team," she says quietly, "but did you *hear* why I'm not anymore?"

I cock my head. I haven't heard, but apparently, a lot of other people on campus have. Do I just live under a rock?

I *have* been a little busy. My entire life revolves around football and dodging the dates my parents schedule for me.

"Tell me," I say.

Her gaze moves past me, to the doorway, then back. I stand between her and her only escape. I don't mean to be menacing, but I want answers. I shift, giving her a better line of sight to the door, and cross my arms.

She heaves a sigh. "*Fine*. I was working on a commissioned mural, and there was a fire, and I couldn't get out on the first floor. The only way I could survive—" Her throat works. "I jumped out of the second-story window. Injured my knee pretty bad, basically ended my hockey career."

I squeeze my eyes shut, imagining the scene she paints. Fire, smoke. Fear. Falling.

Pain.

I know a lot about pain. Especially knee pain.

Her reaction about my hand bursting in flames makes sense now. I'm a dick.

"Were you in here to use the equipment?"

She nods fast.

"You could get hurt if you do it the wrong way." I frown. "I—"

I just need to say it.

"I can help, if you want? I went through my own knee injury. So, I have experience." I clear my throat. "It's probably better than you struggling in here alone, especially if you're prone to fainting."

"I'm not." Her cheeks flame. "I never faint."

"Uh-huh."

"What's the catch?" She steps closer. "You can't go from calling me a jersey chaser and a stalker—"

"I'm sorry," I blurt out.

Her eyebrows shoot up.

"I made a bad assumption based on past experiences. You know what they say when you assume…"

"Right."

"I made an ass of myself," I continue. "And, if I'm being honest, I do have a catch."

She stiffens.

"Date me."

She chokes. "Excuse me?"

"That came out wrong." I turn away from her, swiping my palm down my face. "I don't mean *actually* date me—"

"You saw my tits and now you want to fuck me?" Her voice is hard.

I laugh. "Jesus. No."

"You didn't like them, then?"

My face heats. When's the last time I got this flustered? I spin to face her again, only to find that she's within reach. Her chin lifts, her head tipping back to meet my gaze. She's so fucking *unafraid*, it's a marvel.

"I don't mean sex. Or a hookup. I mean… I need you to pretend to be in a serious relationship with me."

There. It's out in the open.

I wait for the laughter or the immediate denial. That this is a horrible idea, that… I don't know, now *I'm* the stalker or the creep.

It doesn't come, so I press onward.

"I help you in here, you help me out there." I motion toward the door.

"Why?"

I wrinkle my nose. "Why?"

"Yeah, Thorne, *why*? Why me? Why do you need to find someone to fake date you? Why does it have to be a serious relationship? Just—*why*?" Briar's gaze could pin me to the fucking wall.

She's not laughing.

She's so fucking real right now, it makes me want to reel her in and kiss her.

Which is *so* outside my comfort zone, it's not even funny. I don't kiss.

I fuck girls, usually from behind, and they get a limited amount of touching. Sometimes I tie them to the headboard just to make sure they *don't* cop a feel. Their nails down my back or along my arms... I fight off a shudder at the thought.

"You want the truth?" I ask.

She nods emphatically.

I look away. I can't believe I'm about to tell her this. Rhys knows, of course, but everyone else who sees me go on dates with rich, thin, plastic girls? They just think that's my type. And it attracts more of them, like flies to honey, and I can't escape it.

"My parents want me to find the perfect trophy wife," I admit. "They come from old money, and that kind of status demands certain things."

"Like marrying...?"

"Someone of the same class." I wince. "Their words, not mine."

"Gee, Thorne, I'm surprised you're even allowed to play football."

I meet her gaze. Her brown eyes are warm, receptive to my story. She's not judging me. Maybe my parents, but not me. Not yet.

"They don't want me to go pro. They think college ball looks good on a résumé, but even that is bullshit. If I wasn't the quarterback, they wouldn't let me dedicate nearly as much time to it as I do. I'm going to graduate and work for my father. Give my blood, sweat, and tears to the company that's been in our family for six generations, work my way up the ladder, and take over when he's ready to retire. But the Board of Directors will only accept me if I do everything right, and to them? That includes marrying a girl who comes from a family like mine. It means she's going to pop out two-point-five babies who are guaranteed to be blonde brats. A nanny is going to raise them. And it's all about the money."

"And that has to do with the here and now…?"

"They want me to get started on the wife and babies thing." I shrug. My gaze skates away from hers again. "Every week I go on a date with someone who matches their criteria."

She snorts. "Poor you, going on dates with rich girls. Do they all have Daddy issues?"

"I don't want them. I want to focus on playing football. And, well, I met one of the girl's father tonight, and he insinuated some shit about becoming my father-in-law. So I told him there had been a mistake and I was already in a committed relationship."

With you.

Silence.

I can't make myself look at her. I don't often get rejected, and I don't want to be staring at her when she decides to tell me to fuck off. It feels weirdly vulnerable, having admitted all that to her. We're total strangers, save our names. And now, I suppose, pieces of our trauma.

"Let me think about it," she eventually says.

She brushes past me, not quite *fleeing*, but walking faster than I'd seen her. Even with the slight hitch in her step. She disappears out the door.

It bangs shut behind her, and I kick at the blue jersey.

While not outright, her rejection stings all the same.

CHAPTER 11
BRIAR

I CRINKLE the piece of paper into a ball and drop it by my feet. My hockey stick feels foreign in my hands. It's been so long since I've touched skate to ice.

This doesn't even come close to playing hockey, but it still feels good. I swing my stick and send the wad of notebook paper flying into the trash can.

Lydia claps. "Nice."

I smile.

"What's got you so… cheery? You've got energy tonight. Was it the football game? Gave you some school spirit?"

I laugh, but it's sarcastic.

I rest my stick against the wall and slump onto the couch. My notebook is under lock and key in my tight grip. Lydia already thinks I'm half nuts. If she knew I was writing a pro and cons list regarding a fake relationship with Shadow Valley's quarterback, she'll think I've lost my fucking mind.

Maybe I have.

My last relationship ended shortly after the fire, and the breakup was brutal. I swore I'd never date another footballer for the rest of my life, and yet…

Thorne's face appears in my mind.

The angles of his high cheekbones and the golden flakes in his eyes. They're warm and sort of... comforting?

After I came to in the locker room and saw his face, my panic was swept away instantly.

Not only was fainting unusual, but the feeling he gave me was too.

I'm weirdly comfortable with him.

Not comfortable enough to tell him that I was in the weight room to spy on his teammates but comfortable enough to consider fake-dating him.

That's all I'm doing.

Considering it.

"Is that your shirt?"

I glance down to Thorne's shirt, and my heart beats a little faster. My fingers clamp on to the notebook even harder. "Did you know that the men's locker room has a state-of-the-art training room attached?"

Lydia scoffs. "No, but I'm not surprised. They're the favorites."

I sit up a little taller on the couch. "I want to train."

Lydia eyes me cautiously, and bless her soul for keeping her gaze focused on my face instead of dropping to my derelict leg. "Train?"

This is wonderful practice for when I tell my parents that I haven't given up hockey like they assume. I nod at my roommate. Her expression remains even, but I recognize the pity in her blue eyes.

"What do you mean by that?"

My pulse races. "I want to strengthen my leg and play hockey again."

"But—"

I interrupt her. "I know what the trainers have said," And I know what everyone will think if I tell them that I'm training to get back on the ice. "But if I train the right way, I know I can do it."

Lydia paces the living room. She has her thinking face on. The one she wears when she's studying. "How are you going to do this? I thought your parents put an end to physical therapy?"

They did.

They stopped paying for it because the therapist said I'd likely always have a limp and that I'd never play hockey again. Even with my measly earnings from commissioned paint jobs, I can't afford private sessions so I haven't had physical therapy in months. Exercises at home aren't enough, I need *more*.

This isn't all about playing hockey again either. The fear that secretly resides in the back of my head is that much worse with a body that doesn't move as fast as it used to. What if I get trapped somewhere again and can't move quickly? Or what if my arsonist finds out that I'm digging into him and comes to finish the job? How will I fight back or get away?

"I'm going to use the men's facilities," I say.

Lydia stops pacing. Her hands fly to her hips. "What? How?"

I shrug. "I've got an in."

She purses her lips. "An in?"

My nod gets cut short with her gasp.

"Oh my God. Don't tell me you took Ben back."

The disgust on my face sends her shoulders down to their rightful spot. "It'll be a cold day in Hell if I ever get back with him."

Lydia flops on the couch beside me. Her hand falls to her heart. "Oh, thank God. Plus, I heard that he was working his way through the volleyball team."

I roll my eyes. That thought would have stung a month ago, but now, I'm onto bigger and better things.

Like a fake relationship with the captain of the football team, a way to strengthen my leg behind the scenes without anyone dismissing me, and the best part of all? I'll get insider information on the football team.

One way or another—I'm going to feel safe again whether that means I'm strong and able to fight or flee when needed *or* I put a name to the person who's responsible.

All Thorne needs is a fake girlfriend to parade in front of his parents and dutiful girls who they want to set him up with?

Easy-peasy.

I don't have to trust him.

I just have to act like I'm in love with him.

That shouldn't be too hard, right?

"So if it's not Ben who's your in, who is it? Or what is it?"

I smash my lips and turn toward Lydia. We're not the best of friends, but after living with her for several months, I know she's trustworthy. She also gets brownie points for not automatically discouraging me from wanting to play hockey again.

"Thorne."

His name feels funny falling from my lips. My stomach dips, and I don't know why.

Lydia's eyes widen. "Cassius Thorne?"

A laugh erupts from my mouth. "Cassius? That's his real name?"

"Cassius Remington Thorne the third, actually." Lydia shrugs. "I heard his name get called in class once. He turned fifteen shades of red and angrily corrected our professor." She clears her throat and deepens her voice. "*I go by Thorne.*"

I laugh again with her reenactment, which she seems surprised by. Since moving in together, we have never sat on the couch laughing, and just like the Queen herself quotes, *It's me... I'm the problem, it's me.*

"Oh, I cannot wait to call him by his first name," I say through laughter.

"So... are you two friends?" she asks.

Friends? Not a chance. Up until a few hours ago, I hated him.

I nibble on my fingernail. I can say goodbye to the three minutes of normalcy between Lydia and me because after I tell her of my plan, she's going to go right back to thinking I've lost my mind.

"He's going to train me in exchange…" I let my words trail. I think I *have* lost my mind.

Lydia leans in. "Exchange for… do not tell me it's for sex."

"No!"

Her warm, pizza-scented breath fills the tiny space between us. "Thank God."

I quickly blurt out the rest of Thorne's plan. "He wants me to act like his girlfriend."

"What?" Lydia stands abruptly and paces again. She's furiously typing a text message.

I panic and climb to stand. "What are you doing?"

"Calling in reinforcements because you're insane." She says this without pulling her attention from her phone.

"Reinforcements?" My pulse pounds. "If men in the white coats show up to take me to the psych ward…" I'm only half joking.

Lydia smiles while typing. "You *are* insane, but it's admirable as hell. I'm texting Marley."

I sigh. "You're going to try to talk me out of this, aren't you?"

To them, they think I'm just trying to play hockey again.

But to me, it's so much more. I just can't find it in myself to tell them the full truth. Only a handful of people know that someone trapped me in that building. Telling them will only make the pity heavier and their fear palpable.

Lydia clicks her phone off and stares at me from across the room. Her lips turn up at the corners, and she shakes her head. "I want you back on the team, Hart. I'm not talking you out of anything."

CHAPTER 12
THORNE

BILL KEENLAND APPARENTLY WORKS FAST.

Bright and early Saturday morning, the ringtone I gave my father—the Darth Vader theme song—wakes me from a dead sleep.

"A *serious relationship?*" he growls in my ear after I answer his call. "Tell me you're kidding."

"Good morning to you, too," I mumble.

"Cassius Remington Thorne," my father booms.

I wince. All he left off are the Roman numerals that follow *Thorne*. The ones that declare me the *third* of my name. Not my father, though. Just his grandfather, and my grandfather's grandfather. It's tradition to skip a generation, I suppose.

Everyone calls me Thorne.

The only people to ever call me by my first name—or the full name, like now—are my parents. Usually when I've done something wrong. All through school, teachers were quietly and firmly corrected before they even had a chance to do roll call.

So I can get away with no one knowing, or giving a shit about, my first name.

Cassius feels ancient.

Remington feels presumptuous.

Thorne, though? That part felt right. Even as a kid.

"A serious relationship," I confirm. "I was waiting to tell you—"

"Can you imagine how *humiliated* I was when Bill Keenland called to inform me of this? Because you chose to tell him in front of his daughter? The disrespect you show our family." He makes a disgusted noise. "You embarrassed me."

Guilt presses in on me. "I'm sorry."

"Are you going to marry this girl?"

I freeze, gripping my phone tight to my ear.

She hasn't even agreed to *date* me yet.

"Dad—"

"Well. We'll just have to meet her. And if she lasts as long as you think she will, we'll be seeing her for Christmas, won't we?" Except, he doesn't quite frame it as a question.

He hangs up without so much as a goodbye.

I groan.

My door swings inward without warning, and Rhys pops his head in. We've shared a space—first a dorm room, *fuck that*, then an apartment, and now a house—since freshman year. We roped in a few other guys from the football team to join us, splurging on a space where we can have a living area for hosting.

Not parties or anything crazy. I, for one, like to protect my peace. But we're not above beers and tuning in to Monday Night Football. Or vegging on the couch on Sundays, watching the games throughout the day. Or studying our competition on Saturdays...

"I heard the dulcet tones of one Thorne Senior." Rhys ventures farther in, leaving my door open and plopping into my desk chair. "Bit early on a Saturday to have his knickers in a twist."

I sit up and shake my head. "Well, word just got back to him about something I did wrong."

"Naturally." Rhys eyes me. He's in shorts and a t-shirt, his dark hair still wet from a shower he probably just exited. "What did you do this time?"

"I…" I swallow. "Well, you know those dates he's always setting up?"

"Indeed."

"The girl and her dad came to the game last night. My father made sure to let me know that Bill Keenland is some big shot he wanted to impress. When Bill and his daughter came on the field, he made some comment about me being his future son-in-law."

My best friend inclines his chin, clearly waiting for me to get to the fucking point.

"So I lied and told him that there was a misunderstanding and I already had a serious girlfriend."

Silence.

Rhys just stares at me for a solid minute, then tips his head back and bursts out laughing.

My face heats.

"You? A *serious* girlfriend?" He slaps his hand on his thigh. "Fuck, man. So that guy tattled on you. Did you come clean to your dad or what?"

That probably would've been a smart idea.

"I doubled down," I mutter.

He cackles.

"It's *fine*," I snap. I grab my pillow and chuck it at him. "I've got a plan."

"A plan," he repeats. "You have a serious girlfriend hiding under your bed?" He gets down on his knees and fucking checks. When he straightens, there's a shit-eating grin on his face. He checks my closet, then makes a show of opening my window—on the second floor of the house—and leans out.

"Sit down." I stand and pick up my jeans from the floor. "I have a plan in the works."

"This sounds like a fourth quarter Hail Mary." Rhys rolls

his eyes. "A plan *in the works* to get a serious girlfriend? Those don't happen overnight, you know. Or maybe you don't? Since you seem so unfamiliar with the concept."

"Fuck off." I swap my sleep shirt with a clean one. "Briar Hart."

He gives me a blank stare.

"The one who painted the portraits in the locker room."

He stands and comes closer. I squint at him, wary, until he presses the back of his hand to my forehead.

I swat him away. "What the hell are you doing?"

"Checking to see if a fever has made you delusional." He eyes me. "Jury's out. She painted you as the freaking *devil*. How did your proposal go?"

I shift. "It wasn't a proposal."

"It had better be, seeing as how your parents are serious about you getting married." He chuckles. "How did you ask her to be your fake serious girlfriend?"

"Well, I found her in the weight room. And I asked after she fainted at the sight of me." I hold up my hand to stop his onslaught of comments. "Yeah, yeah. I heard how that sounded."

"What did she *say*?"

"That she'd think about it."

He bursts out laughing. "Oh, you're screwed. Have fun with that one, Thorne. I'll be watching with popcorn in hand."

He leads the way out of the room, and all I can do is shake my head.

I didn't even tell him that Dad wants to meet her at Christmas.

————

I didn't realize I was a stalker until I spot Briar exiting an apartment building just up the street. I jog to easily catch up, only slowing to a halt when I'm right beside her.

"Briar."

She jumps out of her skin, lurching away. She stumbles and rights herself quickly, and a flush works its way up her neck and across her jaw.

I like this flustered version of her.

"Don't do that," she hisses.

I raise my hands in surrender.

"Where did you even come from?" She glances over her shoulder, her brows furrowing.

The accusation in her tone makes me think *she* now is considering me a stalker. Which I did just admit to myself, too. So. That's fair.

Not true, but fair to assume.

"I live two blocks down. Same street." I hook my thumb behind us. "Probably why we ran into each other when you were nearly taken out by runaway baseballs."

She gives me a true scowl.

Her black shirt is long-sleeved and skin-tight, showing off her curves. The neckline is high enough to hide her cleavage but leave her collarbones bare. I don't know how she makes wearing a shirt so effortlessly sexy, but there it is. I've never wanted to be a scrap of fabric so bad.

"I suppose you would see it that way." She sighs. "What are you doing? It's Saturday."

"I am well aware." I appraise her. "I'm going to the library."

Her lips turn down. "That's where I was going."

"Great."

We walk in silence, and it strikes me that I should ask her if she's made a decision. I'm not one to shy away from confrontation—part of me is into it, which is probably why my attraction to Briar is so present. She doesn't give a fuck about who I am.

Just that I insulted her a few times.

I match her pace. She doesn't have a pronounced limp right now. It seems to only come out when she's been on her legs for a while. Although she walks slower than some others, I don't really give a shit about that.

It's nice to slow down and smell the roses.

The *Briar* roses?

Fuck off, brain.

I glance at her. Then straight ahead.

I just need to ask her if she's made a decision.

If she'll be my fake serious girlfriend.

Open my mouth to spit out the words…

"You're staring," she interrupts, and I don't get a damn word out.

"No, I'm not. I'm pointedly not staring, grumpy cat."

She snorts, and I smile.

We make it to the library without further conversation, and I kick myself internally when she strides away from me without looking back. I sign in, scrawling my name just below hers, then follow.

She finds a table in the center and drops her bag onto a chair.

I drag out the one across from her and sit.

"What are you doing?"

"Sitting." I tilt my head. "Is this seat taken?"

"Yes." She crosses her arms over her chest. "Go away."

I sigh. "Who's sitting here, Briar?"

"My friend." She shifts. "My friend, who is on their way right now, and—"

"Just one friend?"

"I—"

"There are three more seats." I raise an eyebrow. "Besides, you haven't given me an answer yet, and I'm just trying to get to know you better."

Boom.

Mentioned it.

Now I just wait and try to make it seem like I'm not holding my breath. Although I absolutely am, because I am one hundred percent fucked in the lying-to-my-father category otherwise.

I'm fucked if he finds out I've got a fake girlfriend, too, but that can be solved with a *real* breakup. It's just a matter of getting her to agree.

After a solid thirty seconds of eye contact, in which Briar doesn't even flinch, she nods and sits.

"Okay," she says evenly. "What class assignment are you working on?"

I unzip my bag and take out my laptop. "Research paper on recycled water."

She chokes. "What?"

"What?" I pause. "Recycled water? One of the great inventions that will save millions around the world?"

"You cannot be serious."

I brace my forearms on the table, and the realization strikes hard and fast. I shouldn't be upset about it, but it still stings a bit. Especially coming from her.

"You thought I was a dumb jock," I say.

"What? No, I didn't." Her eyes widen.

It's her blush that gives her away.

"Yes, you did. Briar Hart, *jock* herself, thought I was—I don't even know. Do you think my head is just full of Kermit the frog repeatedly shouting, 'Football! Football!' in my brain?" I rock back and point at her. "Admit it, Hart."

She rolls her eyes. "Honestly? It was more like Hodor than Kermit."

"Hodor." I cross my arms. "From *Game of Thrones*?"

Her chin lifts.

Why the *fuck* does that turn me on?

"If my brain shouts 'football' over and over, what does yours shout?"

She pauses. Her gaze lifts over my shoulder, then sweeps around the room. When she refocuses on me, she clears her throat.

Did something spook her?

"You want to know what's rattling around in my brain all the time?" Her voice drops. "'*Fire.*'"

Before I can answer, she collects her stuff and shoves away from the table.

CHAPTER 13
BRIAR

I'M GOING to have to give him an answer eventually.

I've been dragging my feet—no pun intended. Thorne makes me uneasy, but not in the way the rest of the football team does. There is something genuine about him, even when he's playing football and has that stern, focused glint in his eye.

He has a kind smile. It wouldn't be a bad thing to get close to him so I can watch some of his teammates without hiding behind the bleachers and taking cover in the weight room.

We all know how that worked out last time.

I came so close to telling him yes the other day in the library. I had already made my mind up. My pros and cons list grew exponentially larger after Marley showed up at the apartment. She and Lydia made their own list which matched mine to a T, except all the reasons relating to figuring out who my arsonist is.

But sitting in the library set me back.

A chill zipped down my spine the second I looked past Thorne's adorably messy hair. There was a slip in time, and I panicked. All it took was one glimpse of the student in the back of the library wearing a dark hoodie and I got spooked.

There's a very good chance he doesn't even want me to be his fake girlfriend anymore.

"Let's go." Lydia snaps her fingers at me.

I peek one eye open and see her standing above me. One raised eyebrow later, and she's explaining herself.

"We have plans." She doesn't let me protest, she just continues explaining while gathering her purse and our phones. "The football players are practicing. Marley is meeting us there."

I spring up quickly. "Absolutely not."

She ignores my protesting. A pill bottle rattles, and like magic, one of my pain pills is at the center of her palm with a bottle of water in her other. She offers both to me.

"Do I need to go get the pros and cons list off the fridge?"

I snort.

She literally taped the list onto the fridge when she learned that I had fled from the library the other day. She doesn't know *why* I chickened out, but that's semantics.

I growl under my breath.

There's one teeny, tiny sliver of fear that's holding me back from finding out who trapped me in that building, or at least getting stronger in case I never find him.

Without saying anything, I take the medicine from Lydia and throw it down the hatch.

I swing my sore legs over the side of the couch and sigh at the sight of her pleased face.

"Fine," I say. "But we are *not* sitting beside the jersey chasers."

They go to every practice, and I refuse to be labeled as such.

Lydia laughs. "You don't want to be called a jersey chaser, yet you're about to be dating the quarterback."

Her laughter doesn't fade even as we walk out the door.

———

The crisp air and rigid bleachers are a recipe for agonizing pain. Even with the dose of medicine, I'm still uncomfortable. I refuse to stand beside the group of girls who cheer whenever Thorne so much as blinks, though. So sitting on hard bleachers it is.

"I hope he doesn't expect me to act like them," I whisper.

Marley hides her laughter behind her Styrofoam cup full of hot coffee.

Lydia leans into my space. "He'll expect you to wear his jersey."

Marley glances over. "Yeah, right. Remember when Ben tried to get her to wear his jersey and they got into the biggest argument?"

I shrug. "I played my best game after that argument."

My emotions fuel me, and that night, I was angry.

Lydia bumps my shoulder with hers. "You two have a deal, though. You're going to have to play your part so you can play with *us*."

Nerves roll through me when I peek at the field. Thorne, practicing in short sleeves despite the cool temps, steps back and throws a perfect spiral to one of the running backs.

Screams from the girls on the sidelines ring throughout the air, and he looks over at hem.

My nose wrinkles when they get even more excited from his attention.

"The coach should make these practices private," I mumble.

"If he did that, then this wouldn't happen."

I follow Lydia's line of sight, and my pulse takes off.

"What is he doing?" I seethe.

Thorne, still in the middle of practice, rushes toward the bleachers—and he's staring directly at *me*.

I grab Marley's leg. "Kill me."

She laughs and hides it with her cup again.

Lydia leans backward to talk to Marley around me. "Should I record this?"

My gaze stays trained on Thorne while they have a quiet conversation behind my back. He jumps up, holding on to the rail to haul himself onto the bleachers. He leans over the bar and smirks at me.

"Briar Hart," he muses. "To what do I owe the pleasure of seeing you at my practice?"

Here we go.

My teeth sink into my bottom lip. I am certain the entire football team is staring in our direction, as well as the wannabe cheerleaders.

Lydia elbows me.

"Yes," I blurt.

Heat sweeps against my neck.

Thorne's eyebrows shoot to his sweaty hairline. "Yes?"

His warm eyes move to Lydia and then to Marley before coming back to me. He squints, like he's questioning my answer.

I nod.

Did we just have a silent conversation?

"Ready to make it official, then?" The corner of his perfect mouth lifts on one side.

Hesitation skips up my spine. I pull my shoulders back. "What does that mean?"

His coach calls his name. Thorne ignores it, but for some reason, it makes *me* nervous. I quickly stand and get closer to him. The only thing that is separating the two of us is the metal barrier used to keep the fans away from climbing onto the sideline.

"It means I'm going to make you mine, Briar."

CHAPTER 14
THORNE

COACH ROARS my name from behind me, but I block it out. All I can focus on is Briar, and the cold metal railing under my hands, and the way she suddenly bites her lip like she's fucking *shy*.

She's not shy.

Nervous, then?

"Put my number in your phone," I tell her.

She nods slowly, still shocked at what I just declared.

I recite it when she's done saving my contact info then hold out my hand. Not for her phone. For *her*.

I'm completely aware that this is another test. Not just for her—to see if she'll take it, another acceptance of my proposal —but for me.

Because what if my lack of aversion to her has so far been a fluke?

Then this whole thing will get even more... *arduous*.

But there's no backing down. Not with Coach and my teammates probably all staring at me like I'm the world's biggest asshole, or flake, or whatever shit they'll start to murmur when they think I can't hear. Or they'll just say it to my face.

There has to be a reason she came to my practice. A game —wearing the other team's jersey, no less—is one thing. This is *practice*. The girls who come and watch, giggling like mad or cheering at every throw, drive me nuts.

And yet, Briar sitting here has me confused.

She's not a jersey chaser.

She's not swooning over me—although, honestly? I kind of wish she would. Just once.

After her abrupt departure from the library, I had a calm few days. Okay, that's a lie. They were boring. Eye-wateringly dull. But not *calm*. Because all I could think was what I'll eventually have to say to my parents when my truth comes out.

If Briar says no, that truth will reveal itself sooner rather than later.

My mother called, and I dodged questions about it. I cut my call with Dad short, claiming a meeting with a professor.

So many lies.

And now... she said yes.

She takes my hand.

Her palm slides across mine, her fingers curling. Gripping. Squeezing. My heart damn near lurches. Her skin is warm and dry, at odds with the chilled wind buffeting at me.

Not a single part of me wants to release her hand.

I tug her to her feet, fast enough to surprise her, and reel her in. Until we're face-to-face.

Up close, I can make out every single freckle smattered across her cheeks and nose. Her warm brown eyes bore into mine, widening just a smidge.

"I'm looking forward to this," I say, even though I shouldn't.

We're so close, my lips barely brush hers when I speak. Close enough to be a kiss, but... not. So instead, I bring her hand up between us and press my lips to her knuckles, and the redness that blooms on her cheeks is so worth the reaming I'm about to get from my coach.

———

Three hours later, I walk into the familiar pub. It's got a good selection of food, plus cheap margaritas on Thursdays. And, as a bonus, they rarely check IDs. They won't do anything crazy, like serve someone who could pass for a high schooler.

But everyone else? Free passes, for the most part.

I find Briar already at a booth in the back and slide in across from her.

"Briar," I greet her. My gaze roves over her.

She's changed since earlier. Or maybe I just didn't notice what was under her black jacket. Her black sweater—*not sure this girl ever wears color*—dips into a low V-neck, finally giving me a peek at her cleavage. Her long, dark hair is loose around her shoulders. It has a bit of a wave to it, and even as I watch, she runs her fingers through it.

The sweater seems soft, sure, but her hair looks grab-able.

Nothing better to tug on during sex, directing her head back so I can kiss her as I fuck her from behind…

"Cassius," she replies.

I choke. The sex thoughts vanish. "Don't call me that."

"Shouldn't your girlfriend call you by your first name?" She puts one elbow on the table and rests her chin on her fist. "I thought that was the kind of intimacy we were going for."

"Everyone calls me Thorne," I say, dismissing it without consideration. I don't even know how she discovered my first name, but I think that her throwing around *Cassius* is an automatic flag on the field.

That's why we're here. To set some *ground rules*.

The texts I had waiting on my phone when Coach finally released us—yeah, I was right, we had to do some extra conditioning sprints because of my *lack of focus*—made me smile.

Then frown.

First, a waving emoji followed by the frowning cat. Fitting.

Then, a request to meet up for said *rules*.

She's right, though. They'll keep us straight when all else fails.

"Cassius Remington Thorne the Third," she says under her breath. She leans back and crosses her arms, a smirk gracing her lips. "It has a certain *rich* ring to it."

I scowl. "Stop."

"What?"

"You wanted ground rules? That's the first one. Don't insinuate that you're interested in my money, and definitely don't use my first name in public."

Briar raises an eyebrow. "What if I am interested in your money? What if you picked a gold digger?"

I stare at her.

Truth? It's uncomfortably close to all the other girls my parents have set up with me. They come from money, so they're not wide-eyed about the size of the trust fund, or my future inheritance, but they have expectations.

That, ultimately, is probably worse.

But it's a sore subject all the way around. Most of the school had heard of my last name before I even started playing football here. Money means power, and power is eye-catching. My family has wielded power like that for over a century.

There's a very real possibility that Briar accepted my proposal because of that, and it sits uncomfortably on my shoulders. I didn't think that of her.

Should I have?

"Fine," she relents. "No talk of your parents' money. I'm assuming that also relates back to some Daddy issues?"

My mouth opens and closes, but I've got nothing to say to that.

Our waitress appears, just in time, and takes our order. Briar gets water and a lemonade. I get the same, plus a basket of fries and boneless wings. My stomach growls at the thought of food. And, under normal circumstances, I'd probably have ordered a beer.

But this isn't a date. It's more like a business meeting.

As soon as the waitress is gone, Briar bulldozes ahead with, "*My* first rule is that there's no intimacy."

"Do you mean sex?" I run my thumb under my lip.

She nods once, tightly. "No undressing or under-the-clothing touches."

"Well, duh." My stomach knots. "This is just for show, grumpy cat. I don't really want to fuck in public, so…"

"Great."

"But we do have to have *public* displays of affection," I continue. "Hand-holding. Kissing. My arm around your shoulders. I know smiling isn't your strong suit, but you have to seem happy to see me."

Her throat works. "Kissing?"

Oh, *interesting*. I lean forward. "What, you afraid of a little mouth-to-mouth action?"

"No." The lie comes out too fast.

It's just too unbelievable.

"There's nothing wrong with kissing." I smirk. "I'm quite good at it, if that's what you're worried about."

"I'm not."

"So practicing goes out the window," I muse. "If there's no intimacy in private."

I imagine pressing her up against a wall and getting in real close. I bet her breath would hitch, and her eyes would widen… her pupils would dilate.

"What about the physical therapy help?" She clears her throat.

"Right." I nod to myself. That was part of my pitch, wasn't it? Help her out with the knee. "We don't want to overdo it. And, frankly, my schedule is shit during the season. Three times a week should be good to ease into it."

"I don't want to ease into it."

I shake my head, trying to suppress my smile. I was the exact same way—not that I'd tell her that. The pressure to get better, to fix what was hurting, was all self-driven.

"Three days a week," I reply, more firm. "After my football practices, unless you have something else going on in the evenings? Any late classes?"

She shakes her head.

"What else, then?"

"My two best friends know." She gives me a *look*. "Lydia and Marley. The ones I was sitting with. They know this isn't real."

My chest tightens. "Spilling our secret already?"

"I—" She glances away. "They're a big reason I'm even here right now."

"That's quite existential of you."

Briar frowns and tucks her hair behind her ear. "They're the only ones who can know. I trust them, they're not going to say anything."

I hum. "My best friend, too. Rhys."

"Fine."

I relax.

The waitress delivers the food and drinks all at once. Hey, I never said this was a five-star restaurant or anything. She sets down straws and silverware rolled in paper napkins and disappears without a word.

I pop a fry in my mouth and spear a wing. "Help yourself."

She does, carefully unrolling the silverware and putting the napkin on her lap. She loads her plate with chicken and douses it in ranch dressing.

I press my lips together.

"What?" She glares at me.

"I'm more of a less-is-more person," I admit. "But only when it comes to condiments."

She rolls her eyes. "Lame."

We eat in silence for a minute. There's something else I need to tell her, something that occurred to me on the walk to meet Briar.

And I already know it isn't going to end well.

"My parents." I set down my knife and fork.

This, by the way, is why I like *boneless* wings. There's not such a pressure to be a barbarian and eat with your hands. A reduced chance of buffalo sauce getting smeared across my lips and cheeks, or God forbid, my fingers or chin. It feels civilized.

"What about your parents?"

"You'll probably meet them." I focus on my food. Exhaustion tugs at me suddenly, and all I want is to go home and crawl into bed. "And they can be intense, is all."

And judgmental.

Mainly judgmental—especially about how a girl appears.

But I can't seem to spit out those words, so I leave it at that. There will be time for some sort of makeover at a later date. They like coming to home games, and we're scheduled to be away for the next two. It would be easy enough to coordinate Briar's movements and theirs so that they don't meet until I'm ready.

Or until Briar's ready.

Or… until Briar's wardrobe is ready.

I try not to wince, because what had occurred to me earlier? A shopping spree—for her. To buy her clothes that my parents won't immediately flag as tacky or cheap…

Not that Briar is either of those things.

In fact, I like her all-black ensemble. It shows commitment.

"Hey." Briar taps the back of my hand. One finger against my skin. "I can handle intense, okay? Don't worry about it."

I force a smile and try to believe her.

CHAPTER 15
BRIAR

CASSIUS

You free tonight?

Some guys from the team and their girls are going to grab pizza after practice.

I was thinking it could be a good first outing. We can discuss, of course, but we've got to jump in the deep end sometime.

ME

We're nowhere near ready for the deep end.

Pizza and what? Hand-holding?

Sure.

No kissing.

Roger that, grumpy cat.

I CLICK my phone off and sigh.

The mirror doesn't play tricks. This is as good as it gets. It's been a long time since I've been concerned with how I dress. Even before the accident, I didn't let a date or some guy influence how I wanted to dress, yet my stomach fills with dread the longer I stare at myself.

Black jeans, black oversized sweater, and my black boots. The ones with the loose laces and the orthotics from my physical therapist to help *correct* my limp.

"You look fine."

I eye Lydia leaning against the doorway and turn with a huff. "Good, because I'm not changing."

I don't even know why I'm so concerned over this. It's not like I'm trying to *impress* Thorne.

"I will say…" Lydia enters my room and sits on my bed, which isn't the norm for us. However, since I let her in on my plan to fake date Thorne, we've been much friendlier than usual. My usual grumpiness has gone down a notch. "You are *not* Thorne's type."

I look at the mirror again. "What is his type?"

"Rich girls," she says. "You know, the type with bleach-blonde hair, fake boobs at the age of nineteen, caked-on makeup, and high-end clothes with matching purses."

A choked laugh falls from my mouth. I spin with my eyebrows raised high. "Well he's going to be disappointed to see me then."

Lydia playfully rolls her eyes. "Yeah right, Hart. You're hot and you have this black cat vibe about you. I think you excite Thorne. Whether this is a fake relationship or not."

Yeah, okay.

"Do you want me to go with you?" she asks, softening her voice.

I sigh. "No, it's fine. I have to be a big girl, I guess."

She laughs.

"I'll bring you back some pizza."

"Extra cheese, please."

I shoot her a thumbs-up, grab my bag, and head straight for doom.

———

The pizzeria is packed.

I've been here a few times with Ben, but everything from *before* seems so distant. Almost as if it was another life. The girl I used to be is a fuzzy dream that lies on the outer parts of my brain.

In fact, I completely forget how to act.

What do I do?

My heart skips every other beat as I stand near the door. I'm immobile.

"Briar?"

Oh, for fuck's sake. Really?

I move slightly, and there stands my ex-boyfriend. As if the night couldn't get worse.

I shift in my boots with anger rushing to the soles of my feet. I wonder what he'd do if I just pretended he didn't exist?

He clears his throat. *Fine.*

"Ben." His name comes out of my mouth like boredom.

I look for Thorne. He's my boyfriend. Isn't this the part where he swoops in and saves the day?

"How have you been?"

Out of the corner of my eye, I give him a once-over.

I should ask him how he's been since sticking his tongue down another girl's throat while he was still my boyfriend— just a few weeks after my accident—but instead, I mumble, "Better without you."

"What was that?" he asks, leaning in close.

I back away and hit something hard from behind. Goosebumps cover me from head to toe.

It doesn't take me long to notice that there's a lot of people here.

Every booth is filled.

There are two exits, and I mentally track the path I'd take if there were a fire.

God. Get it together, Briar.

I should be admitted, truly.

"Hey." A sturdy hand collides with mine, and a rush of warmth spreads over my goosebumps. My fingers intertwine against his like they knew it was Thorne before my head did.

"Hi," I whisper.

My breathing is shaky, and he must notice because his attention immediately falls to my mouth.

"How do you two know each other?" Ben questions, still standing entirely too close.

Ready or not, here we come.

Having Thorne's hand in mine, backing me, gives me the strength that I need to get my shit together.

"We're seeing each other." I face Ben again and soak in the shock on his face.

His eyebrows shoot to the sky, and confusion flickers over his features. He swings his gaze to his teammate in betrayal.

"You're dating Briar?" he asks. "Since when?"

Thorne narrows his gaze "Since when do you care who I'm seeing, Patterson?"

I squeeze Thorne's hand, and he quickly glances down at me. He scours my expression, then returns to glare at his teammate.

It doesn't take long for Ben to grumble and walk away.

Or should I say *stalk* away.

Thorne nudges his elbow against my arm. "You want to explain that?"

He smells good. I gulp and ignore the tug in my lower belly.

"Ben is my ex."

"Oh." He seems surprised. His gaze moves across the restaurant and lands on Ben.

Everyone is staring at us.

Ben included.

"This is awkward," I admit.

I try to pull my hand away, but Thorne's fingers tighten against mine.

"What is? The way your ex, who just so happens to be my teammate, is staring at me like I've just stolen something that's his?" He chuckles.

If I'm not mistaken, Thorne rather enjoys this.

I, however, do not.

I hiss between my teeth. "I am *not* his."

Thorne hums. "I suspect some animosity, grumpy cat. Please do tell. Who broke up with who?"

My cheeks warm at the thought of seeing Ben's mouth on someone else's when we were still very much together.

"I don't like the look on your face," Thorne notes.

"And I don't like how everyone in this pizzeria is staring at us." I lower my voice and angle myself toward him. "Do something."

A cheeky grin appears. "Like what? Kiss you?"

I gasp. "What? No! I said no kissing."

He chuckles quietly. "I was kidding. Though, it'd be fun to see the anger on Ben's face afterward."

True, but *no*.

"Should we sit or something?" I ask, desperate to get out of the spotlight.

Thorne, who suddenly seems nervous, nods curtly. "I guess."

"What do you mean, you guess?" I whisper angrily. "You're the one who is supposed to know what to do."

Thorne begins tugging me toward a back booth full of football players and their girlfriends. I recognize a few of the girls but I'm not close enough to any of them to know their names.

"Who said I know what to do?" he asks. "You're the one who's been in a relationship before."

From the outside, it probably seems like we're just talking

quietly to each other. But really, we're arguing like an old married couple.

"So have you!" I argue.

Thorne stops me before getting any closer to his table full of friends. I zero in on the crease of confusion between his eyebrows.

"Says who?"

I pause and try to think. Surely he's had a girlfriend before, right? I search his face, and there isn't a single flaw on there. All I see is hesitation and unease.

"I've never had a steady girlfriend." He glances away, like he's embarrassed. "And I certainly do not consider the girls my parents force me to date *girlfriends*."

Thorne continues pulling me toward the table. He's walking slow enough that I don't have to half drag my injured knee with me. I don't know if he's doing that to save me the trouble, or if he's doing it to save himself the trouble of having a gimp for a girlfriend.

Before we sit and likely make fools of ourselves, causing everyone to question our relationship, he leans in close. "I don't consider the girls I fuck my girlfriends either. So, you're my first, grumpy cat."

A flush works its way up my neck and stays long after his warm breath disappears from my skin.

I hope he thinks I'm flustered because I'm being introduced to his group of friends as his girlfriend and not because I'm affected by the thought of him *fucking* someone.

Unfortunately, I think it's a little of both.

CHAPTER 16
THORNE

BEN FUCKING PATTERSON.

He's not at our table, luckily, but he is close. And he keeps glancing over like he can't put two and two together. It's not so unbelievable that Briar and I are together, is it? She's gorgeous. Yes, she scowls or frowns more than she smiles, and she only wears black, and she seems like she's one snide comment away from ripping your face off…

But she's soft, too. Her hand is still caught in mine, and neither of us have made any move to pull away. She's nervous—but what surprised me was *my* nerves.

It's true: I haven't had a real girlfriend. Never wanted—or needed—one. Until now anyway. Now… I squeeze her fingers, and she squeezes back almost instantly.

The booth we're in is comprised mostly of my offensive end. There's Rhys, obviously, the greatest running back at Shadow Valley. My center, Aaron Jacobs, and his long-time girlfriend. Her name escapes me… I kind of just assumed, when they got together freshman year, that they'd be a fling.

And then they just stayed together, and I couldn't very well admit that I never bothered to learn her name. That kind of makes me seem like an asshole, and I really try not to be.

Names are just not my strong suit.

Patterson is a corner like Stephen McDowell. They're best friends, too. They even kind of resemble each other, in a weird way. You know how people look like their dogs?

That's Ben Patterson and Stephen McDowell.

Ben's the dog in that scenario. Just, you know, for the record.

"How did you two meet?" Aaron's girlfriend asked. "We didn't know you were dating anyone, Thorne."

Shit, that's probably something we should've talked about. Briar and me, I mean. We didn't really talk about what we were going to *say* to people. The lack of experience on my end, about how to navigate this precise situation, makes my heart pound.

I'd rather be staring down a monster than try to figure out the right thing to say in this situation.

"He picked me up off the sidewalk," Briar says.

Her voice cuts through my anxieties.

"Some jerk passed me, and his backpack was open, spilling baseballs all over the place."

I nod sharply. "Anyone would've fallen. It was a hazard."

"You were sure-footed." She turns her gaze on me, somehow softening her eyes—hell, her whole expression seems gentle. "I think I nearly bit your head off when you tried to help me."

I grin. "I was gonna leave that part of the story out."

"It was part of my irresistible charm."

She's right.

"Anyway," She breaks our staring contest and focuses back on Aaron's girl. "He walked me to campus and got my number, and the rest is history."

"Quiet history," one of my receivers says. "Thorne hasn't mentioned you."

"That's on me, too," Briar blurts out. "I didn't want to... I mean..."

"It's a lot of pressure," I cut in. "Dating me can't be easy. We wanted to be sure of where this is going before we made it public."

Rhys nods along, catching my eye. He doesn't do anything to give me away, but he does seem to be enjoying this.

The waitress arrives with pitchers of beer for the table, and I pour one for Briar, then myself. I gulp down half of it at once and lean back in the U-shaped booth. She's on the inside, next to the latest girl my tight end is dating.

I hook my arm around her shoulders.

We said hand-holding and shit. This is the *and shit*.

She doesn't even stiffen, just sinks farther into me, and the conversation moves on from us to something else. I don't really know. It slips in one ear and out the other.

"What kind of pizza do you like?" I ask in her ear.

She tilts her head back to meet my gaze. "Hawaiian."

Pineapple and ham?

Gross.

"Pepperoni and mushroom for me," I tell her, even though she didn't ask. "Pineapple should be found nowhere near cheese."

She snickers. "Uh-huh. Hater."

"Maybe."

"Have you ever actually tried it?"

The waitress arrives and takes our order—and before I can order, Briar does for me.

Us.

"Half Hawaiian, half pepperoni and mushroom, please. Oh, and can I get a personal one with extra cheese to go?" At my questioning gaze, she explains, "My roommate wanted one."

I dip my chin. "That was nice of you, grumpy cat. Maybe you're full of rainbows and sunshine on the inside."

"I thought *you* were the sunshine guy." Her gaze drops to my lips. "And here you are, quiet… almost sullen."

She's got a point.

"How would you be acting if I wasn't here?"

Louder.

More sure of myself, absolutely. It's a little bit funny how withdrawn I feel—and just because of this unstable footing. I lied to my parents, told them I had a girlfriend, and now, by simple agreement, I have one.

A fake one, but still.

And now we have to be convincing, when I've never fucking done this. Never fumbled my way through a *real* date, the kind that included holding hands and walking the girl to her car, going in for a first kiss.

My heart lurches at the thought.

Do I get to do that with Briar?

This agreement has put our relationship on a fast track. We're supposed to be beyond *that*. The awkwardness.

She's right.

While she's had no trouble blending in with my friends, making conversation, leaning into my side, I am stiff.

I nod, both to her and myself, and readjust.

I tune back in to the story Rhys is telling and casually reach for my beer.

Briar threads her fingers through mine, the hand that hangs off her shoulder. Her nails are even painted black, but her skin is warm.

"…and I kid you not, that goose had it out for us." Rhys leans back. "It was fucking *hissing*."

I remember that. I jump in with, "I've never seen Rhys move so fucking fast. You would've thought he was being chased by the whole Crown Point football team."

Laughter.

"*Hissing*," Rhys repeats. "And what did you do while I was running for my life?"

"Recording it." I chuckle. "That is blackmail *gold*, I'm telling you."

"This is why you don't mess with Canadian geese," Aaron mutters. "They're vicious."

"Did you know they have teeth?"

I groan and shake my finger at Rhys. "Don't start."

"Thorne. They. Are. Monsters!"

"They actually don't have teeth," Briar interjects. "Their bills just have serrated ridges."

I throw my head back and die laughing. She doesn't laugh as much, or talk as loud. But the girl knows how to work some comedic timing.

When the pitchers of beer have run out, and our pizzas are gone—minus the extra cheese one in a box in front of Briar—we finally call it quits.

"Are we splitting the bill?" Briar asks.

Rhys quirks his brow. "You guys need to get out more."

I glare at him.

He holds up his hands. "I mean, you know, get out of the house, sex maniacs. A relationship can't be built on fucking."

"*Rhys.*"

He laughs. "Right. What I mean is—"

"I paid," I interrupt. There's no way in hell I was letting Briar try to cover her portion of the tab. Not when my credit card is linked to my parents' accounts, and they have so much money they could lose most of it and still not notice. So what if I pay for my friends' dinners, too? I know that's not the reason they hang out with me, which is why I do it. "We're good to go. Let me give you a ride home."

I take her box and slide out of the booth. The defensive end, at their table, is mostly gone. Ben fucking Patterson and Stephen are still there, though, and the former lifts his head to glower at me. I didn't pay *their* tab. Nothing against Stephen, but I'm not covering Patterson's food ever again.

I curl my arm back around Briar's shoulders and guide her out. I keep my pace slow, aware that her knee might be aching. Mine always twinged after sitting for too long, and I don't know if she was able to stretch it out under the table.

She met me here, but I would hazard a guess she walked. So she doesn't put up much protest—okay, no protest—when I show her to my car.

I open the passenger door for her, and she lowers herself in. Then reaches for the handle, but my grip on the top edge tightens.

I lean down into the opening. "I had fun tonight."

"Are you okay to drive?" Her gaze roves my face.

"Yes."

"Okay."

"Briar?"

She blinks. Big, brown eyes. The moonlight comes in through the windshield, illuminating half of her face. Full lips. No scowl.

"Cassius?"

I sigh. "I told you—"

"The agreement was to not insinuate I was after your money," she whispers. "And there's no one around to put on a show for, is there?"

"There's always an audience." I sway closer to her face. "That's the catch, kitten."

"Kitten." Her nose wrinkles.

"Yeah. Because when you look at me like you are… you're not so much a grumpy cat as you are a kitten. Sweet. Maybe a little spicy." I shrug. "Time will tell."

"I'm losing track of all the nicknames you have for me. And I've got…"

"My real name." I step back, slowly straightening. She doesn't say it the way my parents do, with disdain. She says it like it's the one version of me she wants to know. And I can't even argue against it. No one's seen that side of me in a really long time. "Okay. Keep it, then."

"I will," she whispers, just as I close the door.

At least, that's what I think she says.

Maybe it's just wishful thinking to believe she'll hold on to something as important as that.

CHAPTER 17
BRIAR

THERE'S ALWAYS AN AUDIENCE.

Thorne is right. Now that word has spread that we're dating, I'm catching stares everywhere. It was never like this with Ben. I don't know if that's because Ben isn't as well known as Thorne or if it's because I'm the complete opposite of who Thorne *should* be with.

At least according to what Lydia said.

I won't try and act like I know every last thing there is to know about my fake boyfriend but I think there's a lot more to him than people realize. He isn't a surface level kind of guy, and I can't see him being fulfilled with a rich girl who wears more makeup than a twelve-year-old in Sephora.

Chatter floats down the hallway from the locker room, and my pulse matches the throbbing in my knee. Tonight is my first session with Thorne. I wasn't expecting there to be people around this late at night, but again, *there's always an audience.*

I stop outside of the weight room door, unsure if I should just walk in or if I should wait for him. Standing in a darkened hallway, all alone, puts me on edge, though.

I've been a little more skeptical of the football team since having that foreboding feeling the other night. I've been watching them more, too.

With and without Thorne near.

"Yo, Thorne!" I jump at the sound of Rhys's voice echoing throughout the hall. "Your... *girlfriend* is here."

Rhys winks on his way past. I flip him off because at least I can be myself with him and not pretend to be infatuated with his best friend.

I rest along the door, eager to get started. Footsteps catch my attention. I turn only to be hit with disappointment.

Not that I'm excited to see Thorne or anything.

But I am most definitely not excited to see my ex walking down the hall with his sights set on me.

"Hey, Bry," he says, stopping in front of me.

I scowl at the use of my old nickname. No one but my parents call me Bry, which is where he got it from.

"Hello." My greeting comes out clipped. It's just as harsh as I wanted.

Ben winces. He seems uncomfortable at best; shuffling on his feet, readjusting his bag over his shoulder, running his hand through his damp hair. "So, how have you been? You didn't answer me the other night."

I laugh. It's sarcastic, and he knows it.

"Are you serious?"

He glances away. "Just because we're not together anymore doesn't mean I don't care about you."

I push away from the door, ignoring the twinge in my knee. Ben stares at me from his tall frame. I peer into his eyes and feel *nothing*. Except some animosity, like Thorne had noted the other night.

I guess he's already able to read me.

"You don't get to say things like that, Ben. Not when you made it very clear you didn't care about me when we were together." I roll my lips. "And please don't get this conversation confused with thinking I care about you. In case you haven't heard, I've moved on."

Sort of.

I have gotten over him, but it doesn't really have much to do with Thorne.

"Hey, baby."

Both Ben and I turn to see Thorne heading in our direction. I make no effort to step away from my ex, but as soon as he catches his quarterback glaring at him, he quietly growls and steps backward.

"Everything okay?" Thorne steps beside me. His arm slips around my waist, and suddenly, the conversation with Ben is a little less irritating.

Who knew having a fake boyfriend would give me confidence?

The longer the three of us are in the hallway, the tighter the air becomes. A few football players walk past, eyeing us suspiciously. At the last second, I pull my attention from the silent sparring match between my fake boyfriend and ex and catch the back side of the group of guys.

My eyes are drawn to the one farthest away. He's sporting a black hoodie, and all I can focus on is the hood tugged up over his head.

A darkness works over me, and I lean closer to Thorne.

His fingers dig into my hip, and it isn't until I feel the faintest touch of his skin against mine that I'm brought back to reality.

"I'll just catch you later," Ben says to me while glaring at Thorne.

Thorne replies with a dark chuckle.

He waits until the hallway is empty before turning to glance at me. "You need to tell me why you two broke up, kitten."

I roll my eyes and shove his hand off my hip.

No one is around, so there's no need for him to be touching me.

I stalk into the weight room, eager to work my body. It's a good distraction—just like hockey used to be, and probably like football is for Thorne.

I drop my bag by the nearest wall and immediately go for the stationary bike in the corner.

Thorne walks in a few seconds after me and chuckles when he finds me already heading in that direction.

"You know," He follows after me. "Just because you walk away doesn't mean the conversation is over, right?"

I shrug. "It's over if I want it to be over."

He laughs, and my breath hitches.

It's a nice laugh. A genuine one. It's the type of laugh that has my lips begging to curve.

"I see that I'm dealing with *grumpy cat* this evening instead of my adorable little kitten."

I gag, and his smile widens.

My hands fall to the handles of the bike, and I begin working my knee beyond what it's capable of. I hide my winces from Thorne and bite the inside of my cheek. The taste of metal fills my mouth.

"No."

I snap my attention to him. He's standing with his arms crossed, mere feet from me.

"What?" I act innocent.

He shakes his head and sighs exasperatedly. "Have you even stretched?"

My shoulders slump. Of course I haven't.

"Up," he demands.

The defiant streak that runs wildly inside me wants to refuse. Except Thorne doesn't give me a chance to. He unplugs the bike and holds the cord hostage as he stares at me in an authoritative way.

It's sort of... *hot*. A tendril of his dark, messy hair falls over his forehead, and he quickly tips his sharp jaw, flinging it out of his face. "If you want to get back to one hundred percent, you're going to listen to me."

Heat falls to the pit of my belly with his command.

He didn't ask, and I have a feeling he won't put up with my refusal. This is what I signed up for, right? I just didn't expect him to be so... bossy about it.

I concede and slowly swing my legs to the side of the machine, all while keeping a hold of his stern gaze. It isn't until I'm standing right in front of him that I bend down and touch my toes. If I wanted to be a brat, I'd turn around and put my ass on full display. Maybe it'd set him back a couple of notches.

After a few more stretches, I start back toward the bike, but Thorne clears his throat, stopping me in place.

I spin slowly. His eyebrow hitches, and he moves his finger, wagging it toward him.

"Come here."

My hands fall to my hips. "Why?"

He smirks. "Because you're not done stretching, kitten."

I narrow my gaze and slowly force myself over to him. "If you keep calling me that, I may start meowing."

His hot chuckle distracts me long enough for him to place his hand behind my thigh. His other hand falls to my hip, and before I know it, my bad leg is hanging over his shoulder.

I grunt. "Ow."

The stretch in my thigh is deliciously painful. I gasp when he pushes more while still keeping me steady with his other hand.

"I changed my mind," I say through clenched teeth. "I'm not going to start meowing. I'm going to start *clawing*."

He presses harder, and I glare at him.

"Watch it, kitten. I may like that."

The tug in my stomach shouldn't catch me by surprise, but it does. I don't know if it's from our close proximity, or how I feel safe with his hand wrapped around my waist, or because I haven't been touched since before the accident, but I am learning that I am *very* sensitive when it comes to him.

"Can you let me go now?" I ask through a wince.

Thorne clicks his tongue. "I'll let go as soon as you tell me why you and Patterson broke up."

My spine straightens. "No."

He scoffs. "Suit yourself."

Suddenly, Thorne is staring at my mouth while slowly dragging his hand from the back of my thigh to my calf. Goosebumps trail behind his touch, and even through my leggings, I feel the warmth he leaves behind.

Is he doing this on purpose?

With his other hand splayed on my lower back, he brings me closer to him, stretching my leg even more.

"I'm stretched," I argue.

"I know," he replies. "But you still haven't told me about you and Patterson."

Anger sweeps throughout me, and by the amusement on Thorne's face, he's enjoying it.

"Ah, look at that furrowed brow." He shakes his head. "Someone is prickly at the thought of her ex."

"Of course I am!" I snap.

His eyebrows rise.

I almost lose my train of thought when Thorne massages my calf. His fingers knead the muscle slowly and tediously. It feels good, even with the stretching in my thigh.

"Tell me and I'll let your leg go."

I sigh loudly. My balance is starting to waver, and I'm not sure which of us is more stubborn. In an attempt not to fall, I end up placing my hands on Thorne's shoulders. My fingers dig into his firm muscles, and the longer he massages my leg with his body heat surrounding me, the more I want to give in to him.

"Come on, kitten," he whispers. "Just tell me."

I want to bare my teeth at him.

Or scrape my nails into his shoulders to claw him like I'd threatened.

But instead, I do the complete opposite.

Our eyes lock, and the words slip from my lips in a weak whisper. "He cheated on me a couple of weeks after the fire."

Thorne's fingers stop moving. His jaw flexes.

I glance away because I don't want to see the pity on his face after I tell him the rest. "I overheard him telling his friends that he didn't want to wait until I wasn't *charred* anymore to fuck someone. So I had Lydia take me to one of the parties I knew he was at and I found him with another girl."

The faintest growl rumbles out of Thorne's chest. His brow is curved with anger. A heavy, hot breath escapes him as he places my leg on the floor. He keeps his other hand pressed against my lower back and gazes into my eyes. I brace myself for the apology on Ben's behalf or some sort of sympathetic quote, but to my surprise he flicks his chin at the bike.

"Three minutes."

We break apart, and cool air comes rushing in between us. I quickly make my way over to the machine, because the farther apart I am from him at the moment, the better.

CHAPTER 18
THORNE

RHYS FOLLOWS me through the wide fourth-floor hallway of the Administration building. He keeps opening and closing his mouth like he's going to say something, but so far, no sound has actually made it past his lips.

He probably wants to tell me that of all the girls in the world, and of all the harebrained ideas, mine is the worst.

The girl and the idea.

I just need to keep reminding myself that none of this is real. Briar and I are faking a relationship—of which we haven't had much public-facing time yet, minus the pizzeria —and that means faking glances and pointed looks and touches. It means not *really* reacting when her hand brushes mine or my fingers wrap around her calf to help her stretch in the weight room…

Even when my whole body buzzes at the contact.

I hate it.

"This is a bad idea," Rhys finally mutters. "Are you sure about this?"

I roll my eyes, but I'm far enough ahead that he doesn't catch it. Of course I'm *sure*, but my plan is flimsy at best.

What started as a simple inquiry with Aaron Westin, my

center, turned into a full-blown online investigation. I didn't think I'd be sitting with my coffee at the kitchen table this morning, leaning over his shoulder while he showed me all the drama on social media that I apparently missed.

There was a lot of chatter about Briar a few months ago…

My stomach twists.

I didn't want to read it, but Aaron looked me dead in the eye and said I should know what I was getting into with her. He backtracked, saying she was lovely at dinner the other night, but people are going to *talk*.

What the fuck do I care?

I'm not saying my reputation is untouchable. No—judging by first, the love Briar garnered on the hockey team, then the way the court of public opinion reversed on her after her injury… no one is untouchable.

I just don't want *public opinion* to dictate who I date.

Fake date.

What-fucking-ever.

It's fake, yes, but the hurt in her eyes when she admitted that my teammate cheated on her?

That was as real as it gets.

"Did she ask you to do this?" Rhys jogs a few steps to catch up and grabs my arm. "Don't fall for her manip-ulation—"

"Do not." I shake off his grip. "She wouldn't ask this of me."

And I'm doing it anyway.

I reach the right door and stop dead. Through the narrow vertical window in the wooden door, I can see the students in class.

There's Briar, her head down over a notebook, her pen scribbling furiously. And farther back, her ex.

The cheating snake.

The time ticks closer to the top of the hour, and finally, the professor releases his class. Briar doesn't rise when the rest of the class does. Everyone seems to scramble to put their laptops back in their bags, to pack up and hurry out, while she moves much more methodically.

"Grab him when he leaves," I say over my shoulder.

Rhys groans.

I cut through the tide of students exiting and slip up the aisle. I lost sight of Ben, but he was one of the ones packing in a hurry. Somehow, sticking around to be the last one out of the room doesn't seem like something he'd have the patience for.

Did he rush her after the accident, too?

Or did he just stop giving a fuck entirely and leave without her?

I force my jaw to unclench and drop into the chair in front of her.

She jerks her head up, her eyes narrowing—then, shockingly, softening.

"Hey, kitten." I smirk. "How was class?"

"Fine…" She glances around. "What are you doing?"

"I figured I'd walk you to your next one. Or lunch, if you're free." Because I don't have her class schedule memorized… *yet*.

She nods once. "I don't have class until three."

I can't stop the bright smile that takes over my face. I grab her bag and sling it over my shoulder, then offer my hand.

She takes it, and I gently help her to her feet. And I keep the hand, just because she lets me.

That lasts until we get into the hallway, anyway, and come face-to-face with Ben and Rhys. While my best friend isn't *holding* Ben, in the physical way that I was hoping for, he does seem to be doing his best effort to keep him distracted.

"Patterson." My voice comes out like a whip, and Briar immediately stops in her tracks.

My teammate glances from Rhys to me, and his expression flattens.

"Show him what we found," I tell Rhys.

"What are you doing?"

"Making a point." I squeeze her hand.

Rhys shows Ben his phone, and he goes still.

"That goes public if you so much as *peek* at Briar again," I tell him. "No glances. No stopping to check up on her. Those days were over the moment you fucked her over."

He looks from me to Rhys, then back again. "What is this, some sort of shakedown? You want to blackmail me?"

I release Briar's hand and get up in his space. It takes a lot of effort to leave my hands by my sides instead of balling my fists in his shirt. Slamming him into the wall would probably feel real fucking good.

"What do you think Coach would say about your flagrant cheating? We have a code of ethics, Patterson. And honestly, I'd love nothing more than to see you kicked off the team. But since you're good at your fucking job, you get one more chance." I stare him down.

Finally, his gaze shifts away. "Okay, fucking hell. Fine."

I smile.

We watch him walk away, and I turn back to Briar, expecting her to be furious with me.

Because I didn't do it *for* her—I did it because of her. Because of the gleam in her eye. Although I highly doubt she'll see it that way.

Instead, she seems... *gleeful*. "What the hell did you find to make him shake in his boots like that?"

I lift one shoulder. "Just proof that he pays someone to write his papers. His GPA sucked freshman year, but it got better. Now we know why."

"Holy shit. Do you think he'll leave me alone?" She bounces on her heels, then winces. Then smiles.

A true smile.

"I think he likes football enough to not test me."

I hold out my hand again. She takes it, and I reel her in.

There are plenty of people around. Plenty of witnesses.

It seems only right to kiss her in this moment.

Our lips touch. Brief but *holy shit*. She pulls away too fast, and I mask my frown.

"Sorry," she murmurs. "I wasn't expecting that."

My dick twitches in my pants. "We're going to have to work on that. After all, practice makes perfect."

CHAPTER 19
BRIAR

"OW." I clench my jaw and raise my leg again.

"One more."

I grumble under my breath. I do as Thorne says, though, because he *does* know what he's doing when it comes to strength training. My leg thuds to the mat like it weighs three hundred pounds when I'm finished with my final rep.

He laughs and takes a seat beside me. Our legs brush against each other. I can hardly feel it through my leggings, but heat still moves through me.

It's because he kissed me.

It was the briefest of brief kisses. Like, a split second. I pulled away because I was surprised over the fact that he went straight in *and* because of the zip of butterflies that came with it.

Even thinking about it causes my head to spin.

It left me feeling… curious.

"Has Ben cornered you or anything since I threatened him?"

My heart skips a beat with the thought. *Cornered.* Trapped. They're too similar in meaning, and it forces me to think of a certain *someone*.

"He has, hasn't he?" Thorne's lips flatten. "I'll take care of it."

"No." I'm quick to reach my hand out and place it over his. I think he's just as surprised as I am because we both snap our attention to it. "He hasn't talked to me since."

Thorne searches my face. His golden eyes narrow, like he thinks I'm lying.

I give his hand a squeeze. "I'm telling the truth. I may be a grumpy cat as you like to say, but I'm not a liar."

His lip lifts into a smile, and I'm pretty sure I feel a few butterflies flying around my stomach—which I will continue to ignore.

"You don't lie, huh?"

I jerk my hand back because I'm not sure I like the way his honey-colored eyes darken with something enticing. "No."

Thorne leans backward onto his hands, appearing cool, calm, and collected. He has this nonchalant attitude that I crave to have. Instead, I'm "prickly" and "uptight", according to those around me.

"Okay, tell me this." Thorne turns and gives me no room to look away. "What did you think of me kissing you the other day?"

My nostrils flare.

Shit.

Heat burns my cheeks, and I'm sweating even more than before. Thorne shakes his hair off his forehead and waits for my answer.

I shrug. "It was fine."

"Then why'd you pull away so quickly?" he asks, smirking.

Because.

"I told you." I climb to my feet and start packing my things. "I was surprised."

"Surprised?"

My breath hitches when I realize he's also climbed to his

feet. I move quickly and see that he's standing no more than a foot away from me.

I nod. "Well, yeah. How was I supposed to know you'd lean in and kiss me in front of everyone?" My words come out too fast. I'm nervous.

He thinks I'm amusing. A full smile slides onto his face, and I kind of want to slap him.

"What?" I roll my eyes and put my back to him. I start pulling things out of my bag again, only to shove them back inside. I don't even know what I'm doing other than attempting to distract myself from my nerves.

Thorne's hands land on my hips, and the room is spinning. We're face-to-face now.

I'm flush against him with my palms splayed over his chest.

"What are you doing?" I ask through ragged breaths.

He inches his chin to the door. "I saw someone walk past."

My heart beats faster. I glance toward the window in the door to see. *What if my arsonist is spying on me like I'm attempting to do to him?*

"Oh," I manage. "Are they gone?"

Thorne doesn't answer. He bounces his gaze back and forth between mine. The longer we stay like that, the harder his heart beats against my fingertips.

"Do you want me to warn you next time?"

I swallow when his attention drops to my mouth. I've kissed guys before. I don't need a warning.

Nonetheless…

"Yes," I say. "That way I can act accordingly—"

"This is your warning, kitten."

Wait. Wha—

My brain sizzles out.

My body does not.

Thorne's lips press against mine, and I fall right into his kiss. My eyes shut the moment our mouths touch, and when his hands squeeze my hips, I move even closer and let his tongue sweep inside. Every part of me that I thought was dead comes back alive, and it's burning brighter than it ever has before.

Thorne drags his hand up the side of my body, skimming over every last curve, until his fingers delve into my hair. He tips my head back, and the kiss grows hotter.

Holy shit.

A little whimper escapes, and it's enough to break me out of the trance.

I back away, and my quiet gasp spills into the open space between us.

Thorne unburies his hand from my hair while keeping a hold of my gaze. I'm too stunned to speak.

That was a *good* kiss.

Like really fucking good.

It swept me right off my feet, and now I'm left wanting more.

"There," he whispers raggedly. "Consider that practice."

I think I need more practice.

I remain quiet because I'm at a loss for words. All I can manage is a quick nod.

"You good?" he asks, smirking. "Don't tell me… that was the best kiss of your life?"

Thorne is dangerously hot. His smirk is inviting but cocky at the same time.

I try to cover my tracks. I scoff and busy myself with grabbing my bag. I peek over my shoulder at him and shrug. "It was okay."

Thorne's laugh echoes around the empty weight room. I hide my smile by keeping my back to him. My lips flatten together to keep from showing him all my cards. He reaches over my shoulder and snatches my bag from my grip but lingers for a second with his mouth hovering beside my ear.

"It's going to be awfully entertaining getting you to admit that I'm the best you've ever had."

Desire flies to the spot between my legs, and my nipples have entered the party.

Traitors.

Thorne steps away, and when I move to follow him, I swear he's carrying himself more confidently after the kiss.

I won't admit it out loud, but it's warranted.

———

My mouth still feels branded.

Like it isn't mine anymore.

Thorne's face comes into view—those golden eyes that twinkle with amusement but also have a depth to them that puts my body on high alert. His hands on my hips and the way his smooth whisper sounds in my ear. *God.*

Frustration backs my every move.

I dump my bag onto my bed and begin gathering my sweaty clothes. I gulp the rest of my water bottle and push Thorne out of my head. Lydia comes home but I keep my door shut so I can have a few minutes to get myself together before having to act like Thorne isn't taking over my mind.

Throwing my workout clothes into the bin in the corner of my room, I start clearing my bed off. I pause when I smell something... strange.

Is that gasoline?

My nose turns upward. I walk around the room sniffing the air like a dog after a bone. The closer I get to my desk, the stronger the scent is. My heartbeat pounds violently inside my ears.

I stare at a piece of notebook paper that's soggy around the edges.

It isn't mine.

I'm much too neat for something like this.

My hand is shaking. I reach for the note, and the closer I bring it to my face, the stronger the gasoline is.

What the hell?

My legs grow weak. I slip to the floor.

The note is lying in front of me. I read it until my vision blurs.

Stop looking.
Or you'll be the one soaked in gasoline.

I don't know how much time has passed, but when there's a knock on my door, I move quickly. The note is buried underneath my bed, and I climb to my feet, ignoring my sore muscles.

Lydia storms inside, all dolled up for some party, I'm sure.

"Hey—" Her smile falls. "What's wrong?"

"Huh?" Even my voice is shaky.

Shit.

"I'm fine."

Lydia cocks her perfectly arched eyebrow. Her arms cross against her low-cut shirt. "That's a lie if I've ever heard one. You look like you've seen a ghost."

I shake my head and hope it covers up the fact that my entire body is shaking. "I'm fine, really. What are you going?"

Lydia eyes me closely. "The hockey house for a party. I wanted to see if you wanted to come with."

A party right now?

I can't.

My gaze falls to the floor. I still smell gasoline.

"Sure." The word rushes from my mouth, and we both pause.

Surprise flickers over her pretty features. "That was way easier than I thought it would be." She claps her hands excitedly and walks over to my closet. Clothes fly through the air and land on my bed. "Snap, snap, Hart! Marley is waiting for us."

I fake a smile and nod.

When she leaves the room, I exhale.

The hockey house is the last place I want to go to, but it's either that or I sit in my room, obsess over the note, and become paralyzed with every noise I hear.

He knows where I live.

And that does *not* sit well with me.

CHAPTER 20
THORNE

RHYS

Get your ass to this party, Thorne. You're not gonna want to miss this.

I SCAN THE TEXT AGAIN, then shove my phone into my pocket. Rhys sent it almost an hour ago, followed by an address, and I had to work up the nerve to climb out of bed and throw clothes on.

My body hurts from a particularly grueling practice. An ice bath would probably do the trick on my sore muscles, but I just can't find it in me to do that tonight. Instead, I climb the steps of the front porch and get hit with a wave of loud, pulsing music.

I grit my teeth and continue onward. I haven't seen Briar since our workout session last night, though not for lack of trying. Today was a full schedule for me. Classes, a meeting with my academic advisor, a late team lunch, and then evening practice. I don't think I stopped moving until I pitched myself into bed... but even that was short-lived.

Once I'm *in* the house, though, my mood lightens. Some teammates bump my fist as I pass. I catch a glimpse of one of the hockey guys whose house we're in and nod a greeting. Evan Mitchell is a pretty cool dude. We only know each other in passing, though.

If half the football team wasn't here, I probably wouldn't just show up.

"What are we celebrating?" I ask one of the other hockey players.

"We won our third straight home game!"

I grin and clap him on the shoulder, then push deeper into the house.

Honestly, I have no idea what the 9-1-1 from Rhys was about, and I don't see him anywhere. Someone shoves a cup into my hand, and they yell something in my ear about my girlfriend.

Girlfriend?

Briar is here?

My head swings around, but there's no sign of her in the front rooms. Or the kitchen. Finally, in the dining room, I spot her.

Black, long-sleeved shirt—*typical*. Black jeans. Chunky jewelry.

Her hair is in a high ponytail, and a few pieces around her face have escaped the tie. She seems to be sweating slightly, because strands stick to her forehead.

She's at one end of a beer pong game, her tongue slightly poking out, an eye scrunched up. She tosses the ping-pong ball and howls when it goes into one of the cups.

Jealousy churns my stomach.

Why didn't she tell me she was going out?

We had plans earlier that she blew off. Not a huge deal, I figured time just got away from her. If there's one thing I *can't* be, it's clingy.

At this moment, though? I want to be. I want to be glued to her side.

I want to be her beer pong partner.

I want to kiss her again. Pick her up, have her wrap her legs around my hips. Press her against a wall and—

"Thorne!"

I tune back in to the present just in time for Briar to pitch herself at me. I catch her—*of course I fucking catch her*—and let her momentum swing us around. Her arms wind around my neck, and she plasters her chest to mine. I barely manage to keep from spilling my cup, but it doesn't matter. I've got her.

One hand across the small of her back, the arm with the cup against her side.

Her eyes are huge, glassy, her pupils huge.

"I'm so fucking happy to see you." She grabs my cheeks and drags my face down, and she plants a sloppy kiss on my lips.

My brows furrow when she leans back. Her palms are hot on my face.

"You okay?" I ask.

"So much better now that you're here." She grins. "Can you help me win? I think I'm losing."

She releases my face and latches on to my wrist instead. She tows me to her side of the table, where a guy across from her waits expectantly.

There's only one cup left in front of us, and four on the other end. I grimace and wet a ball, tossing it fast.

It goes in.

The guy across from me drinks without complaint, then tosses the ball. It sails into the final cup without so much as a wobble, and Briar reaches for it.

"I've got it," I say. I pluck out the ball and gulp down the beer. "What now?"

"Now..." She bites her lip.

I want to bite her lip.

"We should dance!"

I quirk my lips, but I follow her. Again. I'm captivated by her, but I don't even care. We find the section of the house that's been designated a dance floor, and she shoves her way through. She's not limping—which probably means she's going to feel it tomorrow—and she doesn't seem to mind the crowd pressing in on her.

But I'm not going to turn down the feel of her body against mine, so I plunge through the crowd after her and grasp her waist. I pull her close, and we move to the music. She inches closer, until my knee is between her legs, and she grinds on me.

Her head tips back, and she lets out a groan.

"What did you take?" I ask in her ear. I nip her lobe.

"Oh, fuck." She tilts to the side, giving me more room. "Just a little…"

"A little what?"

"Can you feel that?" She runs her hands down her front, her fingers dipping into the waistband of her jeans. "There's electricity between us, Cassius."

I grab her hand and twist her around. Her ass in my groin. My dick comes alive, stiffening in my jeans, poking into her ass. She rolls her hips and leans her weight on me.

"I think we need to find a room," she pants. "Right now."

"But I'm not done with you." My lips trail across her jaw and down her neck. "I thought you wanted to dance."

"I…"

I suck at her skin. Kiss. Suck. *Nip.*

She groans.

"What did you take, kitten?" I ask again.

"Some girls were doing X in line for the bathroom." Her gaze crashes into mine. "To be fair, I didn't know what it was until after I took it."

X, as in… ecstasy.

No fucking wonder.

"You took a random drug from a stranger without asking a few questions first?"

She giggles. "Sorry."

Oy.

I steady her when she sways a bit too much.

"You okay?" I ask, my lips at her ear. To be heard over the music, obviously.

"Just a bit lightheaded." She blinks hard. "It's fine. I'm fine."

Her knees buckle, but unlike the last time she passed out on me, I'm not across the room. I swing her up into my arms before she can hit the floor. She giggles again and loops her arms around my neck.

"My savior."

Heat works its way up my neck, but I smile down at her anyway. We garner quite a few looks as I carry her out of the party. I put her in my car, grateful I didn't drink more than that quarter cup of warm beer from the game, and slide behind the wheel.

Her hands immediately reach for me.

"Kitten," I admonish quietly, the darkness almost making her more alluring. I catch her hands and thread my fingers through hers. "You're not in your right mind."

"Doesn't matter," she argues. "I want you."

I groan. My dick twitches in response, but it's out of luck.

I drive us home one-handed, the other keeping her wandering hands in her lap, playing with my fingers. She traces a nail around my knuckles, humming to herself, until I park in my spot at the house.

"Oooh, are you going to take me to bed?" She smiles. "Ravage me like one of those wicked jersey chasers?"

"If you were a jersey chaser, I would've left you at the party."

Her smile widens.

I shake my head and get her out of the car, keeping an arm around her waist to make sure she doesn't eat shit on the way inside.

Upstairs.

I nudge her toward the bathroom and quickly shed my shirt and jeans, changing back into the sweats I wore before Rhys's text. Now, I'm infinitely glad I heeded his advice and showed up.

Where were her friends? They weren't anywhere near her, keeping an eye on her, that's for sure. Or they saw me and backed off… and let me just carry her out of the party?

I press my lips together, unsure which thought is worse.

Briar enters the room and throws something at me.

I barely get my hands up in time to catch her shirt, and my breath catches. "Briar."

Her jeans follow a second later, and I let out a growl.

"I want you," she says, a repeat of earlier. She reaches back and slowly undoes the clasps of her bra. "There's so much tension between us, Thorne. So let's just fuck and get it out of our systems."

"I did not anticipate this," I mutter, more to myself than her.

She drops her bra, and I'm greeted with the sight of arguably the best tits on the planet. Her nipples pebble in the cool air, her areolas are light pink, and I itch to take her breasts in my hands.

Not while she's like this.

I know what regret feels like—and I would die if we woke up the next morning and she was ashamed of what we did.

I snag a shirt out of my dresser and motion her closer.

She smiles at me, batting her eyelashes, and reaches for the waistband of my sweatpants.

I ignore her until I can get the shirt over her head.

"Hey—"

"I mean it." I guide her arms through the sleeves and catch her wrists from any more groping. I walk her backward to the bed and give her a light shove onto it. "Sleep this off."

Her body bounces, and she stares up at me. "Alone?"

"I…"

"Where will you sleep?"

"On the couch." I grit my teeth. I don't love that idea, but...

"I'll keep my hands to myself." She shuffles back to the edge of the bed. "Just..."

"What?"

"Stay."

The sudden vulnerability in her gaze has to be alcohol or drug related, right? But she blinks once, twice, and her eyes flood with tears.

Shit.

"Okay. Okay, yeah, no funny business." I motion for her to scoot back again. "Stay here."

When I finish in the bathroom, she's in the exact same spot. On the far end of the bed, her legs pulled up and her arms wrapped around them.

There are scars all over her leg—

My heart squeezes.

She wears long pants everywhere. Even to the gym, she's in leggings or yoga pants. I've never seen her in shorts, and now, her gaze seems heavy. She's hurting—not physically, not yet, but emotionally. Because she stripped, and now there's this extra *something* between us.

It feels fragile.

Maybe not quite trust, but...

I sit on the bed and draw up the blankets, motioning for her to get under them.

She blinks, then slowly unfolds. Her scarred leg disappears under the sheets.

I climb in, too, then flick off the lamp. In the darkness, I roll onto my side to face her.

The questions burn in my mind. I know how it happened —there was a fire, she was trapped, she jumped out of the second-story window to survive. The rumors about why she was in the building in the first place were never answered.

Some say she was there doing a job, painting one of the walls with a mural for the new owners. Others say she used to bring hookups there, or do drug deals, or...

"Come here." My voice comes out gruff, and she winces. "Come on, kitten."

She scoots forward. I meet her in the middle of the bed and wrap my arms around her. Her face is inches from my bare chest, her warm breath coasting across my skin.

Goosebumps rise in its wake.

She brings her arms up, one tucked between us like a safeguard, the other tentatively pressing to my sternum. Then up to my shoulder, down my arm.

"It's okay," I whisper. "I've got you."

She sighs, and something tells me that maybe nothing is okay.

But I can do my best to fix it in the morning.

CHAPTER 21
BRIAR

I FLING my legs out from under the covers. My head throbs, and my body buzzes.

I must've slept because it's hard to open my eyes. They feel heavy, just like my head, but the rest of my body feels light.

The room is hazy and dark, though there's a little bit of light peeking through the window. I make a noise, and it sounds like a whimper. I turn onto my side and cradle my stomach while hitching my leg higher. There's warmth nearby. *Skin on skin*. It feels good.

Really good.

A lustful sigh falls from my lips, and I move closer to the warmth.

It takes me a few seconds to come to my senses.

Who is beside me?

My eyes spring wide open. Anxiety plows into my chest, and I fly off the bed. I thud onto the floor and scramble to get away.

"Briar."

I slip and land on my knee. My teeth sink into my lower lip as I take in the pain radiating down my leg. I see the door, except it looks like it's moving. I try to focus, and when I do, a tall shadow stands in front of me. Panic ensues, and I'm suddenly back in that burning building. "Get away from me!"

"Shit, Briar. It's me."

Large, warm hands fall to my hips. Why do they feel *so* fucking good? I'm tingly all over.

"I know what you did!" My voice is raspy. I want to pull away but I also like the way his fingers feel digging into my waist, which is so fucked up.

Am I dreaming?

"What?"

My cheeks are trapped with his firm grip. The light from the window shines a streak onto his face, and I'm mortified.

"Oh my God." My gaze bounces back and forth between his worried eyes.

"Are you back?" he asks, flexing his jaw.

I nod once, and he visibly relaxes.

"Sorry," I mutter. "I got…" I try to think back to last night. The memories flash in and out. I remember the gasoline note and going to the party.

Then the football players showed up, and I spiraled with fear.

I took something to *calm* me. In hindsight, that was a terrible idea.

It did calm me. It calmed me enough to get closer to the football team so I could see if any of them smelled like gasoline, but it also made me antsy, too.

The more I think about the night, the blurrier it becomes.

I remember Thorne showing up, and how happy I was. How *trusting*.

"Trying to recall what happened?" He drops his hands from my cheeks and slowly skims them over my body until they're resting on my hips again.

My stomach dips with heat.

I nod, and he slowly pushes me backward onto the bed.

He forces me to sit, and the thoughts going on in my head are dangerous at best. I'm not acting like myself. My legs beg to open, and my pulse races. There's a plea on the tip of my tongue for him to touch me.

I'm turned on, and I have no idea why.

Thorne drops to his knees in front of me, and I pant. My hairline prickles with heat, and I breathe faster.

His touch is intoxicating. The palm of his hand moves against my thigh until it lands at my knee.

"You took X last night," he admits, rubbing the spot that hurts the most from falling onto his floor.

"I… what?"

No fucking wonder.

Thorne peers at me from below, and I feel *seen*.

"Did we…?"

I'm not wearing pants. My scars are right there for him to see.

His hand tenses on my thigh. "No."

I breathe a sigh of relief.

"But you wanted to."

My face is hot. I pull my leg back quickly so I can put it back under the blanket, but Thorne's fingers dig into the flesh, keeping me still.

"Are you embarrassed?" His voice is soft and smooth.

My nipples harden, and there's a rush of lust flowing between my legs.

"Being turned down after throwing myself at you? Yeah, you can say that." I try to move my leg again, but he keeps me trapped.

"Why are you trying to escape me right now, kitten?" he asks.

I look at my leg. My scars are ugly. The ones from surgery are long and rigid around the edges. Then when you move down to my calf, it's bumpy and discolored from the fire.

It's gross.

It's no freaking wonder he turned me down.

I haven't been with anyone since the accident.

Ben was too impatient for me to heal, and now I'm too ashamed to let anyone else see.

"Stop looking at yourself like that."

I glance away and try to escape the pressing glare in his eye. He seems angry with his heavy brow line and flexing jaw.

It turns me on that much more.

I'm all over the place.

Hot and bothered, ashamed and embarrassed, angry yet still vulnerable.

Thorne's sigh is followed by a quiet growl. "Now I need you to stop looking at me like that."

"Like what?" I ask.

"Like you still want me to put you out of your misery."

God, but I do.

"I can't help it." I pull away harder this time, and he lets me go. "My body is..." I stand on wobbly legs and head for the door. "Wired."

My breaths are choppy, and the room is spinning.

I have to get out of here.

Finally, my gaze lands on my jeans that are bundled on the floor. I rush over and try to turn them right side in, all while avoiding Thorne's hot gaze from across the room.

He commands my attention on any good day.

Today?

I can't help but follow through.

"So what's your plan?" He leans against the door with his arms crossed.

Is he blocking the exit?

"You going to leave my room and go home to get yourself off until the X is out of your system?"

The longer I stand in his room without curbing the need I feel, the more frustrated I become.

"Well, I can't have you do it!" I snap. "You rejected me once. I can't really remember how it made me feel but I know I don't want to relive it."

Thorne scoffs.

I roll my eyes. "I can't go off and fuck someone either. You're my boyfriend." I pause. "*Fake* boyfriend."

Thorne's arms fall to his sides. He quickly advances on me, stalking across the bedroom until he traps me.

"If anyone is getting you off, it's me." His warm breath floats against my lips, and my eyelashes flutter closed. "I turned you down last night because you were completely out of it. I wasn't going to take advantage of you."

I lean against him. My nipples harden from the feel of his firm chest, and I shake. The arm around my waist traps me, and without knowing what I'm doing, my leg hitches around his hip and I'm pressing into him.

His other hand weaves into my hair, and my head tips backward. I open my eyes, and his pupils are dilated with need.

I've never craved someone like this.

"Considering you're sassing me, I know you're back in your right state of mind."

My lips part, and all I want to do is kiss him.

"I am… but my body isn't," I rasp.

I'm acting desperate but I feel like I'm going crazy. My nerves are fried, and my skin tingles.

"I feel…wild," I admit.

"I know, kitten," he whispers. "I'll help bring you back down to earth."

Oh, thank God.

"Only if you promise to never take unknown drugs at a party again."

"Never," I rush out. "I promise."

"That was awfully fast," he whispers. "I wonder what else I can ask of you."

My entire body trembles with the heat of his breath fanning over my neck. His teeth latch on to my earlobe, and he gives it a quick tug.

"I'm sure you'll think of something,"

He smiles against my mouth. "That I will, kitten. Now get on the bed."

CHAPTER 22
THORNE

BRIAR SITS on the bed and stares up at me. I take a second to make sure the door is locked—Rhys would probably pick this exact moment to burst in otherwise—then return to her.

She's so sexy it hurts.

I run my hands up her legs again, this time hooking my fingers around the waistband of her panties when I reach her hips. I slowly drag the black fabric down, carefully removing it and tossing it to the floor beside me.

"Grab on to the headboard," I order.

Her eyes widen, and she reaches over her head. Her tits strain against the t-shirt I put her in last night, and I make a mental note that next time, I'll pay them the attention they deserve.

Right now, though, I must be between her legs.

Immediately.

I spread her legs and lean down, running my nose and mouth up the inside of her thigh. All the way up, up, up, until I can smell her arousal.

"Oh God—"

I swipe my tongue through the folds of her pussy and barely suppress my groan. When the tip of my tongue trips over her clit, her hips jerk. I smile to myself and do it again. My hands wander in, and I slide one finger inside her.

"Fuck," she hisses above me.

Her hands stay locked around the edge of the headboard.

"Good girl," I croon. "Now just come on my fingers and tongue and I'll give you what you really want."

In her heightened state, it doesn't take her long. I curl my fingers inside her, pumping as my lips fasten around her clit. Her legs clamp around my head and tense with her climax. Her back arches off the bed, and she twists away from me.

"One down," I tell her. I straighten and shed my sweatpants, pausing only to grab a condom from my nightstand. I kneel between her splayed legs and roll it on, enjoying her heaving chest.

It would be better if it was brighter in here... and if she wasn't wearing a shirt.

I push the fabric up, exposing her chest, and my dick gets even fucking harder.

My hand joins hers on the headboard, and the other guides my cock to her entrance. She's slick, with her cum and more arousal, and her wide eyes are locked on my face.

I meet her gaze, *pause*, then thrust into her.

We both moan. Her muscles tighten, pulsing around me, and I have to stay still for a moment so I don't completely lose my shit.

I'm supposed to be good at this. I mean—I *am*. I've fucked my fair share of girls. But she feels different. Closer to heaven than anything else I've experienced.

A slice of guilt drops through me at that thought. I shouldn't compare her to other girls.

But there it is.

"You feel so good," I tell her, slowly withdrawing until just my tip is still encased inside her.

I push in an inch at a time, and her eyes roll back. Her muscles tremble, her abdomen tensing. My self-control is hanging on by a thread, but I'm going to fucking milk it until it snaps.

Slow. Torturous. Teasing.

In and out. One hand on her hip, one on the headboard. My fingers are so close to hers, but just barely not touching.

"More," she finally says. "Please, Thorne, *more*."

I close my eyes briefly, then nod.

I can do more.

"Hold on tight, kitten."

I pull out and slam into her harder, and the whole bed jerks. I do it again, and pleasure radiates up my spine. I chase that feeling, bent over her, while her hips rise to meet me. Her heels dig into my ass, and she releases one hand from the headboard.

I watch its path down her body warily, but she slides it down her abdomen and touches herself. Her fingers stroke her clit in fast, tight circles, until she's gasping and falling into another orgasm.

Her pussy clenches and releases, waves of her orgasm seeming to go on forever. I'm *right there*, too, my balls tightening, my muscles burning, until I tip over the edge.

I still inside her, groaning through my teeth, until it finally stops.

I slip out and climb over her, then pause.

This is the part where I would dispose of the condom, *maybe* get the girl a towel or something, and then wait for their quick exit. But then again—it would be midnight, or three in the morning. Not *seven* o'clock in the morning.

She already spent the night.

I remove the condom and tie it off, chucking it in the trash in a wad of tissue, then climb back over her before she can move.

Her eyes widen. "What are you doing?"

"Making sure you're satiated." I eye her. Do I kiss her? Is that crossing a line?

"I… yeah." Her cheeks are red. "Thanks for the help."

"Anytime, kitten."

"Well, no." She shakes her head. "This was a one-time thing."

My body hovers over hers. Barely touching, except our hips, and her breasts against my chest. But at that, the ice comes crashing down on me.

Of course she would see it that way.

"Right." I clear my throat. "Then…" I roll off her.

Her gaze drops to my cock. She stares at it for so long, it grows half-mast under her attention. Then, slowly, to full hardness.

"You want another round?" I ask. "Or maybe you should take a picture. It'd last longer."

She shakes her head and staggers to her feet. "I just need to pee."

Her limp is more pronounced, and I sit up fast. She hobbles into my bathroom and closes the door, and I swear under my breath.

What the fuck is *wrong* with me?

This is fake.

This is *fake*, and worse, it was my idea. I can't be the one to fucking immediately catch feelings for her when she's clearly just humoring me.

I find clean boxers and jeans. I rummage around for my phone, which still has a charge on it. There's a text from Rhys, which was just the flame emoji—guess he saw me leave with Briar, even if I didn't actually see him while I was there—and another from my dad.

Sent only a few minutes ago.

FATHER

> Your mother and I are coming into town for your next game, Cassius. We want to meet your girlfriend.

"Fuck."

"What's wrong?"

My head whips up. Briar reentered the room, and she stands in the middle of it with a t-shirt clasped to her chest.

"I…" My mouth goes dry. "Um."

"Cat got your tongue?" She cocks her head. "You look like you're spooked."

I am spooked.

"We're screwed," I say softly.

Her brows furrow. "What? Why?"

I show her the text from my father. "We need to get our stories straight. We need to—we need to be able to be affectionate in public without freaking out. We need to be able to tell them our first date, and each other's favorite color, and our coffee orders. And movies! What if they ask about what you like to watch? Do you even *like Star Wars*? Not that they would give a shit, really, I'm pretty sure my dad turns up his nose at that kind of thing—"

She grabs my face. "Thorne? Breathe."

I take a long, ragged inhale.

Her palms are warm on my cheeks. "You're freaking me out."

"Yeah, well, I'm freaking myself out. They're…" I wince. I can't say it.

"They're what?"

Shaking my head, I lean down and grab the shirt she dropped. "I think we need to discuss this over breakfast. Get dressed."

———

The diner down the street is technically open twenty-four hours, but the prime people-watching time is from seven to ten in the morning, give or take. It's when they're at their busiest with people in all the stages of life.

You've got the corporate people in suits. The blue-collar folks getting ready to start their shifts—or, in some cases, just coming off them.

And then the students.

Grad students, looking harried and stressed.

Undergrads, half-asleep in their giant mugs of coffee after a long night out.

And us.

I wouldn't say Briar and I stand out, by any means. We fit in amongst the harried and half-asleep, tucked into a booth at the back. I took the side with my back to the wall, because some thoughts have filtered through my brain about how to make my parents accept this fake relationship, and I don't think Briar will like any of them. So I've been avoiding her gaze by people watching.

"Just spit it out," she eventually says.

"Spit what out?" I focus on her.

Her lips press in a flat line, and I get the sense that she's one lie—or omission—away from getting up and going home.

Not that I can blame her.

It suddenly occurs to me that she had her own freak out this morning. And I reacted the same way she did to mine, grabbing her face. Helping her calm down.

"Let's talk about you," I suggest. "Who did you think I was this morning?"

Her face reddens. "No. I'll tell you that later—*if* you can just say what you've been stewing on since you read that text."

Right.

I shift in my seat. "Well. My family has, uh, generational wealth."

She blinks. "Obviously."

"Like, they're really fucking rich." My voice stays low. "And I know, this is *literally* the definition of a first-world problem. Or a one-percenter problem, I guess. But the rich tend to only socialize with... themselves."

Briar glares at me. "Thorne, I'm going to be honest, you're driving me crazy."

I hold up my hands in surrender. "Fine. They're judgmental, okay? To a neurotic degree. They judge me, they judge their peers..."

"They'll judge me," she finishes. "I gotta say, I was expecting this."

I pause. "You were?"

"All parents are judgy assholes. That is not groundbreaking."

I rub the back of my neck. "Well, I think we have some ways to, uh, stave off the immediate ordering of our breakup."

Her warm brown eyes narrow.

"Just a little makeover, is all," I mutter. "For the game."

She scoffs.

"You don't have to change *how* you dress..." I make a face. "You just have to change how expensive the clothes are."

Her eyes bug out. "You've got to be kidding me. I can't afford—"

"Kitten, I am *not* saying this is going on your credit card." I tilt my head. "Don't you want to spend some of my parents' money before they act like witches toward you?"

She considers that. Then, slowly, her lips curl into a smile.

CHAPTER 23
BRIAR

THREE SHOPS LATER, and all I left with is a complex.

I know it's not that Thorne thinks I *need* a makeover, but it still makes me feel like I'm not good enough or something.

Which to his parents, I'm likely not.

It's no surprise by any means, but it's still offensive if I think about it.

"Thorne, I look stupid."

He grins, and I want to rip the stupid tennis skirt from my body and throw it at his feet.

"Fine, grumpy cat…"

I stand near the dressing room and watch as he pursues the racks of some high-end store that I'll never be able to afford with my art degree—at least according to my parents.

"What about this?" He comes back holding a black miniskirt, a maroon sweater—that matches the color of his jersey—and a black puffy vest that has a price tag hanging from the zipper that makes me do a double take.

"Remember this is my parents' money," he reminds me.

I sigh and snatch the clothing from him and pop back into the dressing room.

I'm half-naked when he moves closer to the curtain. His

shoes peek from below, and his voice sounds like he's inside here with me.

"What are your parents like?" he asks.

I straighten the skirt on my hips. "Normal, I guess."

He chuckles. "What's *normal*, kitten?"

My cheeks ripen with heat. That nickname doesn't seem cute anymore after he used it during our quick fuck session. I don't know if it was because I'd taken something to enhance everything—which I'm still beating myself up for—or if it was because it was *him*.

Either way, hearing his raspy chuckle makes my stomach twist.

"Uh..." I pull the sweater over my head. *It's so soft.* "They're your typical, hard-working middle-class family. My mom is a receptionist at a doctor's office, and my dad makes cabinets for a living." I glance at the price tag again. "They are by no means *rich*."

Thorne sighs loud enough for me to hear. "That sounds like a dream."

"They're good parents, but being an only child and middle-class comes with certain limitations."

After shrugging the vest on, I smooth out my hair. Thorne's finger hooks around the black curtain, and he pulls it back slowly to make eye contact with me in the mirror. "Like?"

I glance at my bumpy leg. I'll need tights if I wear this.

"They want what's best for me, but to them, that means no more hockey, and they're not really a fan of my art degree either." A sadness lingers. "They're disappointed in me, I think."

Thorne comes up behind me and places his hands on my shoulders. He gives me a light squeeze and shakes his head. "I don't know them, but I don't know how they could be disappointed in you."

I half roll my eyes at his sweet comment.

Thorne isn't what I thought he was. I judged him too harshly.

That doesn't mean I'm in love with him or anything, but he's just… *good*.

"We're going to have to lie to my parents, though," he adds, stepping away. He sits on the bench in the dressing room and stares at me.

"About?"

He seems uncomfortable. "About your parents' jobs. That won't be good enough for Andrew and Helena."

I laugh sarcastically. "Too poor for their liking?"

Thorne is deep in thought. He taps his finger on his chin. "Instead of your mom working as a receptionist at a doctor's office…let's make her a Physician's Assistant? My parents won't follow up on that, and it's still in the same field."

I nod.

"And your father…"

"An architect?"

Thorne's lip twitches. "Close enough, I guess. But let's make it to where he designs medical buildings or something. I don't want my father to get a wild hair up his ass and think he can contact your father to build some skyscraper somewhere for his business."

"Got it."

I put my arms out and gesture to my new clothing. "Well? I'll need tights, but is this expensive enough for your parents?" I mentally add up the prices and the fact that he's about to spend almost five hundred dollars on one outfit is beyond me.

Thorne drags his gaze over every inch of my body. He takes his finger and spins it in the air. I act unbothered and do as he says, turning around.

He clears his throat, and I glance at him in the mirror.

A wave of lust hits me. He's staring at my butt while flexing his jaw.

"Like what you see?" I tease.

He snaps out of it and catches my attention. The look in his eye is that same one he had yesterday morning when he lifted my shirt up and saw at my breasts. *Hunger.*

"We need shoes." he grunts, standing and leaving the dressing room.

I quickly undress and put everything back onto the hanger. It doesn't take me long to find him near the shoes. He's rubbing his hand against his chin as he stares at the shelf lined with boots.

"I like those." I come up beside him and point to the shiny Doc Martens calling out to me.

Surprise flickers over his features. "Yeah?"

I nod happily, like a kid in a candy store.

Or better yet, a girl in an expensive store with a credit card that doesn't belong to her.

Thorne walks over and tells the clerk something. She comes strolling over to me within a minute with a size eight.

He thanks her and grabs the box from her hands.

"Sit," he tells me.

I take a seat, and he bends down below.

"How did you know what size I needed?" I ask, curious.

After slipping my Converse off, he peers at me with those warm, honey eyes. "Because I pay attention, kitten."

Well, shit.

Cat's got *my* tongue.

I say nothing as he works the boot onto my foot and laces it up.

When he's done, he grabs my hand and pulls me to stand. I wobble, because my knee is sore, but I catch my balance.

"You hurting today?" His tone brinks on the edge of worry.

I brush it off. "I'm fine."

"I'm putting you in an ice bath later."

I scowl. "I hate ice baths."

He leans down and whispers in my ear, "I'm leaving you in there extra long for lying to me about being fine, too."

I try to step on his toe with my new boot, but he moves away at the last second.

He laughs at my expression. "I know you better than you think."

"Oh, whatever." I roll my eyes and turn away, only to be spun right back around.

Thorne's forehead is burrowed, and his jaw is tense.

"What's wrong?" My curious gaze works its way around the store.

Thorne's hot breath fans against my face with a heavy sigh. "My father's client."

"Okay…" *So?*

A tight swallow works against Thorne's neck. "That one whose daughter I had dissed by telling him I was in a committed relationship with someone else."

Ah. Now it makes sense.

I latch on to Thorne's wrists. His fingers squeeze my hips from the touch.

"That someone being me, I'm assuming?"

He nods and stands taller. His spine straightens, and every one of his muscles are stiff with stress.

I smile softly at him and attempt to calm him down. "Don't worry. Just play along. Consider it practice."

Confusion fixes itself onto his face, but when I get closer to him, the worry lines disappear.

I flutter my eyelashes. "Kiss me."

He doesn't even blink before his mouth falls to mine. I shut my eyes, and for once, I let myself *feel*. There is no rushing between us. We kiss slowly, and from the outside, I can only assume it appears real because it *feels* real. The sweeping of his tongue against mine is slow. It sends a gush of something warm into my chest, and I reciprocate.

We get lost in the show.

It's only after I hear a clearing of a throat that we break apart.

Our eyes lock, and our chests are heaving.

That was... a lot.

"Hello, Cassius."

I back away from Thorne, only for him to pull me in closer. Our hands clasp at his side. The man responsible for our *fake* relationship stands in front of us in his expensive suit, staring expectantly.

"Mr. Keenland, sir." Thorne inclines his chin. "Good to see you again."

I squeeze Thorne's hand because his tone is clipped. He squeezes it back and then rubs his thumb against my skin in a comforting way.

It feels natural, even if we are practicing.

"Yes," Mr. Keenland says. His gaze cuts to me. "And who is this?"

"My girlfriend, Briar." Thorne smiles at him. "The one I told you about."

"Nice to meet you," he says gruffly to me.

Thorne asks about some business deal that Thorne's father is in charge of, and that carries the conversation away from me.

After what feels like ages, they part ways. He made no move to inquire further about me, but I consider that practice, too.

After all, I can only assume that Thorne's parents will be the same. It won't matter if we make up some story about how I'm actually some rich girl who has no real ambitions like playing hockey again or pursuing a career in art.

"I think we need more practice," Thorne finally says after we're alone again.

I eye him suspiciously.

He seems back to his normal, relaxed self.

"Do you now?" I drag out my words after unclasping our

hands. I place my fists on my hips and raise an eyebrow. "I think you just want to kiss me again."

He looks right at my mouth, and a flush works up my neck.

"I think you're right, kitten."

CHAPTER 24
THORNE

"THIS IS FINE," I tell Rhys. And myself. And Briar, perched on my bed. "This is all fine. We're fine. You're fine, I'm fine—"

"He's freaking out," Rhys says to Briar.

"Obviously," she replies.

"I'm not."

"This is like when Coach asked you to throw a Hail Mary pass and none of our receivers were free, so you did this dance in the pocket, twisting and dodging, until you could finally let the ball fly." Rhys snickers. "And remember how that turned out?"

"I got sacked." I frown. "And a concussion. I was out for three weeks. Thanks for that reminder."

"Yeah, but your perfect spiral landed in what's-his-face's hands, he scored a touchdown, and we won the game." My best friend smirks. "So what if you got a little knocked around?"

"I—"

"He's probably trying to say, you got the job done even though it seemed impossible," Briar interrupts. "Just like now. I'm your, uh, receiver. Just throw me the ball, baby."

I groan through my teeth.

We've got an hour until Rhys and I need to be at the stadium, and then I have to play while Briar is left unattended in the presence of my parents... and *then* we're going out to dinner.

So, basically, fuck my life.

Not to mention I haven't been able to scrub the thought of fucking *her* out of my mind. Every time I close my eyes, I see her face as she came. And every time I lick my lips, I swear I taste her arousal.

"Rhys, get out."

I focus on Briar, who stares down my best friend with her arm lifted, finger pointing to my door.

He blinks at her, then slowly nods. He closes the door behind him, and then it's just us.

"We've been over this a hundred times," she says, pushing up from the bed and coming closer. "We've got this. I'm wearing the fancy shit we bought, you know what my parents fake do for a living, and I'll survive them without you."

Yeah, right.

"I probably won't even see them until after the game," she says. "Lydia and Marley are going to sit with me."

"Oh. Good. But if you see two people in expensive outfits looking like they don't really belong—"

"I'll say, 'Hello, Mr. and Mrs. Thorne,'" she finishes with a wicked smile. She steps into the bathroom with me, using one finger on my chest to back me up. "Now, Cassius Remington Thorne the Third... you seem a little stressed. I think I can help."

Her fingers trail down my dress shirt and hook on the waistband of my slacks. Her eyebrow rises, and I slowly nod.

This is not part of the plan.

But I'm sure as fuck not going to stop her.

She unbuttons my pants with deft fingers and drags the

fabric—and my briefs—down my thighs. As it goes, she lowers herself.

"Your knee—"

"Is fine," she murmurs. "For this? It's fine, Cassius."

I open my mouth to protest her using my first name so much, but then she wraps those fingers around my cock—which is quickly waking up—and my brain stops working.

She can call me whatever she wants.

Thorne. Cassius. *Baby*.

"Briar—"

"Just lean on the counter and enjoy it." She meets my gaze and winks. She strokes me to full hardness. Her tongue pokes out between her red painted lips. "Mmm, hello, friend. Long time no see."

"It's only been—"

"Shh," she interrupts. "I'm getting reacquainted to the one that made me see stars the other day."

I huff out a laugh, but she keeps stroking, twisting her wrist and squeezing around the tip like a damn expert. When she leans forward and takes me in her mouth, I just barely stop my hips from jacking forward and pushing deeper.

I grip the counter to keep from threading my hands through her hair.

She licks and sucks at the tip while her hand keeps jacking me off. Her tongue flicks at the underside of my cock's head, and I'm torn between wanting to take over and let her continue to tease me like this.

"You're so fucking sexy on your knees." I stare down at her. I can see down her shirt, to the dip between her breasts. "Fucking hell, Briar."

Her mouth lifts away from me. "My real name?"

"*Kitten*," I growl. My dick feels like it's going to explode. "I'm a breath away from taking over and fucking your face until tears stream down those pretty cheeks."

"Hmm." Her tongue pokes out again, and then she slowly licks at me. "Sounds like fun."

My body tenses. "Is that—"

"Show me what you're made of," she goads.

Oh, fuck.

I reach out and run my knuckles across her cheek. Then, well. My fingers plunge into her hair, and I guide her mouth back to my cock. Her hands come up to my thighs, her manicured nails digging into my skin lightly.

She takes more of me into her mouth, and I let out a hiss of breath when I hit the back of her throat. I stay there for a second, then withdraw. When I push back in, she sucks. Her cheeks hollow, and her tongue curls around me.

Pulses of pleasure zap up my cock, through my balls, and up my spine.

Slowly, I increase my pace until my words come true. The intensity brings tears to her eyes. She gags around me, and it only makes me want to push deeper. When she reaches up and cups my balls, I see stars.

It's game over at that point.

I release her hair. "I'm gonna—"

She doesn't pull away, and I explode in her mouth. My vision goes white for a second, my cock twitching with each pulse, until I've got nothing left.

Only then does she carefully withdraw, licking her lips. She presses a finger to the corner of her mouth.

I haul her up and set her on the counter. Legs parted, me between them. I run my fingers under her eyes, catching the remnants of tears.

"That was something else, kitten." My voice holds wonder. "I…"

"When you win, we'll add that to your pre-game ritual." She winks.

I kiss her.

I can't help it.

I *really* don't care that she just swallowed my cum—maybe it's even because of that. Because she really didn't have to. Because we're alone, and we can't seem to stop from breaking our own damn rules. But our lips part, and our tongues tangle, and my heart fucking skips.

When we break away, we're both breathing hard.

I step aside and clean myself up, towing my briefs and slacks back into place. I tuck in my shirt, but my gaze keeps straying back to Briar. She sits immobile on the counter, watching me until I'm done.

Then, she hops down—landing mostly on her good leg—and swivels around to assess the damage in the mirror.

"Oh, fuck," she laughs. "I need to redo this."

I wince.

"It's okay, Thorne. I knew what I was getting into. I'll see you after the game, yeah?"

"On the field," I confirm. I find the special access pass I got for her and hook the lanyard around her neck. "You're going to be okay?"

"Of course." She presses a kiss to my cheek, then rushes away.

I watch her ass on the way out and chuckle to myself.

But I'm not alone for long.

Rhys comes in a second later, and he rolls his eyes at me. "You two are so fucking screwed."

"What?"

He snorts. "Fake dating, my ass."

I ignore him and grab my keys and phone. I don't have to bring anything with me since it's a home game. All our gear is already at the stadium. My wireless headphones are in the car. They make us walk down a hallway, and the social media team takes photos of us. It's a bit nerve-racking, not knowing what kind of shots they're getting. And, of course, they go everywhere for promo. Having headphones to block out the noise helps.

Walking in with Rhys helps, too.

"Let's go," I order. "Anyone else riding with us?"

"Nah. They know you have some fancy dinner with your folks tonight."

Great.

I check my phone and shoot Briar a quick text.

ME

Thank you for letting me get my anxiety out.

To my surprise, the little bubbles of her typing pop up right away.

BRIAR

Make it worth it, hotshot. 😉

Rhys gags. "You guys are kind of cute, I'll admit. But seriously?"

"Shut it."

A new text comes in, and I'm smiling before I even read it. But just as fast, my smile drops.

FATHER

We have reservations tonight. Let's make sure this is a celebratory dinner and not a pity one, yes?

"He's an ass."

"You've got to stop reading my texts over my shoulder." I shake my head. "But, yeah. He is."

Rhys claps me on the shoulder. "Let's go fucking win a football game, then."

CHAPTER 25
BRIAR

I TOLD Thorne I'd be fine, but the truth is, I'm antsy.

Thankfully, I'm good at putting on a front, which is going to come in handy when it's all said and done and we're broken up. After spending time together, and touching all the time, I'm afraid that my off-limits heart is going to be full of little thorns by the end.

Pun intended.

"You look… nice," Lydia muses.

Marley laughs. "One year ago, I never would have guessed that I'd see you at a football game wearing *that*."

"Stop it," I hiss. *Do I seem totally out of place?*

"Don't get me wrong." Marley scoots into the second row, and Lydia and I follow after her. "You look freaking amazing."

"I look like I always do."

It's true. Sure, the sweater is soft and warm, but it's not that much different from the rest of my sweaters.

"Wow, someone got a makeover," someone says from behind.

We all three turn, and I catch the eye of some girl I

couldn't point out in a lineup if I had to. She looks like the rest of her girl gang.

Girl gang because they're all four scowling at me with their bright-red lips and caterpillar-like eyelashes.

A harsh laugh falls from my mouth, and suddenly, everyone is staring at me.

"Sorry." I smash my lips together.

Marley and Lydia both snicker quietly.

"Don't you... like... play hockey or something?" one of the lookalikes asks, staring at all three of us.

I swear my knee aches at that exact moment.

"They do." The blue-eyed one points at Lydia and Marley, purposefully signaling me out. "But she doesn't... *anymore.*"

A flicker of red and orange flames loom on the outer part of my memories. I squeeze my fists tight to stay calm.

"Oh, why not?" one asks.

The blue-eyed girl shoots me a cruel smile, and that's when I notice she's wearing Thorne's number. *Oh, this ought to be good.*

She whispers loud enough for everyone to hear, which turns out not to be a whisper at all, "She's the girl who burned in that fire last semester. Remember?"

There's a collective gasp, and I'm red hot with embarrassment.

Anger comes next, and if it wasn't for Thorne's parents being in attendance, I probably would have acted irrationally and pulled her by her hair to teach her how to keep her mouth shut.

"Tell us you're jealous without telling us." Marley doesn't bother to hide her laugh.

A huff that comes out more like a shriek catches everyone's attention. "Jealous? Of *her*?"

I smile sweetly at the group of girls that I'm certain Mr. and Mrs. Thorne would much prefer their son to take to dinner instead of me. "Well, you are wearing my boyfriend's number." I plop my lower lip out and show her some fake pity. "It's kind of cute that you're such a fan, even if he doesn't know your name."

"He does, too!" She stomps her foot like a brat, and I reach forward to pat her arm.

Only I don't get a chance to because she flinches away from me. She flicks her blown-out hair over her shoulder and leaves her seat. Her friends skitter after her like little ducklings.

When I see that they're gone, I finally exhale. I glance back to the field and try to calm my racing heart.

Practice.

That was practice.

The real test is coming, after the game when I'm face-to-face with Thorne's parents.

Lydia leans in and shouts over the crowd's growing volume, "That was impressive. I've never seen you hold such restraint. On or off the ice."

I shout back to her while staring at the opening on the field that I know Shadow Valley is seconds from running through, "I have a job to do."

Unfortunately, this is just the beginning.

———

My throat is sandpaper.

It's like I'm back on the ice with my team, screaming for us to get our shit together to win the game.

Shadow Valley is one field goal ahead of Wilder U, and the clock is ticking. One of the Wilder U players gets injured, and I take that as my opportunity to rush to the restroom before I head to the field with the pass that Thorne gave me.

"I'll be back. I'm going pee," I say to Lydia and Marley. "If the clock ends before I get back, I'll see you later."

Lydia squeezes my hand. "Good luck at dinner with Mr. and Mrs. Priss."

I laugh and turn, heading in the opposite direction.

It takes me longer than most because of the soreness in my leg. Thorne has created an entire strengthening regimen that I follow to build the muscles along my legs to help support the pain in my knee. It's working, even if my thigh feels strained from all the toning I'm doing.

I slip inside the restroom. There isn't a line for once, so I finish my business in record time. After I run my fingers through my wavy hair and apply some lip gloss to prepare for a full-body examination from Thorne's parents, I leave and rest along the chain link fence near security.

I show him my pass, and he nods, letting me stay near the opening of the field.

I find number thirteen right away, and it doesn't go unnoticed that I have butterflies.

He's standing on the sideline, more focused than I've ever seen him. The edge of his jaw grows sharper when Wilder U gets the first down. I nibble on my lip and glance back and forth between the game and his rigid stance on the sidelines.

Wilder U makes it to field goal range, and there's a collective sigh from Shadow Valley fans.

I don't even have to look on the field to see that they've gotten a field goal. I can tell by Thorne's frustrated posture. He pulls his helmet back on with force.

"Thorne!" I shout.

The security guard shakes his head. He likely thinks I'm some jersey chaser, trying to garner the quarterback's attention.

But I'm not.

I'm his girlfriend.

Or his fake girlfriend.

Whatever.

When Thorne finds me, he pauses. Surprise replaces his frustration, and I smile.

"Remember that pre-game ritual, baby." I wink.

I watch him try to hide a grin. He chuckles and points at me, winking right back.

My cheeks are warm to the touch. I shuffle on my brand-new boots and flick my chin to the field.

Get out there and win.

As if he can read my mind, he nods.

Before he heads out, he glances over my shoulder, and his smile falls.

My heart races.

I don't know why I expect it to be my arsonist, as if Thorne would even know about that, but I'm on edge anyway.

I turn and glance behind me.

Ah.

The parents.

Before greeting them, I send Thorne a reassuring nod. *I've got this.*

He has no choice but to trust me. He rushes the field with the offensive line, and I pray he can throw a touchdown or at the very least, get another field goal to put us ahead before time runs out.

I brace myself for the vetting process I'm about to go through. I spin and fake a smile.

Mr. and Mrs. Thorne are standing alone. Not that I blame anyone for keeping their distance. When Thorne said they'd look out of place, he was right.

His mother, Helena, is wearing a long fur coat and heels that will no doubt sink in the field, and his father is sporting a suit that is freshly pressed and too expensive to be wearing to a college football game.

I approach them slowly. My guards are up.

"Hi, Mr. and Mrs. Thorne! I'm Briar, Thorne's girlfriend."
Fake girlfriend.

Helena acts surprised, but you can hardly tell due to the Botox. I'm certain she already knew who I was.

"Oh, hello!"

I wouldn't do this on any other day, but I lean in and give her a hug because I know it's something that a brainless rich girl would do. They'd probably cut off a limb to get close to their future mother-in-law.

She smells like Chanel and… money.

I swear.

After I back away, I glance at Andrew, who I choose to refer to as Mr. Thorne because it's very obvious that he expects respect. "Mr. Thorne," I say, placing my hand out. "It's so nice to meet you both."

"Likewise." His grip is firm, which is no surprise.

The crowd roars, and I pull my hand away to clap. Thorne threw a thirty-yard pass, and they're in field goal range.

"Let's see if he can manage not to screw this up," his father grumbles.

I feel Helena's eyes on me, probably adding up how much each article of clothing costs. Never mind the fact that their money bought them.

"He won't," I say. "Not with you here."

He scoffs. "I highly doubt my son cares if I'm here or not."

"Not true," I lie. "He's happy you're here to watch."

"Oh, *please*." Helena laughs lightly and grabs my arm. "I think he's just excited to show you off. When he told us he had a girlfriend, we didn't expect… you."

I fake a giggle, even though I feel a bit like throwing up. "I hope that means I've exceeded your expectations."

Mr. Thorne glances at me out of the corner of his eye. He turns away to watch the game. He's too hard to read. Helena, though, she has a twinkle in her eye.

"The babies you two would have!" she rejoices. "You're much prettier than any girl he's ever introduced us to."

Never mind the first part of her sentence. I'm too focused on the irrational jealousy I'm swimming in thinking about Thorne introducing another girl to his parents.

"Don't embarrass me, Cassius!"

Both Helena and I twist to Thorne's dad and his completely discouraging shout from the sideline.

Either Thorne didn't hear him or he's ignoring him.

I shout, too. "Let's go, Thorne!"

As soon as I cheer him on, the ball snaps. Thorne catches it and backs up, searching for an opening. Wilder U is good at hockey and apparently football, too.

The crowd holds their breath, and I find myself doing the same. At some point, I've moved closer to the fence, and although it's been a few seconds, it feels like hours by the time he throws the ball.

I follow it through the air, praying it makes it into the hands of Rhys. He catches it at the last second, both feet touch down in the end zone, and the fans lose their minds.

"Yes!" I jump up and down. My knee buckles so I grip the fence and keep myself steady.

It's even better that Rhys was the one who caught the ball, because he's one of the only other football players who I feel that I can trust.

I'm skeptical of the rest.

I rush the field with my pass as soon as the buzzer sounds, forgetting all about Thorne's parents.

My only saving grace is that the act of running into Thorne's arms is something a loving girlfriend would do so at least I make our relationship believable.

It feels awfully believable, too.

CHAPTER 26
THORNE

THE HIGH OF winning is eclipsed only by the sight of Briar making her way through the crowd. I shrug off Rhys's arm from around my shoulders and cut a path toward her.

The sweater, skirt, and black tights combo is deadly on her, and I am suddenly grateful that we spent the time on shopping. She wasn't thrilled for most of it, but at the end... As I told her, it wasn't about giving her a whole makeover. I *like* her style, even if it's overly monochromatic.

It was just about giving my blue-blood parents a hint at wealth.

Or class.

Or what-fucking-ever they decide.

It won't be enough, of course. They'll probably take one look at her and make a decision based on something inane. Her hair or makeup or just the way she smiles. Or the limp.

The thought of putting her in an ice bath bubbles to the forefront of my mind. I still need to do that... and make it enjoyable for her.

But then there's no more time for other thoughts or distractions. There's just Briar in front of me.

I wrap my arms around her, and hers come around my

neck, as I lift her feet off the ground. Her gaze burns into mine for a split second, then our lips crash together.

It sizzles between us, of course, but I'm aware of everything else around us. My teammates and fellow students, the coaching staff, the media. It's probably why I don't deepen the kiss, and instead keep it close-lipped.

When we break apart, she gives me a dazzling smile, and I can't help but mirror it.

"You were fucking incredible," she tells me.

"Thank you, kitten."

"Cassius!" A woman's voice, unmistakably my mother, cuts through the noise.

Briar's smile tightens.

"Did you meet them?" I ask in Briar's ear.

"Yeah, it was fine."

Fine.

I suppress my scoff of disbelief and slowly lower her so her feet touch the ground again. The boots we picked are sensible, at least. Nothing high-heeled—no doubt her knee would protest that, even if it would be sexy as fuck.

Still, I keep my hand on the small of her back when we face my parents.

"Good game, sweetheart," my mother says. She comes in close.

I lean down and let her press her lips to my cheek. It's been a while since she was able to reach without assistance. She's shorter than Briar by at least four inches, and the points of her heels sinking into the grass don't help.

"Son."

Dad extends his hand, and I shake it. His grip is always crushing, but this time it seems even more so. He squeezes hard, and I get a glimpse of the anger in his expression.

So he hasn't calmed down any since our phone call the other week.

Lovely.

"We have reservations in an hour," he adds. "We'll meet you out front."

"Of course." My fingers tense on Briar's back. "I've got to get changed. Walk with me?"

She glances up at me and nods. I lead her away, stopping only twice for reporters followed by cameramen.

I give run-of-the-mill, media-training answers, and then they let us pass.

"Is it always this hectic?" Briar asks in the tunnel. She keeps glancing around like someone's going to jump out and grab her.

"What? Yeah, I guess." I drop my hand from her back. "Are you okay?"

"Of course."

"You—"

"Thorne!"

I pause and glance back. Stephen McDowell jogs toward us, only slowing when he's even with Briar and me.

"Nice throw to win it," he says. "Our defense was sweating when they made that field goal."

I lift my shoulder. "It happens."

Stephen eyes Briar. "You escorting your girlfriend to the locker room?"

I force a laugh and shake my head. "No, just giving her an escape route from my parents."

He sticks his hand out. "Stephen."

Friends with your slimy ex, I almost say. Patterson has done a good job at avoiding me—and, I think, Briar. At least, she hasn't said anything else about him showing up or running into her.

"Briar." She shakes his hand, then quickly withdraws. She wraps her arms around her stomach and stares straight ahead.

"I'll see you around," I tell Stephen.

A clear *get the fuck out of here.*

He takes the hint and hurries on, while I slip my fingers around Briar's arm and stop her. I press her against the wall and plant my forearm next to her head, leaning in.

"You're jumpy, kitten."

She's looking everywhere but at me. I put my finger under her chin and direct her face up toward mine.

"Just, uh, I don't want to be seen by the wrong people."

The wrong people?

Seen? With me?

I drop my hand and step back. Hurt ricochets through me, louder than it should. Who are the wrong people? The whole point of us was to be seen...

But that was my plan, wasn't it?

"Come on." My voice comes out more gruff. "There's a room you can wait in up ahead that'll be out of sight."

She follows along behind me. "I didn't mean it like that."

I shake my head. I don't know how she could've not meant it. I direct her to the assistant equipment manager's office and leave her there. It's been unoccupied since the summer, so I doubt anyone will accidentally walk in on her.

Then, pushing aside the sudden bad taste in my mouth, I head into the locker room to prepare for what will probably be the most awkward dinner of my life.

———

My mother hasn't stopped talking.

The restaurant we're in is nice. It has a Michelin Star—or two or three, I don't know—and the service has been top-notch. The lighting is bright, the chatter amongst other tables a low babble in the background of my mother's rambling.

We're doing courses. Five of them.

The server returns with the first, which is a cold soup. I missed the *cold* detail, though, so when I blew on my spoon, my father glared at me. And then I put it in my mouth and realized… and almost gagged.

Mom's steady chatter provided a commentary on what life has been like back home. An interior decorator and her crew were in for their seasonal change. The house decor has to match, after all, and we're quickly slipping into winter.

"And we're so excited to have you join us for Christmas, Briar," my mother adds.

Briar chokes.

I mentally curse. I probably should've mentioned that.

"That remains to be seen," Father interjects. "Christmas is a long time away."

I grit my teeth. "I thought it was your idea to have us home for the holidays, Dad."

He waves his hand and picks up his glass of wine. "Well, that was before I *met* Brianna, Cassius."

Briar lifts her chin. "It's Briar."

"Briar," Mom repeats, glancing at her husband. "A lovely name. I'm sure he'll have it down by Christmas. So, tell me, do you go to all of our son's games?"

My fake girlfriend sets down her silverware. Her soup bowl is empty.

Only four more courses to go.

"I try to go to all of them, yes," she answers. "And my friends and I saw a few of his practices."

"How lovely," my mom echoes. "Do you have any hobbies of your own?"

"*Mom*," I whisper.

She frowns. "What?"

"You—"

"It's okay." Briar rests her hand on my wrist. "I understand what you meant by that, Mrs. Thorne. I do have hobbies of my own."

"Hobbies are important." My father meets my gaze. "Hobbies like football are great for exercise. And luckily, Cassius chose to be a quarterback, which lends to his excellent leadership abilities. That's why we allow it, quite frankly."

My chest tightens, and my attention falls to my now-empty bowl of cold, shitty soup. Before I can come up with a retort, the server has returned to clear the table. They whisk away the empty bowls and return with a fresh bottle of wine.

Football is not a hobby.

It never has been.

Briar's fingers drum on my wrist, lightly, dragging my attention over to her. She flicks her hair over her shoulder and smiles at me.

She's calm in the face of all of this. But why shouldn't she be? At the end, when this is over—when our fake relationship has run its course—I will be stuck with my asshole parents, and she'll get to walk away.

And I hate that.

The next course and the third pass with little incident.

It's between the third and fourth course that their conversation turns back to us.

Well, Briar.

"You mentioned hobbies." Father focuses on Briar. "What exactly are those?"

She sits up straighter. "I paint. And I used to play hockey."

"Hockey," he repeats slowly.

"Painting," Mom interrupts. "What kind of painting? Portraits? We hire a wonderful artist every few years to give us an updated family portrait. Of course, getting Cassius to sit still long enough was always the challenge…"

"She painted the locker room mural," I say quietly. "It came out beautiful."

"Thanks," she whispers. To my parents, she adds, "It goes along with the art degree."

They both pause.

"Art degree?" Mom tilts her head to the side, narrowing in on Briar.

The thing about my mother... she's fickle. She has a kind heart *sometimes*. Like maybe, initially, she gave Briar a chance. But as soon as she hears something she doesn't like, a switch flips.

"Yes." Briar raises an eyebrow. "I know it's not very practical, but I decided to focus on doing something I love."

My heart squeezes.

"Well," Mom pats at the corner of her mouth with her napkin. "I suppose your taste in men will make up for that... salary difference. If this is the lifestyle you're going to accustom yourself with, attaching yourself to the Thorne name."

"*Mom.*"

She ignores me, focused on Briar. "At least the women in our circles know what they're getting into."

"That's enough," I say. "Briar knows what she's getting into with *me*. But I should've better warned her about you."

"I'm fine," Briar says softly. "I know what I want to do with my life, and I am free to do it."

"Your parents must be very..."

"Supportive," Briar finishes.

"Of course, dear." Mom turns to me. "Cassius, I completely forgot. I ran into Vanessa Keenland and her daughter, Cynthia, when I was getting my nails done earlier this week. Cynthia was asking about you."

I stare at her. "I... okay."

"I'm just saying. For when this blows over, you know, it didn't scare her away. She was saying what a gentleman you were on your date, and I know that sometimes you go too hard in the *wooing* department, especially if you bring them home after—"

My face heats. "I don't—"

"Oh, it's fine, honey, we know you're an active young man. Your father was the same way your age."

Gross.

Briar wrinkles her nose and slowly sets her napkin on the table. "Excuse me, I'm just going to use the ladies' room."

She gets up and strides away from the table, and it takes everything in me to not leap up and follow her.

"Can you at least pretend to be nice?" I lean forward. "Would it kill you?"

"I just don't see what the big deal is." My mother's expression sharpens. "She's an art major? What do her parents do, Cassius? Work in *retail*?"

I recoil.

"I'll be right back," I snap. I toss my napkin down and head in the direction Briar went. The bathrooms are down a darker hallway, and I pause in front of the first door. It's open, revealing a single-person one.

Which means she's in the other.

Without thinking, I go to the closed door and rap my knuckles against the painted wood.

"Briar? It's Thorne. Let me in."

Silence.

She could totally be rejecting me right now. She could wait me out—how long would I stay here? Looking a little desperate or a lot foolish?

But then the door knob turns, and it swings inward.

I immediately step inside, all the anger of sitting there listening to my parents *shit* bubbling up.

Briar's expression is resolute. Her jaw clenched, her lips pressed together.

Can't have that.

I approach her, and she backs away. I feel feral, but my hand is gentle when it reaches for her. My palm settles on her throat, and I continue to walk her to the far wall. Her heartbeat thrums against my fingers.

"Are you mad at me?"

She exhales. "No."

"Maybe you should take it out on me anyway."

I kiss her before she can reply. I kiss her until her lips part for me, and my tongue can sweep into her perfect mouth. I withdraw and bite her lower lip, tugging until she gives me a reaction.

A groan.

My fingers tense on her throat, and she makes another noise. Something caught between a whimper and a moan.

"What are we doing?" she asks, her lips brushing mine.

"Just a little balm," I reply, my voice too ragged. She tears me to pieces without even trying. "Let me make us both feel better so we can go back out there together. Okay?"

"Okay."

So that's exactly what I do.

CHAPTER 27
BRIAR

I'VE NEVER DONE this before.

I mean, I wouldn't really consider it public indecency. No one is around. It's a one-person bathroom. *But* it is in a public place.

"Thorne," I whisper over his mouth. He bites my lip and tugs on it.

This is hot.

Like, can't-hide-how-much-I'm-turned-on hot.

It feels sort of wrong because his parents are waiting for us.

But it feels sort of right, too. Because let's face it. They are complete fucking assholes.

"Put your hands on the sink, kitten."

Thorne turns me around swiftly, and I do as he says. His mouth hovers over my ear, and goosebumps rush to my skin. "We're going to have to be quick."

I whimper when his hand falls between my legs.

His hiss pulls my attention to the mirror. *Holy shit.* He's dangerously hot with his hooded eyes and his fingers tugging on my panties.

"Fucking hell, kitten. You're in thigh-high stockings? Later I'm going to fuck you with only those on."

I whimper again.

I'm desperate for the ache to go away. For something to ground me and calm my fizzled nerves.

"Ahh." My hands clamp on to the sink when he rubs his knuckle against my clit. I thrust backward, eager for him to ride this out with me.

"You want me to fuck you now, kitten?"

His mouth lands on my neck, right behind my ear. He sucks so hard, I see stars.

"Please."

God, I even sound desperate.

But for some reason, I'm okay with it.

I'm okay with it because it's Thorne.

Wait, do I trust him?

"Come for me, then I'll fuck you quick. My parents are probably wondering where we are."

"Fuck your parents."

The rumbling of Thorne's chest vibrates my spine. His finger moves in and out of me while his thumb rubs fast circles over my clit.

"That's it," he encourages, kissing on my neck again. "Those noises you're making are so fucking sexy, Briar. Hurry up and come so I can feel you squeeze around my—"

I throw my head back and combust. My hands slip, and my knees buckle. A hot tremor of pleasure zips through me as Thorne catches me by the waist, hauling me up to his chest.

"Look at how perfect you are when you come, kitten."

I open my eyes slowly.

The bathroom is hazy, and we're a blurry mess in the mirror.

Thorne kisses the spot on my neck that's sore. "Let me correct myself." His hand lands on my chin, and he squeezes it tight until I'm staring at us both in our reflection. "Look at how perfect you are when *I* make you come."

A blissful sigh falls from my mouth, and I lean forward again. I inch my skirt past my hips and press myself on to him. "Well, are you going to make me come again or what?"

The condom is already halfway on by the time I get my hands on the porcelain.

The tip of his dick is inside, and I'm already clenching around him.

We both turn to the knock on the door and freeze.

"Cassius?" His mother's voice sounds from the other side, and Thorne curses quietly. "Are you in there? Please come back to dinner before your father has a conniption. He's already angry, and you disappearing from dinner is disrespectful."

Thorne growls and pulls out of me. I quickly adjust myself and turn to lean against the sink. He places his hand flat on the door and speaks through it. "And the way you talked to my girlfriend is disrespectful."

God, his parents are awful.

I replay everything they said during dinner and cringe. It's no wonder he was so nervous about this evening.

Without putting much thought into it, I erase the space that separates us and wrap my arms around his waist from behind. I rest my ear on his back and hear his pounding heart.

"I will refrain from *offending* that girl as long as you come back."

That girl.

I squeeze him tighter. His hand falls to my arm, and he rubs this thumb slowly on the inside of my wrist.

"We'll be right there, Mrs. Thorne." I'm proud of how sweet my tone is.

Thorne drops his head, and after a few seconds of silence, he starts to laugh.

I smile against his back because it's a nice sound. I like it. "Why are you laughing?"

"Because..." He tugs on my arm, and I move in front of him. He takes the back of his hand and rubs his knuckles over my cheekbone. "I'm still fucking hard."

I immediately glance at his pants.

"You're the only girl in the entire world who has the power to keep me hard as a fucking rock with my mom right outside the door."

I giggle, and Thorne grins. We stare at each other for a few seconds, and it's difficult to tell what's going through his head, because surely it isn't what my heart is tricking me into thinking.

"Let's go before I make my father even more angry."

He brings my hair in front of my neck to hide the hickey he gave me and then quickly adjusts himself. After a moment, he opens the door to an empty hallway.

We walk hand in hand toward his parents. I feel lighter after our little bathroom escapade and I'm pretty sure that isn't the orgasm talking.

———

I stare at the dessert placed in front of me.

I'm thankful it's the final course of our excruciating dinner with Thorne's parents but I'm not sure I can eat whatever the *hell* this is.

I glance at the waiter, who is sweating due to Thorne's father scolding him for not grabbing our empty plates fast enough.

He must want this dinner to end just as quickly as I do.

"Poached Pears Belle Helene," the waiter says, quickly scurrying away.

Thorne's hand falls to my leg under the table after I continue to stare at the pear covered in *chocolate*?

"Why isn't she eating?" Mr. Thorne refuses to look in my direction.

Thorne squeezes my thigh. I clear my throat, saving him from the trouble of making up some excuse.

"I'm trying to watch my figure," I answer, glancing at Helena next. "Us girls have to stay in shape so we can keep our men happy, right?"

I hear the faintest growl from Thorne, but surely he knows I'm just trying to appease his parents. They want some Barbie-like wife for Thorne so that's what I'll act like if it'll get them off his back.

"Well then, you're dismissed."

I slice my attention over to the head of the table. Andrew Thorne doesn't even glance at me. Instead, he glances at his watch, like he has somewhere else to be.

Thorne scoots his chair back but stops as soon as his father slaps the table. "Not you, Cassius. *Her.*"

Now it's my turn to grab Thorne's thigh. *Calm down.*

"And how do you expect her to get home?" he grits between clenched teeth.

"She'll find a way. You and I have business to discuss."

I can tell Thorne wants to argue, but instead of letting him, I drag my palm up his leg and latch on to his hand. Two squeezes later, and I'm placing my napkin onto the table and standing upright.

Coming to stand behind Thorne, I place my palm on his shoulder and glance to both of his parents. "Thank you so much for dinner." Thorne reaches up and softly touches my hand. "It was so nice to meet both of you."

Not.

Helena says some fake-nice remark, and Andrew grunts followed by a curt nod.

"I'll see you later," I whisper, placing a kiss on Thorne's cheek.

I don't breathe again until I'm outside.

Thorne texts me almost immediately.

CASSIUS

Uber is on its way. Check the license plate before you get in.

I send him a thumbs-up emoji.
He texts again.

CASSIUS

I'm sorry... for the entire night.

ME

Don't be.

The truth is, I'm sorry for him.

CHAPTER 28
THORNE

BRIAR'S ROOMMATE, Lydia, meets me at the door with a raised eyebrow and pursed lips.

"I know," I say, holding up my hands in surrender. "If she told you anything about the train wreck my family is…"

She sighs and holds her apartment door open wider, allowing me to pass. "She's sleeping."

"I figured." I rub the back of my neck. "Thanks for not slamming the door in my face."

Lydia points to the coffee table, where two phones sit. "She left her phone out here when she went to bed, and it kept lighting up rather insistently with your texts. So…"

Right.

I did go a little crazy with the texts as soon as my father was finished. Just more bullshit about how embarrassed he was with this girlfriend *stunt*, and then about how I'd better enjoy my last season of football.

Because, according to him, my time to fuck around is coming to a close.

One more year left of school, but no football?

He said he would buy the university a whole building to

keep me from playing. What administration will be able to resist that? Millions of dollars, just to bar me from the field.

My dreams flushed down the toilet.

I push away my anger and leave Lydia behind, creeping down the hall and entering Briar's room carefully. I nearly trip over a black pot placed right in the opening. It has a few metal utensils balanced on it. One touch and it would cause quite the ruckus.

My brows furrow.

I click on my phone's flashlight and illuminate the room, curious about the booby trap. I close the door behind me and step farther in, first taking in Briar's still form buried under the blankets, then the rest of the room.

A mini hockey stick catches my attention. It's wedged into the upper portion of the window to prevent the lower pane from opening. There's an actual hockey stick leaning in the far corner. A gleam of gold in the light pulls my attention, and I move to her desk.

It's a trophy.

I lean down and scan the plaque at its base. She won Most Valuable Player last year.

Wow.

Of course she did. She's fucking impressive.

Which makes me want to wake her up and *tell* her she's impressive. Not just for the hockey award, although that is cool. But also for being herself, and not caving to my parents' bullshit, *and* for surviving dinner with a smile intact.

And also, I wouldn't mind finishing what we had started earlier...

I peel back her covers and lean over her. She looks so peaceful, I almost don't want to disturb her. Almost.

I touch her shoulder.

She wakes immediately, but her gaze doesn't focus on my face. Her lips part, her eyes widen. Instead of shrinking away, she grabs my wrist and *hauls.*

Not expecting it, I lose my balance and topple. She grips my shoulders and uses her legs, twisting, and suddenly I'm on my back, and she straddles me.

Her breathing is ragged, and something sharp presses into my throat.

Holy shit.

"Briar," I rasp. "It's me."

My palms land on her thighs, sliding up to her hips, then her waist. The prick of pain wakes me up, but she doesn't seem to understand—or see.

"Kitten. Focus on me."

She blinks, focusing on me. My phone lies facedown somewhere to the side, the flash illuminating the room. It helps me see the moment she realizes what she's done.

I wrap my fingers around her hand and the knife, moving it away from my throat.

"Thorne," she gasps. "Oh God."

"It's okay. You're okay."

"You're bleeding!" She tosses the knife and stares down at me. "And I…"

"Performed some cool moves," I finish, attempting humor. I move her back a little, until she's sitting on my thighs, and sit up. "I've gotta say, though, I'm concerned about why that's your first reaction to someone waking you up."

She stiffens.

I tuck her hair behind her ear, then carefully straighten her shirt. Her shorts are twisted, too. Once I'm done fussing, she lets out a sigh. She climbs off me and stands beside the bed, her expression wary.

I scoot back until I can rest against her headboard, then pat my lap. "Come back here."

"I just… you're bleeding."

I touch my throat, and my fingers come away dotted with blood. "I'm not going to die from a scratch. Come. Here."

She exhales and relents. She crawls toward me and slowly

swings her leg over my lap. My hands automatically find her bare thighs, and my fingers creep down toward her knee. We've been working on strengthening exercises, and it seems to be helping. Forward progress is usually slow in the beginning—excruciatingly so. But she hasn't given up on me.

I find the rough, scarred skin, and she shivers. It doesn't bother me—not how she thinks.

It *kills* me that this happened to her.

But I've never been disgusted by her scars. The thought that someone made her think they should be hidden twists my stomach.

"So." I knead her legs. "The pot and forks? The mini hockey stick?"

She bites her lip.

"Do you trust me?"

"Yeah," she whispers. "I don't know why, but I do."

"Then *trust* me." I lean in and steal a quick kiss. "And that's *my* lip to bite, kitten."

Her breathing hitches. "Bossy."

"If you want *bossy*, then tell me what's going on." The need to know is going to drive me insane.

"I…" She shudders. "You know about the fire."

"I do."

"Well… it wasn't an accident."

I straighten. "What?"

Her gaze slides away from me. "There was someone there that night. They started the fire and they—they saw me coming, trying to get out, and slammed the door in my face."

Tears fill her eyes.

I tug her to my chest, the horror echoing through me. I cannot imagine what that would've been like. The fear of it.

I know fear.

My father made me an expert in fear.

But this? To be alone…

"The building filled with smoke and fire so fast, and there

was no choice. I ended up back in the room I was working in, and then I just…"

"It's okay." I cup the back of her head, her cheek on my chest. I try to remember to breathe. "He can't hurt you."

She pulls back slowly. "That's the thing, Thorne. He *can*."

My confusion must be apparent, because she scrambles off me and goes to her desk. She rummages around in one of the drawers, then flicks on the lamp and returns to me. She holds out a note sealed tight in a Ziploc bag.

Stop looking.
Or you'll be the one soaked in gasoline.

My heart beats faster. "Someone left this for you?"

"Not just someone. The guy who freaking left me to die." She balls her fists. "He got in here—I—"

"Hey." I set the note aside and catch her hand. "Hey, hey. He snuck in like a coward when you weren't here. But *I'm* here now, kitten."

She swallows. I've never seen her look so forlorn.

"I just don't want him to hurt you, Cassius."

I close my eyes. I hate to admit that I like it when she says my first name. It's like a balm instead of the rough reprimanding tone my parents use.

Speaking of parents…

"I hope the dinner didn't scare you away."

She meets my gaze, and the corner of her lips lifts. "Me? Scared of some rich old snobs? Never."

"Good." I run my thumb across her knuckles. "Then you need to get naked immediately."

She backs away from me and grabs the hem of her shirt.

She lifts it slowly, revealing her toned abdomen, then her bare breasts. I swing my legs off the bed and scoot forward, but I manage to keep my hands to myself—for now.

Briar swivels around, giving me a view of her back, and hooks her thumbs in the waistband of her sleep shorts. She leans forward and drags them down. I swallow hard, the view of her perfect ass almost too much.

My dick is standing at attention, pressing against my sweatpants.

I stand, too, and kick them off. Along with the rest of my clothes.

She meets me in the middle of the room, and she puts her palm on my abs.

"A six-pack just isn't fair," she murmurs.

I flex harder, grinning.

"Make that eight." She sighs. "Fuck me."

"That's the plan, kitten."

I skim the side of her neck and catch her hair in my hand. Using it to pull her head back, I lean down and kiss her hard. My other hand palms her breast, and I pinch her nipple. Roll it between my fingers. She moans into my mouth, and I shift forward. My dick brushes her stomach.

Beds are overrated.

I release her breast and hair and grip her hips, lifting her. I cross the room and put her back against the wall next to the door—barely missing the pot contraption—and raise her higher.

She wraps her legs around my waist. The heat of her cunt is an almost unbearable turn on, and I groan when the tip of my cock slips through her arousal. I do that a few times, teasing us both, then carefully notch it.

"Ready?"

She nods, the movement quick and jerky. "Please get inside me."

I grin.

Thrust.

Her warmth envelops me, and I sit in it for a second. Then draw out and slowly push back into her.

"Fuck me." Briar holds on to my shoulders, but her hands slip toward the back of my neck, then into my hair. Her nails scrape at my scalp. "You stretch me so good. I could die of happiness."

"You? Happy?" I continue my slow movements. "That might be the best thing you've ever said to me."

She sighs.

I kiss her neck, finding the sensitive spot I was working on earlier. I suck at it, then skim it with my teeth. I want her marked for the whole school to see. I want to do a lot of firsts with her.

Public affection.

Spend the night in her bed.

Call her mine for good.

Don't get ahead of yourself.

I drag my lips down, over her collarbone, to her breast. She gasps when I suck her nipple into my mouth, flicking it with my tongue. My hand returns to her other one, paying it just as much attention, until she writhes against me.

To my shock, her body tenses, and her head falls back. She clamps around me, the orgasm sweeping through her body.

"Holy shit." I raise my head. "Did you just come from me playing with your tits, kitten?"

She blinks at me, slow and dazed. "That, uh, hasn't happened before."

Fuck yeah.

Another first.

"Cassius?"

"Yeah?"

"You stopped fucking me."

Right.

"Sorry, kitten."

I resume, my pace quick. I chase my pleasure and hers, my fingers going straight to her clit. Some part of me is after the release—but another, more selfish part, just wants her to say my name again. In wonder. In ecstasy.

I roll my hips, hitting a new angle inside her, and her eyes flutter. Her nails dig into the back of my neck. We wind tighter and tighter until—

There.

Her mouth opens, her eyes squeeze shut. Her cunt pulses around me, and it's just enough to push me over the edge, too.

It isn't until I'm spent, my body pressing hers to the wall, that I realize I didn't use a condom. I pull out of her and slowly lower her feet to the floor.

"Briar—"

"I noticed," she whispers. "I'm on birth control. And, um, I'm clean."

My shoulders snap back. "I am, too. Clean. Not on birth control."

She cracks a smile, but it's tired. I follow her into the bathroom and wash up while she uses the toilet.

It's weirdly not weird.

And after that, I hand her shirt back to her, turn off my phone's flashlight and the lamp, and climb into bed with her.

It feels like the most natural thing in the world.

And that's what makes it so goddamn terrifying.

CHAPTER 29
BRIAR

MY LIP IS raw from chewing on it. The sun is just barely breaking through the clouds, and I've been up for hours with Thorne's arm wrapped around my waist, keeping me safe.

He believed me.

Not that I thought he wouldn't, but without the fire department investigating and determining that the fire was arson, the university was hesitant to take my word for it. Even after the fire department ruled it as arson, the dean had questions.

As if he thought I would start a fire, trap myself in a building, only to jump out and injure myself.

Sure I'm a little callous but I'm not suicidal.

Thorne shifts in his sleep, and I take a second to stare at the side of his face.

A smile tugs against my lips when I trace the curve of his relaxed jaw.

My heart races.

This is getting too real.

It's becoming easier and easier to trust him. Not only with my body but my secrets and heart, too.

I've been through hard shit.

I'll be fine when we *break up*. Right?

"Kitten." My pet name slips from his mouth. His voice is a sleepy rasp.

"Cassius," I reply.

He peeks one eye open.

How can someone look so... *good* first thing in the morning?

Humor works itself onto his face, and I start to question if I said my thoughts aloud.

"Is my fake girlfriend blushing at the thought of me being in her bed first thing in the morning?"

Key word: fake.

"What?" I put my back to him. "No."

He chuckles. "It's okay. This is a first for me, too."

His arm clamps over my hip, and he pulls me closer to him. We're spooning, and I can't ignore the feel of his hard length against my backside.

"Who said this is a first for me?" I tease.

He makes a noise. "Right. I forgot. *Ben*." He says his name with disgust, and I wrinkle my nose at the thought of waking up beside my ex.

"Is this really a first for you?" I ask. Surely that's not true.

His warm breath coats my neck when he sighs. "Yeah, kitten. It is."

I blink in disbelief. "How?"

There's a long pause. He's holding his breath, I try to turn toward him, but he keeps me in place and exhales. "I don't like people touching me."

I'm skeptical. "I touch you."

His nose skims the inside of my neck. "You're not *people*."

I flop onto my back and find him staring down at me with a furrowed brow. Eventually, he flops onto his back, too.

"I've never told anyone this," he starts.

There's a slip in his voice, like he's nervous. I intertwine our fingers but stay lying on my back so I don't put too much pressure on him.

"But I have this... aversion to touch. I've been like this since I was a child."

"Aversion?" I press.

His hand squeezes mine. I'm not even sure he realizes he's doing it.

"Whenever someone touches me for too long, I start to panic." He chuckles quietly and tries to pull his hand away. I keep it trapped until he relaxes. "It's embarrassing, honestly. I'd actually hyperventilated from it a few times when I was younger."

"More embarrassing than me being afraid to cook because of the open flame?"

He glances over at me but then turns away to continue.

"I didn't really understand why until I was old enough to put two and two together. It's because of my father."

My heart races.

I hate him even more now.

"He used to say he was teaching me to face my fears, but I think he just wanted to control me."

"What did he do?" My voice is more of a croak.

"He forced me to face whatever fear I had. Swimming? He held me underwater until I passed out."

I try to hide my shock, but Thorne shifts at the sound of my parting lips.

"Afraid of monsters under my bed? He turned the lights off, shoved me underneath, and kept me there until I stopped fighting him."

My heart hurts.

It protests inside my chest. Like if it could crawl from my body and go into his, it would.

"There's more, but I'll save you the trauma." He shrugs away his emotions. "The more he did it, the more I hated being touched. It made me feel... smothered." A chill works through his body.

I slowly move to my side and get closer to him. I drape my leg over his and place my hand over his racing heart. "I get it. I feel the same when I'm in a crowded room without a direct view to the exit."

Thorne nods, like he understands.

We may be in a fake relationship, but I don't think either of us can deny the connection we have.

"I'm glad I don't make you feel that way when I touch you," I whisper.

He angles himself, and our mouths are a breath away. My lips part, and his hooded gaze falls to them.

"Me, too." He cups my cheek and tugs me in close.

The kiss is tender but real.

At least it feels that way to me.

We kiss for what feels like hours, only coming up for air every few seconds to discard our clothes on my bedroom floor. I press my lips to the cut I left on his throat before I climb on top of him. I slowly brush my fingers over his bare chest.

His cheeks are flushed. He watches with rapt attention as I touch every part of him. The more I touch him, the tighter his grip gets on my hips until he's pressing himself into me. I gasp when he fills me. We fuck slow.

We don't say a single word.

Only hot noises, heavy breathing, and whimpers that fall onto his mouth from mine.

I know it's wrong.

I think *he* knows it's wrong.

This definitely doesn't feel fake, but neither of us put a stop to it. We move against each other, sweat coating both of our bodies, until we're fully sated and breathless.

I've never had sex like that.

And by the way he's gazing at me from the bathroom, I don't think he has either.

———

Thorne is watching me like a hawk.

He trails my every step.

By the end of my second rep, I spring up from the mat and give him a look. "You're making me nervous."

He smirks. "Wouldn't be the first time."

I roll my eyes.

"Why are you staring at me so intensely? I'm surprised you haven't told me my form is wrong."

He walks over to me and holds out his hand to haul me to my feet. I wobble a little, but he steadies me with his hands on my waist. I peek at him, and his brow is furrowed.

"I didn't realize I was showing my thoughts on my face."

I cock my head.

I know exactly what thoughts are going through his head.

"You're thinking about what I told you, aren't you?"

He huffs. "How could I not?"

My heart races. I push his hands away and drop back to the floor to finish my reps.

"There has to be more we can do." He paces in front of me, and I try my hardest to focus on the burning in my thigh instead of the worry I've inflicted onto him.

"The police are handling it." I say in between breaths.

They are.

Sort of.

I'm pretty sure they've run out of leads.

Thorne stops pacing and stands above me. "Did you tell them about the note?"

I glance away.

"I don't see the point." My stomach hurts. Worry is

gnawing on my insides. "The gasoline would have likely taken the fingerprints away."

Thorne's lips flatten into a straight line. His gaze traces over my face. I try my best to smooth my features but I'm certain he knows me well enough now to know that I'm worried.

"Up," he demands.

I slowly rise to my feet. He cups my chin, and my worries start to fade.

Not enough to slow my heart but enough to calm the shaking of my legs.

"You're tense," he states.

I swallow. *Of course I am.* Not to mention, I still haven't told him that the arsonist is on the football team.

"It's a hard workout," I say, lying right through my teeth.

He grins. "I have the perfect remedy."

My eyebrow arches with my thoughts going right to the gutter.

He laughs and rubs his thumb over my bottom lip. "Patience, kitten." He leans in close, his lips tickling my ear with his whisper. "I'll reward you after."

CHAPTER 30
THORNE

I DUMP the fifth bag of ice into the tub and snicker to myself.

She's *so* not going to enjoy this.

"Have you ever done an ice bath?" I call over to her.

She's cooling down on the treadmill, taking it easy as I directed. Following orders for once.

"I've iced my knee before," she replies.

That's not the same thing.

The treadmill beeps, and I dip my hand into the water. She grabs a water bottle and comes my way, her eyebrow raised. The water has a nice bite to it, just a few seconds stinging my fingers.

This is going to be fun.

I motion to her body. "Might want to strip down."

"Thorne!"

I snort. "I don't mean completely. The sports bra and your panties can stay."

Because I don't want to know what I would do if someone walked in and got an eyeful of her tits. I'd probably lose my mind…

My chest tightens. I've been avoiding my own thoughts

regarding our relationship. Mainly, that it's all pretend. Except it's starting to not feel quite so fake, and that terrifies me.

I wasn't lying to her the other night. I haven't done this before. Haven't held on to a steady girlfriend, haven't cared about anyone more than football to give them the time of day. No sleepovers, no public displays of affection, no repeated dates.

Anyway. Now is *not* the time to start thinking about such things.

"There's something I didn't tell you," she says in a low voice.

"Tell me when you're in the ice bath." I point to the tub.

She frowns, but she does as she's told. She steps up to the edge and lifts her good leg, gripping the edge to keep her balance. She slowly lowers it into the ice water and sucks in a sharp breath.

"Yep, I know how that feels," I say. "Keep pushing."

She says something under her breath and lifts her other leg in. The water barely touches her knees.

"Now sit."

"Fucking hell." She white-knuckles the lip of the tub and drops down inch by inch.

That just makes it worse, really.

Finally, the water rushes over her hips, then her abdomen, and she gets all the way into a seated position. She's barely breathing, her chest not rising or falling as usual. And she's so fucking tense...

I cock my head and count backward from ten, anticipating her cop-out.

And sure enough, she hauls herself up almost immediately.

"O-o-okay." Her teeth chatter. "That was fun."

I shake my head. "That was not good enough, grumpy cat."

She scowls and doesn't move.

"You really are like a cat. Afraid to get wet." I shed my shirt and shove my sweatpants down, revealing my boxer briefs. I set a timer for three minutes on my phone and step in behind her.

"W-what are you doing?"

I ignore the feel of the water and focus on her, running my hands down her arms. "Helping. Obviously."

She exhales.

"Now we sit." I lower myself and spread my legs, leaving a space for her. The coldness leaves a familiar tightness in my lungs, a steal-your-breath iciness that I force myself to relax into.

She looks at me, then slowly comes back down. She settles between my legs and leans against my chest.

I immediately wrap my arms around her waist, holding her hostage. Her skin feels hot, even with ice cubes bumping into us.

"Breathe," I say in her ear. "Focus on relaxing every individual muscle."

"Y-you do this on the r-r-regular?"

"After practices a few times a week." I nip her ear. "*Relax.*"

My hand slides lower, down her abdomen, and slips under the waistband of her panties. Her breathing comes faster when I stroke her clit.

I lean over and check the timer on my phone. "Two minutes left, kitten. Think you can slow your breathing a bit?"

"Not with you d-doing that."

My finger rubs a lazy circle. "I was going to wait until after to reward you, but I think I'll start now."

She groans. Her head tips back and rests on my shoulder, and I watch her struggle to unclench her muscles. And take a deep breath. Then another.

When she does, I increase the pressure of my rubbing.

"Fuck," she moans.

"I wonder if you'll come like this," I muse to myself.

"Y-yeah, just—"

"You're getting tense again."

She blows out a frustrated breath and sags on me.

"There." I push two fingers inside her.

She immediately arches up, but I don't care. There's thirty seconds left on the timer now, and I seem to be in competition with myself. A race against the clock.

I pump in and out. My other hand comes down and flicks her clit, all while she's trapped between my arms. If I wasn't in ice water, I'd have an erection the size of Texas. As it is, I can feel my heartbeat in my groin.

The timer goes off, the noise shrill, but she's *right there*. She grabs my wrists, holding my hands hostage, and I continue until she tips over the edge. She rides it out, her hips moving, her mouth parted.

When the climax subsides, she releases me and hauls herself out of the water. I follow more carefully, my gaze sharp on her red skin.

I climb out and offer my hand to her, then snag one of the two towels for her. I use the other one to dry off and smirk at her.

"That wasn't so bad, was it?"

She shakes her head. "You're impossible."

"We're going to add that into our routine," I continue. "It'll help."

"If every ice bath goes like that, then… maybe."

My smile widens.

"But…" She fiddles with the corner of the towel. "I didn't say what I have to tell you."

"Right." I face her. "I'm listening."

Fear flashes across her expression, and she glances around. As if someone snuck in while we were distracted?

"The arsonist," she whispers.

"What about him?" I inch closer.

"He's on the football team, Thorne."

Fuck.

———

I sit in Rhys's room, debating how much to tell him.

If anything.

This feels a *little* like bad luck, running to tell my best friend a secret of my fake girlfriend's. But I can't face this alone. How the fuck am I supposed to walk into the locker room, or onto the field, every day knowing that one of my teammates tried to kill Briar?

But unfortunately, Rhys knows me too well.

The second he walks in and finds me waiting at his desk, he drops his bag, closes his door, and says, "Spill."

For the record, neither of us gossip. We just keep each other appraised of things going on in the school if it's necessary. Or interesting.

Okay, so, maybe that's a form of gossiping.

"If it's about one of the hockey girls hooking up with Ben Patterson, it's already gotten out."

I freeze. "What?"

"Oh. Did you not hear? I think it's a revenge plot against Briar, honestly. But he clearly has a type, and that type is *scary*. No offense, dude. I've seen Briar's scowl, and it's not something I want to cross. I can only imagine that her thighs are thick enough to crush my skull—well, *your* skull—"

"Shut up," I snap. "What the fuck is his problem?"

Rhys laughs. "You, obviously. And Briar… together. Do you see where I'm going with this?"

I wave him off. "That's not what I wanted to talk to you about."

"Something *else* happened?" He sits on his bed and grabs

a notebook from his bag, flipping to a blank page. "I'm ready, Professor. Fill me in."

"Put that shit away," I groan. "You're impossible. And this has to stay in the vault. It's serious shit."

To his credit, he *gets* serious. He tosses aside the notebook and focuses more fully on me.

"Remember the fire that nearly killed Briar?"

He rolls his eyes and nods.

"Well, it wasn't an accident. Someone set the building on fire with her in it." A lump forms in my throat just thinking about it.

"Holy shit." Rhys' eyes go wide. "How—"

"She saw the guy. Kind of. Not enough to identify him completely, but she *was* able to ascertain that..." I press my lips together.

Do I tell him this?

It's not a matter of trust—I trust Rhys with my life, no questions asked.

But do I trust him with Briar's trust?

Something uncomfortable snakes through me.

"Please spit it out," Rhys says, interrupting my internal debate. "What did she see?"

"It's someone on the football team," I blurt out.

"Fuck." He echoes my earlier sentiments. He gets up and paces in front of me. His hand goes to his hair, and he pulls at it while he ponders everything I just said. Finally, he stops and looks at me. "Okay, so, what's happening?"

"What do you mean?"

"Like, are the police on it, or...?"

"Yeah. There's an open investigation, but Briar hasn't heard anything. She thinks they've run out of leads, which would make sense. A fire tends to destroy all the evidence, and I'd guess whatever incendiary device was used was too common for them to narrow down."

"If this guy has even done it before," Rhys muses. "I

mean, he went for what he *thought* was an abandoned old warehouse, right? Key word: abandoned. If I had a fixation on fire, I'd probably start somewhere that felt safe to practice on."

I smack my palm to my forehead. "That makes sense."

"This guy didn't come ride to the rescue either, so he's not one of those guys who creates an incident just so he can save the day." He frowns. "I think I've been watching too much *Criminal Minds*."

I chuckle. "Yeah, well, it's probably going to come in handy while we figure this out."

"Just call me Special Agent Derek Morgan." He strikes a pose holding an imaginary firearm. "I *am* the handsome one out of the two of us."

"Great." I stand. "Hone those skills, Morgan, because we're going to be profiling our teammates at practice until we figure out who our arsonist is."

And we're going to keep Briar as far away from this as possible. The arsonist already knows her face. He got into her room, left a threatening note. He warned her to leave it alone, to stop searching.

Well, as far as he's concerned, she has stopped.

But me and Rhys have only just begun.

CHAPTER 31
BRIAR

"IS THORNE MEETING YOU THERE?" Marley puckers her lips in the mirror a few times, then turns toward me.

I shrug. "Not sure."

Lydia makes a face at Marley, but unbeknownst to her, I see it in the mirror. She shakes her head, as if she's telling Marley not to ask me about Thorne. Which means that Lydia is much more observant than I give her credit for.

He hasn't been back over to our place since after dinner with his parents, and our texts have been short and to the point. Aside from a few of our PT sessions, we haven't really spent much time together. He's not shying away from touching me when we are together, but something is off.

I'm starting to second-guess my decision to tell him about the arsonist.

Did I scare him off?

Or is it that I'm too invested in our fake relationship? Sure, we've broken some rules along the way and we can't keep our hands to ourselves, but I need to remember that we're still in a *fake* relationship.

When Marley, Lydia, and I show up to the warehouse, I pull my phone out to text Thorne.

It feels wrong not to text him.

But it doesn't feel right to text him either.

Fuck. I'm confused.

I decide to text him anyway. Because regardless of what I'm feeling, we're still boyfriend and girlfriend to our peers and his parents. That was our deal.

ME

> I just wanted to let you know I'm at the warehouse party with Lydia and Marley.

I shoot him the address because it's not at any of the typical party spots and I'm not sure if he's been to one of these. One of the lacrosse players likes to engage in cage fighting on the side, and that's tonight, apparently.

Thorne doesn't text back.

I pretend not to be disappointed and let Lydia and Marley tug me along with them toward the cage. I glance around nervously. The warehouse isn't too far from campus, and there are several windows, all within my sight, so I take a deep breath and try to remain calm.

That only lasts ten seconds into the fight, though.

Because as if I wasn't already feeling antsy, I spot a few football players.

My spine stiffens.

I back away and move closer to the door.

Just in case.

Lydia glances at me over her shoulder, and I mouth that I'm okay. The truth is—I'm not.

I'm even more frustrated when I find zero messages on my phone.

My attention bounces over every football player, lingering on a few familiar faces who I've seen talking to Thorne a time or two.

None of them seem to notice me.

It's fine, Briar.

I yelp when an arm wraps around my waist.

"It's me."

My lungs fill with air. I tilt my head back against his chest and slow my breathing. Thorne's warm eyes are like a safety net.

"You didn't text me back," I note.

His brows crowd. "That's because as soon as I saw your text, Rhys and I rushed over."

"Worried about me?" I tease, but also, *is he?*

"After you cut me with a knife, I'm not sure I need to be." His chuckle rumbles over my back. "But yeah, kitten. I am."

It shouldn't make me happy to hear him say that, but *God*, it does.

"You've been quiet," I state, moving my attention back to the cage in the center of the warehouse.

"I know," he whispers in my ear. "I'm sorry."

I shrug, playing it off. "Don't be. I just figured your parents finally forbade you to see me."

He grunts. "I wouldn't listen." I flinch when the lacrosse player lands a hard hit to the other guy. *Jeez.* "They did try to set me up on another date, though."

"Oh, did they?"

Thorne takes a beer from Rhys, who comes to stand near us. He seems more serious than usual, like he's about to jump in the ring next.

"Yeah, I told them that I'd make sure to run it past my girlfriend and get back to them."

I snort. "I'm sure they loved that."

"I'm not sure I care."

Rhys leans over to Thorne and says something in a low voice. It's too echoey in the warehouse for me to hear what he said, but Thorne's arm around my waist tightens, like he's afraid I'm going to slip away at any second.

Maybe I should.

Just to see if he'll chase me.

Wait, stop it.

I'm losing focus on the real goal here—finding out who the hell tried to burn me alive.

Rhys leans away, and I peek back at both guys. Their jaws are tight, and they're staring out into the crowd. Neither of them are watching the fight.

"What are yo—"

Broken glass catches my attention, and I instantly slip through Thorne's grip and fall to the floor. I cradle my knees and shut my eyes. *No.*

The sound vibrates throughout the open space, and people yell. I'm paralyzed on the floor with fear so heavy, I can't even hear Thorne shouting my name. It's only when he bends down in front of me and grabs my face that I realize I'm in a full-blown panic.

"Briar, baby."

His voice soothes me. I suck in the air he's giving me and nod sharply. My nails dig into his forearms, and he hauls me to my feet.

Rhys's eyes widen as he moves from me to Thorne. "Fire."

Fire.

"Go get Marley and Lydia!" I shout to Rhys. "They're near the front!"

Thorne nods, and Rhys is gone. He's working against the crowd to get to my friends. He makes it to them quickly, and as soon as Thorne sees them heading in our direction, he hauls me upward and into his arms.

"Don't panic. Just look ahead. I'll get you out."

Remnants of smoke float around us, and it doesn't take much to shoot me back to that night. I shake in Thorne's arms and wrap my arms around his neck. "I'm slowing you down. Put me down."

"No."

Fear sends me into a complete frenzy. The building isn't engulfed in fire by any means. It's not like it was doused in gasoline like the note, but it's still a fire. Orange and red flames flick aggressively, cutting in and out between the rustling of air from everyone leaving. I see a few guys trying to put the fire out but turn away when I start to cough.

"Bury your face into my shirt."

I do as Thorne says and keep my face there until the cool night air brushes against my neck.

"Get in!" Rhys's voice perks me up. He's in his car, Lydia and Marley already tucked away safely in the backseat.

I hurriedly climb in the back, ignoring the bite of pain in my knee.

"We've got her." Lydia slips the seat belt over me and buckles it.

Thorne jumps in the front seat in record time, and Rhys speeds away.

The sound of sirens catches my ear. Lydia's hand falls to my leg, and she gives it a squeeze. "You okay?"

I nod but stay silent.

"You're all staying at our place tonight." Thorne doesn't turn around when he says this. His voice is low and resolute.

None of us argue.

I know what he's thinking.

This isn't a fluke.

It's another threat.

And if *this* doesn't scare Thorne away, then maybe I'm wrong.

Maybe our fake relationship isn't fake to him either.

CHAPTER 32
THORNE

RHYS MEETS ME DOWNSTAIRS. The girls are staying in my room for the night, and I don't think there's a chance in hell I'm going to get any sleep. Judging by the way Rhys stares at me, his whole body tense, he's thinking the same.

That's fine—we can plan.

"Shame about Cross," Rhys mutters. "I was anticipating his fight."

I shrug. Cross Lopez is a beast on the lacrosse field, but he also strikes me as an angry person. He found a useful way of channeling his rage, though. The guys who organize the underground cage fighting ring pay their fighters well. There was a rumor a while ago that he fights so he can pay for school.

Anyway, I've never actually talked to Cross, but I heard that he is an impressive fighter. While I mirror Rhys's sentiments about the night being cut short, a warehouse fire isn't going to stop him.

We'll have a chance to go again.

"Let's focus." I grab a water bottle and drop onto the couch. "Who did you see in the warehouse? From the team."

He names off a few, then pauses. "Are we excluding them

because they were there, or including them because of the same reason?"

I frown. "It would be kind of dumb for them to show their face, then go and set the fire, right?"

"Unless it was a spontaneous thing because of..." He mouths Briar's name.

I scowl at him. "She got that creepy note, and then she goes to the warehouse. And, what? The arsonist sees her and decides to freak her out even more?"

He rolls his eyes. "It's the same reason you dragged me out of the house as soon as you got her text. Even you were worried."

"I was *not*—"

"Don't lie to yourself, hmm?"

I sag back into the cushions and cover my face.

The worst thing is—he's *right*. I've been trying to put a little distance between Briar and me. We keep our interactions outside of the *fake relationship* short and to the point. I haven't been over to her place since after the dinner, and beyond stolen touches when we work on her exercises, or the very pointedly public ones...

Nothing.

It's better that way.

Rhys clears his throat, and I drop my hands.

"Fine," I snap. "I was concerned."

And my *concern* is affecting everything.

"What if her ex is the one setting the fires?" Rhys asks suddenly. He leans forward. "Think about it—he knew she was going to be painting the mural last spring. It could've been an honest-to-God attempt to actually kill her. And then when she survives, he freaks and breaks up with her. But *then* she starts sniffing around the football team, so he tries to get close again."

My stomach flips. "It would make sense," I allow. "Did you see him tonight?"

"Not before the chaos." He frowns. "And after, I was too busy trying to find Lydia and Marley, then keep us all from being trampled."

Right.

"I only saw Aaron and his girlfriend." I think back. "He was kind of near us, though, and he took her hand and got the fuck out quicker than we did."

"Good thing," Rhys mutters. "Because he lives with us."

Well, yeah.

"We suck as detectives," I add.

He laughs and leans forward, holding out his water to tap against mine. I shake my head and do it, chuckling under my breath.

Maybe the police will have better luck with this one.

———

"Thorne, wake up."

I open my eyes and groan. Bright sunlight streams in through the living room windows, creating a halo effect around Briar's head. It takes a second to realize that I fell asleep, and I shoot upright.

"Whoa, easy." She grasps my shoulders. "You okay?"

"I didn't mean to…" The sound of snoring draws my attention.

Rhys is passed out on the other end of the couch, his mouth open.

She giggles. "Yeah, well, you did."

Her laughter does something to me.

Something bad.

The feeling from last night, the sick-with-panic feeling, comes back. Briar being scared devastated me, and I've been doing everything in my power to help her. The same as she's been helping me with my parents.

But that hasn't really been working, has it?

None of it has.

This fake relationship isn't serving its purpose anymore. My parents still want me to date other girls of their choosing —and even when I say no, like I did the other day, they tell me I should still have dinner with them as friends. Just in case.

And Briar...

All I can think about is her. Her expression. Her eyes. The way she bites her lip. Her perfectly timed scowls and scoffs. The little gasps she makes when she's on the edge, and the whimpers as she comes. Her body tensing around me.

The smell of her.

The taste of her.

It clashes horribly in my mind when I realize I haven't cast a single thought about my upcoming football game. Our opponents are formidable, but have I watched any of their tapes from this season? Have I done any fucking research?

No. Practice has been practice. But around it, when I should be leading my team through example, I've been burying my dick in her pussy. I've been trying to catch a *maybe* arsonist.

So just... stop.

I take a breath. It's like being on the field, with a minute left in the fourth quarter and one last play. One last decision to make.

I stand, forcing her to step back. "I was so fucking worried about you last night."

She tilts her head. "I... I know. I'm sorry I freaked out."

I can't do this.

"Do you know what I've been doing at practice almost every fucking day this week?" I move around her, needing some distance between us. When she doesn't reply, I tell her. "I've been asking subtle questions of my teammates. Checking if anyone had a freaking alibi for the night of the fire. Wondering if anyone was going to act suspicious."

"Thorne—"

"My only dream is to make it pro, Briar." I cross my arms. My stomach feels like it's turned into a pit of snakes. "Football has been *it*. And I know it's not in the cards for me, according to my parents, but it doesn't make the dream any less real."

Her expression flickers. "I know that."

"No, you don't." Panic constricts my chest. "I've been so distracted lately."

"By me?"

"*Yes*, by you." I force myself to stand still. To look her in the face, even when I want to run out the door and hide from this conversation. "This is a fake relationship, and it feels—"

"Real," she whispers.

"Yes." *Yes*. It feels fucking real. "And I can't do it."

Her eyebrows lift. "Excuse me?"

"I can't do real, Briar." Fuck, why does this hurt so much? "This is my last season playing football, and I am not even thinking about the game. I'm thinking about *you*. And I just need it all to fucking stop for five seconds. I won't do this. I don't even care that my parents didn't believe our ruse. I'm losing sight of what I love most in life because of you."

She stares at me. And stares and stares and stares.

My heart cracks. "Please leave."

"Cassius—"

"*Leave*," I order, throwing my hand out, one finger pointed toward the front door.

She bolts.

My gaze falls to Rhys, who is doing an admirable impression of a sleeping man. The front door slams, and his eyes crack open.

I let out a sigh, somehow feeling eight hundred times worse than I did two minutes ago. If I thought this was going to make me feel better... I was dead fucking wrong.

CHAPTER 33
BRIAR

"AREN'T YOU DATING THORNE?" someone asks in passing on their way to the game.

I stop dead on the sidewalk and scowl at her, already annoyed that this random girl is wearing his number. She looks me up and down, as if she has no idea why he's dating me.

Apparently, neither does he.

I don't know how to answer her question. Am I dating him? Fake-dating, I mean? After I shoot her a dirty look, she stares at me strangely and scurries off toward the stadium.

Am I supposed to be going to the game and acting all lovey toward him like before? He said his parents didn't believe our ruse, but I'm not sure if that means he's calling it off or if he's only wanting to act like we're a couple in the public eye. Does it really matter? His parents are still trying to actively set him up on dates. They don't really care if he is dating me.

I skipped out on our last PT session. He didn't question it.

Instead of going to the weight room, I did exercises in my bedroom.

I don't need him.

Hurt tangles my heart. His rejection stings. But what did I expect? This isn't on him, it's on me. I let myself get invested knowing that our relationship wasn't going to last. It was based on a lie, a ploy. Yet, why does it hurt more than when I walked in on Ben cheating on me?

My phone buzzes as I walk in the opposite direction of the stadium.

I lose my breath with his name on the screen.

CASSIUS

Are you coming to my game?

The first thing I type is, *No, I wouldn't want to be a distraction.* But I quickly click the backspace and refrain from acting hurt over this.

ME

I wasn't sure if I was supposed to. Are we still fake dating or not?

My heart skyrockets when I see that he's typing. I'm not sure what's worse: him breaking up with me and us having to deal with the campus gossip, or still having to fake our relationship in front of everyone when really, I'm feeling the sting of rejection every time he crosses my mind.

CASSIUS

Yes. My parents may not care, but dating you gives me an excuse not to go on these dates they're setting me up on.

An excuse. That's all I am.

Great.

I slip my phone into my pocket and turn around.

Marley and Lydia said they'd save me a seat if I decided to come to the game. I blamed not going on a paper that was due.

There is no paper.

I finished it the night before when I couldn't sleep.

I pass by the girl who asked if I was Thorne's girlfriend and *accidentally* nudge her with my shoulder.

She gasps.

"Oops, sorry." *Not.*

Once I arrive at the game, I'm the only one in regular clothes. Everyone is dressed in maroon or gold, sporting their Shadow Valley attire. I'm in my black jeans, Converse—because I refuse to wear the Docs that Thorne bought me—and a thick black sweater. I look like a black cat, which is exactly what Thorne refers to me as.

"Hey!" Marley scoots down. "I didn't think you were coming."

I shrug. "I finished my paper."

She and Lydia both stare at me for a second too long. They can tell something is up but they know me well enough not to ask.

Throughout the game, I fake clap and cheer to keep my role as Thorne's girlfriend going.

By the last quarter, my cheers aren't fake.

Even if I am hurt by his rejection, I still want what's best for him, and that means winning.

The buzzer sounds, and Shadow Valley continues their winning streak.

Lydia, Marley, and I join in the crowd with our cheering. Some girls have taken their shirts off and stand in nothing but bras, waving the cotton around and yelling out various players' names.

I hear a lot of *Thorne* but I block it out as I walk down the steps to the gate.

It doesn't take long for him to spot me standing with my friends.

He's in the middle of the field, giving an interview when he stops in the middle of speaking and smiles at me.

He makes it seem so real.

I have butterflies and I hate that.

Ugh.

He places his hand on the reporter's arm and nods over to me. The camera pans and *shit, I'm up.*

I smile warmly and wave.

I'm certain this is for a show in case his parents are watching.

My heart races as soon as he heads over to me.

I do my best to play it cool when he leans over the fence to bring me closer. His long arms reach me easily, and his hands fall to my waist.

His lips are soft against my cheek. "Thank you for coming."

"Gotta keep up our charade," I say cooly.

Why does this hurt so much?

He pulls back, and although his face is smooth without any expression, I can see the concern. "You didn't come to our training session."

"You told me I was a distraction. What did you expect?"

Thankfully, it's so loud with the roaring crowd that no one can really hear us. This time, he doesn't hide his unease.

"Kiss me and go." I'm desperate to put space between us and I'm even more desperate to leave.

Any minute now, my potential killer could walk out of the locker room, freshly showered and ready to burn me alive again. And this relationship is fake. After Thorne's dismissal of me the other day, I have no problems keeping that in the forefront of my brain.

His jaw flexes.

He glances at my mouth, and I hate myself for craving him.

I reach up on my tiptoes, ignoring the radiating pain from my hip down to my foot, and let him kiss me.

It's a light kiss but it lasts far too long, like he didn't want it to end.

I'm the one to break us apart.

"I'll see you later," I say, trying my best to keep my voice neutral.

He nods and turns.

I do the same.

Only I *won't* see him later.

CHAPTER 34
THORNE

I FOLLOW our kicker down the hall. For the past two days, he's been acting a bit off. He missed a field goal at the game last night—an oddity in and of itself—but he also hasn't been as engaged in the locker room. I've been watching him, and he just seems checked out.

His hands were wrapped, too, which seems out of character.

Did he burn them starting the fire?

"Hey!" I call. "Jack!"

He stops and turns. He plucks earbuds out and raises an eyebrow. "Sorry, Thorne. I was jammin'."

"What are you listening to?"

"Paul McCartney." He holds up his hand. "Don't start to give me shit."

"I won't. Just wanted to say that you did a good job today."

"He scowls. "Yeah, right. I've been missing some easy thirty-yarders lately."

Well... yeah. I point to his bandaged hand. "What happened?"

"Got into a disagreement with my brother." He tugs aside

the part around his knuckles, revealing deep-purple bruises. "Our parents raised us to deal with that sort of shit ourselves and not complain, which generally results in punching each other a few times. I didn't want Coach spotting it and benching me, so…"

"Jeez." I stare at him. "That kind of makes me glad I'm an only child."

He chuckles. "Yeah. So, did you need something?"

"Nah. See you tomorrow, man."

He leaves, and my shoulders drop. That was a fail. I was *sure* he was going to be added to the list of suspects, but his grumpy mood was because he thought his performance was subpar.

I fish out my phone, automatically checking for texts from Briar.

Nothing.

Her expression from when I kicked her out floats in front of my eyes, only to be replaced with the flash of hurt right before I kissed her on the field.

Fuck. She's still helping me, and what am I doing?

Not a lot, that's for sure.

I open my conversation thread with Rhys.

ME

Meet me at your car.

RHYS

10-4, Captain.

I roll my eyes. He's been picking up more and more television cop show lingo. I have no idea if police actually say half the things that come out of his mouth. I follow in the same direction Jack went and step out into the cold evening.

The parking lot is mostly empty, and I zip up my jacket on the way to Rhys's car. He comes from another exit. He remote starts it, then unlocks it for me, and I climb in fast.

The cold weather makes my knee ache. I know it's probably nothing compared to Briar's, and another freaking pang goes through my chest.

"What did Jack say?" Rhys practically falls into the driver's seat.

"He showed me his bruised knuckles and told me some story about solving problems with his brother with his fists." I sigh. "So, we're nowhere."

Rhys points to the glove box. I open it and take out the small notepad we've been using for our list. It has everyone who we saw from the fight on one side, then everyone *else* on the other. If they have an alibi for not being at the fight, they got crossed out.

If we saw them after the fire started—like, for example, Aaron—they get crossed out.

"There's got to be a way to narrow this down," I say, drawing a line through Jack's name.

Rhys talked to Willow, Aaron's girl, who told us a few other guys she and Aaron went with. And, when pressed, she insisted that they were with them the whole time leading up to the fire.

"I don't like that we haven't crossed out Ben's name," Rhys says. "Let's work on him."

I glare down at the list. "He'd see straight through me if I question him, and you probably blew your cover, too."

He hums, thinking it over. I buckle my seat belt, and he pulls out of the parking lot.

"Okay," he finally says, when we're nearly home. "He's besties with Stephen McDowell."

"Right…"

"So we ask *him*." He glances at me. "Obviously."

That would make sense. Especially since they're together a lot. Questioning Stephen on where he *and* Ben are would probably be pretty plausible, and less likely for Stephen to get his hackles up.

"Let's talk to him tomorrow," I suggest.

My phone buzzes in my pocket. I hit the side button without removing it, silencing the vibration. It's probably my mother, up in arms once again about going on another date.

She keeps mentioning Cynthia Keenland, which is driving me nuts. She had nothing special going on underneath the layers of Botox and filler. Just her daddy's last name.

Briar is so much more than that. One, I don't think she's even considered filler, in her lips or other places. Two, she has a mind of her own. She does what she wants—

"You've got that sad look in your eye," Rhys interrupts.

I scowl. "No I don't."

"Were you thinking about Miss Heart of Thorns?"

I punch his arm, but he only cackles.

"Get it? She's head over heels for you, and you're *Thorne*—"

"Fuck off." I get out of the car and slam the door, leaving him behind to hurry up and get inside. My phone goes off again, and I growl louder as I fish it out.

Not my mother, though.

Lydia?

I swipe to answer it fast, my heart picking up speed. "Lydia? What's wrong?"

She pauses. "What makes you think something is wrong?"

"I—"

"Okay, okay. Heartbreak aside, I think you're the only one who can help us."

"*Us*?"

"Briar," she corrects. "The women's team was finishing practice, Coach left, and then suddenly Briar passes us all laced up."

There's a distant *whoosh* in my ears. She's on the ice? *Skating?*

"Tell her to stop," I demand.

She's not ready. We've been working on conditioning, but

skating is a whole new beast. One sideways movement could derail everything. It could set her back months. A year, even.

"We tried." Lydia sighs. "I stepped off to call you, but Marley keeps trying to talk sense into her."

"And?"

"It's not working. She's frustrated."

Clearly.

"And angry," she adds.

At me.

"I'm on my way." I hang up on her and pivot, nearly crashing into Rhys. "Be back later."

"Uh-huh." He narrows his eyes at me, but I don't fucking care.

I drive like a bat out of hell to the arena. I park at the end of the row and rush inside, down the long, darkened hallway. Lydia stands on the mats that line the hall from their locker room to the rink, her hands planted on her hips. She's still in skates and pads, the practice jersey boldly showing the Shadow Valley U Knights on her chest.

"Is she—?"

"Still out there," Lydia clips out. "If she hurts herself—"

"I know. Just… give us a minute." *Or a few.*

She makes a face. I ignore her and head to the rink. The door is open, giving me a view to the ice. Briar is at the far hash marks. Marley passes her a puck from the blue line, and she takes a slap shot.

Just watching her twist makes me cringe.

I step onto the ice and grit my teeth. The Zamboni hasn't come through yet—probably because of Briar's continued activity—so the chewed-up ice at least gives me a little friction.

"I'll take over," I tell Marley.

Briar's head shoots up. "No."

"Yes," I snap, my voice booming across the distance. "You want to fuck your knee up? You do it with me."

I hold my hand out, and Marley passes me her stick on her way off the ice. I can't say I've played much hockey—and this, with no skates, definitely doesn't count—but I'm coordinated. I glare at Briar when she slaps her stick on the ice.

"What?" I bark at her. "Is that caveman for pass you another puck?"

"Fuck off, Cassius."

I roll my eyes and drop Marley's stick. I kick a puck at her, and even though it's slow, she takes a shot.

"There." I point. "That hurt, kitten?"

"No," she lies.

I laugh and storm closer. She moves to pass me, but I snag my fingers in the practice jersey she donned. She's not wearing padding, though. I yank her around. With her skates on, she's almost my height. *Almost.*

I hold her tightly and resist the urge to shake her.

"Let go of me." She pushes at my chest.

I shake my head. "No."

"Let *go.*"

"You're being a brat," I snap in her face. "Don't hurt yourself because you're pissed at me."

She struggles harder, and I can't do it—I'm going to lose my balance, and this fight, if I keep going like I am.

So I haul her over my shoulder, pinning her thighs to my chest, and slap her ass. Once, *hard.*

It takes her by fucking surprise, enough that I manage to get us off the ice. Lydia and Marley stand in the shadows.

"Locker room empty?"

Marley nods quickly.

"Keep it that way," I order.

A shiver runs through Briar, and I dig my fingers into her thighs. I kick the door open and storm through, then drop her carefully back to her feet.

"Give it to me." I motion to her.

"Give you what?"

"Your anger." I shake my head. "Your frustration. Your helplessness that you seem to need to take out on yourself—or prove it doesn't exist? I don't know. Don't hurt yourself. Hurt me."

She stares at me for a long moment, then goes to one of the benches in front of a cubby. She unlaces her skates, her movements too jerky. I just stare at her in silence, my own anger building in my chest.

"I don't want to care." My words slip out, but it doesn't break the growing tension. "I don't want to care that you're going to freaking hurt yourself doing stupid shit like this."

"Then don't." She yanks her feet out of the skates and sets them aside. Rising, she strips out of the practice jersey, revealing a black skin-tight long-sleeved shirt underneath. And leggings under the pants.

"You make it impossible." I step forward. "Look at me."

She straightens and faces me.

"I need to think about football. You heard my father—"

"You don't have to bow to your parents' will!" she shouts. "My father this, my mother this, trust fund fucking *that*. Who gives a shit? Who are you without your money?"

My mouth opens and closes. "You've got to be kidding me right now."

"Your head is up your ass." She scoffs. "I'm going to skate again."

I clench my jaw. "Not if you injure yourself first. Doing things wrong, rushing into it—"

"God, you're impossible." She yanks the tie out of her hair, shaking it loose. "You're infuriatingly talented, and *kind*, and I hate you for it."

I stalk closer. My heart drums against my ribs, and I reach for her. I can't help it. My fingers slip through the silky strands of her hair, cupping the back of her head, and I pull her into me.

My gaze burns into hers, and I suddenly need to know the truth.

"Do you really hate me?"

Her eyes widen, but she doesn't soften. Who would Briar Hart be if she *softened* for me?

"Yes," she says.

"Liar."

Her hands are at my jeans, unbuttoning them. Her gaze dips down, then back up, and a challenge gleams in her eyes. "Let's find out."

CHAPTER 35
BRIAR

MY PLAN IS GOING to backfire.

I can feel it in my bones and I most definitely can feel it between my legs.

He wants to challenge my hatred for him?

Fine.

After shoving his pants down, I cup him through his boxer briefs, relishing in the control I have. His head falls backward, and I stare at his bobbing throat.

I don't hate him. But I need to in order to save myself from more heartbreak.

I push on his chest until the backs of his legs hit the bench. He sits and grips me around the waist.

"You're doing a pretty shit job at showing me how much you hate me, kitten."

I say nothing. I drape myself over his lap and straddle him. The hard metal of the bench presses against my throbbing knee, but I don't care.

"Fuck," he mutters. "I love seeing you like this."

Heat brews between my legs, and my bra feels too tight.

Do not give in.

I'm putting myself through hell, for what? To prove to him that I don't need him? To drive my hatred for him?

To protect your heart, Briar.

Right.

My fingers grip the cotton of my long sleeve. I tug it up and over my head only to drop it on the floor near my skates. Thorne gazes at my spilling breasts like he wants to take a bite out of them, and I'd truly love nothing more.

His hands grip me so hard around the waist, there's a sting against my skin. He peers at me through hooded eyes and a slightly parted mouth. I drop my hands to his shoulders and start grinding.

He helps me and presses his hips to dull the ache we're both feeling.

"If this is you hating me, I hope you never stop," he rasps.

My mouth goes to his neck. I suck, nip, and lick him until he's out of control with need. He moves me over him, our clothes causing so much friction, it burns my skin.

"Do you want to fuck me, Thorne?" I ask, whispering my seedy breath into his ear.

My plan is to get him twisted up, burning with need, completely desperate for me, and then demand he leave.

Just like he did to me the other day.

But maybe I should let him fuck me first.

No.

He repeats his name quietly. "Thorne?"

I cup him around the neck and lean back to stare into his eyes.

His warm, golden-speckled eyes.

Safe. I feel safe when I gaze into them, even while mending my bruised heart.

"Answer my question," I snap, frustrated with my thoughts.

"Why did you call me Thorne?" he asks, still moving me back and forth.

I'm highly aware of every little thing.

The tension, the pulse between my legs, the scent of his cologne mingling with the faint smell of ice.

I'm breathless. "Answer... my... question."

He peers up at me with sad eyes. As if he knows what I'm about to do.

"I'll do anything you want me to do, kitten. Want me to fuck you? I will. Want to hate-fuck me to make yourself feel better? Go for it. I told you to take your anger out on me. Now do it."

I dig my nails into his skin. He pauses and stares at me.

"This is me proving to you that I hate you." I climb off his lap, grab my shirt, and slip it back on. I stare at him from across the locker room. He's still on the bench with his pants undone, flushed cheeks, and an angry glare in my direction.

I cross my arms. "Get out."

His head tilts, but he makes no move to listen to me.

"I said, get out." This time my voice is a little more firm. So firm, I don't think he noticed the quiver toward the end.

Thorne drops his head. He's white-knuckling the bench but then he chuckles.

I'm hot with anger.

God, maybe I do fucking hate him.

"I get it," he says. "You're trying to give me a dose of my own medicine."

"No—"

Thorne stands abruptly, and words die on the end of my lips.

He stalks over to me too quickly, and I freeze.

It seems like I'm holding my ground, but really, I'm not.

His hand gets lost in my hair with the forceful tipping of my chin. "You want me to chase you, kitten? Prove to you that I care about you? Tell you how wrong I was for pushing you away to focus on something that couldn't in a million years be more important than you and your safety?"

I remain quiet. My lip wobbles with unshed emotion.

"Stop fighting me," he pleads, dragging his thumb across my bottom lip.

I angrily whip my face away. "Why? So you can just throw it in my face that I'm just this big distraction to the thing you love the most? I gave you an out, Thorne! But here you are, showing up like fucking Prince Charming."

Thorne grips my chin again and forces me to look at him.

"I was wrong."

My jaw clenches.

"I didn't think I could love something more than football, and then you came along with your cute little scowls and all-black clothing that only you can pull off. You stuck through the worst dinner of your life, took being openly offended by my parents, and *still* fucking came to my game after I fucked up and hurt you." His brow furrows, and the grip on my chin gets heavier. "The truth is, it scared the hell out of me to see you terrified. I freaked out because this thing between us isn't fake to me."

Thorne's face grows blurry. The knot in my throat tightens.

"You can stick to your guns, kitten. Pretend you hate me, claw my back, run just so I'll chase after you—" My head flies backward with a harsh tug on my hair. "Because I will, Briar. I'll fucking chase you."

The locker room is hazy.

I can't think straight.

I was so dead set on hurting him like he hurt me, but I can't do it.

Some people are worth the heartbreak. And I think he's one of them.

Thorne steps closer, and I move backward. We do this until my back hits the wall behind me.

"What'll it be, kitten?" He cups both of my hands in one of his, bringing them up and over my head. He traps me. I couldn't run even if I wanted to. "Are you going to soften for me? Let me break through that wall you've thrown up to keep me out? Or pretend like you still hate me?"

I stare at his perfect mouth.

"I guess we'll see after you fuck me," I whisper.

His knee goes between my legs, and he spreads them. "Challenge accepted, *kitten*."

I grow weak with his kiss. It's hot and sloppy. His tongue flicks inside my mouth, and I arch my back, pressing into him.

I whimper when he takes his hand and trails it down the front of my body until it rests above the waistband of my leggings. One finger swipes under the fabric and stays. I sink my teeth into his lip and pull.

He hums against my mouth. "You really are a little black cat, aren't you?"

I suck in a breath when he moves his hand lower and swipes my clit. I'm so needy it hurts.

"I want you to beg for it, kitten." He tugs on my earlobe.

Never.

I make a noise, and he eats it up, touching my clit again and again until I'm forcefully trying to free my hands from his grip.

"Beg."

Another whine escapes past my lips. "N…no."

He smiles against my mouth. "That's fine. I'm patient."

"Cassius."

"Oh, we must be getting close. You used my first name." His finger slips inside me, and I lose my footing.

"I w…wo… won't beg."

God. It feels so good yet so tortuous.

"Yes you will, kitten. You're going to break just so I can piece you back together. The sooner you soften for me, the quicker I'll let you come."

As if he has the control?

His finger disappears. My eyes spring open, and he's staring at me with a hungry gaze. His mouth curves and it's the best thing I've ever seen.

"Beg, Briar."

He never calls me that.

His tongue slips out of his mouth, and he runs it over his swollen bottom lip. A rush of heat washes through me, and no matter how much I try to protest, my body gives it away.

I'm ready to beg for it.

CHAPTER 36
THORNE

SHE FEELS SO sweet against me, I can barely stand it. It takes everything in me to not hurry. Everything feels like a rush, and I want this to be different. In a sweaty locker room, with the harsh fluorescent lights overhead, she's never looked more beautiful.

I release her wrists and offer her a smoldering expression.

"Take out my cock."

A thrill goes through me when she does, shoving the fabric down. I've been hard since I threw her over my shoulder, but now, under her gaze, precum oozes out.

Without warning, she drops down and licks it.

"Fuck," I groan. "No. I don't want your mouth on me—I want your cunt squeezing me while I kiss you to death."

She lifts her head, her tongue poking out between her lips. "To death?"

"It'll be a heavenly experience." I smirk. "Although the sight of you on your knees is doing something to me, kitten."

"Good." She takes me in her mouth again.

She's too skilled in the blow job department.

I grab her and haul her up, pushing her harder against the lockers. I *was* going to play nice. In a way. But now? I catch her wrists again, in one hand, and yank her leggings down with the other. She kicks them and her panties away, her gaze hot on my face.

When I raise her leg and hook it around my hip, she automatically lifts her other. I keep her supported against the wall, her wrists in my hand… and my other now free to travel. It goes between her legs, and I tap her clit.

Her hips jerk.

"Hmm," I murmur. "I don't hear much begging."

"I'm waiting for my heavenly experience," she retorts.

I snicker. "Yeah?"

"The sex, the kisses…"

"You already know my kissing is supreme."

She rolls her eyes.

"Now." I lean in until my lips hover over hers. "You seem like you need a reminder."

Besides kissing in public—the quick, close-mouthed kind, we haven't really kissed. Not since we put more distance between us… the night after the party.

In all honesty, I feel like I need to be the one begging. I'm the one who freaked out, who kicked her out of my house. I'm the one who feels rotten about it, and who has come crawling back.

So I don't make her beg. I'll give her exactly what she wants.

Needs.

As soon as she leans forward a hair…

Her warm brown eyes meet mine, and her breath coasts against my lips. She seems to be deciding something. Maybe just peering into my soul through my eyes.

My cock is *right there*, between her legs. It found its place naturally, notched at her entrance, as if I needed any more proof that this thing was never fucking fake.

She kisses me.

I part our lips and take a taste of her mouth, at the same

time thrusting up into her. I catch her moan, her body trembling around me. Her hands curl above us, but I only tighten my grip.

Then, quickly, I pull away from her.

"I told you I have an aversion to touch." Our noses brush.

"Yeah," she whispers.

"That's why…" I look up at her trapped wrists. "I've done this to you a few times."

"I know, Cassius." She slow-blinks, her pussy clenching around me. "I know. It's okay."

"No, it's not. Because you're not…" *You're not any girl.* Slowly, one finger at a time, I release her hands. "Touch me. *Please.*"

She lowers her arms. Her fingers skim along the side of my neck, down to my shoulders. Then lower, between us, until she can lift my shirt up and off. Her palms brush my chest, and I close my eyes at the sensation.

No horrid memories of my father, no crushing anxiety. No skin crawling.

Just lust… and maybe something deeper. Something more permanent.

She kisses me, dragging my mind away from where her hands are going. She nips my lower lip, and the pain zings straight to my cock. I groan into her mouth and start to move. Quick. Everything in me wants this *now*.

I've waited.

We've been apart for too long, for my bullheaded comments, for her stubbornness…

"Harder," she moans.

I'm right there with her. I slam into her over and over, and she clings to me the same way I cling to her. Nails digging into skin, our chests pressed together. She kisses me like I'm the last breath she needs.

My fingers thread in her hair, my palm at the back of her head so she doesn't knock it against the wall. Her body tightens, tensing around me, and I chase her high. I rub her clit through our frantic movements.

Our kiss pauses when she comes. A wordless, open-mouth cry, her lips still on mine. I fuck her through it. My balls lift, the pleasure spiraling out, and I follow her over the cliff.

———

We get a round of applause when we arrive, hand in hand, back at her apartment. Lydia and Marley are on the couch, and their cheers make Briar smile.

So I smile, too.

She releases me and goes over to them, and I can't stop thinking about the thought that popped into my head mid-sex.

More than lust.

Love.

I love her.

It doesn't seem scary. It doesn't seem wrong. It doesn't even worry me that I'd choose her over football. This time, I'm ready for that thought, and I don't let it destroy me.

The difference between her and my parents, though, is that she would never ask me to choose.

It's okay to have more than one true love.

A sport and a girl.

She finishes her conversation with them, and I follow her down the hall to her room.

"I have to tell you something," I say once the door is shut.

My gaze automatically takes inventory of her room. The mini hockey stick wedged in the window, the pot and forks tucked against the wall for use later. The knife on her nightstand.

"What's that?" She sheds her shirt and glances over her shoulder at me.

I bite my lip and keep myself back.

"I…" My mouth goes dry. "Rhys and I have been trying to find your arsonist."

"*What?*"

I wince.

She stalks toward me. "Cassius Remington Thorne the Third, please tell me you have not been putting yourself in danger—"

I catch her hand and reel her in the rest of the way. "Me? Never."

"You just said—"

"Well, we've been subtle about it."

Kind of. I mean, the arsonist would probably have figured it out, if he was one of the players we've talked to. But so far, all of the ones Rhys and I managed to *delicately* question have been ruled out.

"You might be subtle, but Rhys?" She eyes me. "He's…"

I exhale. "You might have a point there."

She cracks a smile, but it's a little wobbly. She glances around her room, seeming to take in the same details I did. Or maybe just checking that everything is as it should be.

"Hey, kitten?"

She looks back.

I nod to her chest. "My brain is going to scramble if you stay shirtless."

Her gaze drops to her breasts, then swings back to me. Her grin is wicked.

"Oh? And what about if I…" She drops her leggings and panties then plants her hands on her hips. "Oops. I'm naked."

Nothing I can do about that but get naked, too.

CHAPTER 37
THORNE

IN THE END, Briar negotiates to be included in whatever schemes Rhys and I have. She's an excellent negotiator when she has her hand on my dick, but I digress...

She comes with Rhys and me to a party, but we're not there to have fun. She views it as a mission, the same as us. I keep her tucked under my arm, her all-black attire fitting for the occasion. I'm in the same, my black hoodie and black pants giving burglar vibes instead of cool vibes.

Rhys is in a black sweatshirt and dark-wash jeans, a black cap pulled over his head.

"Remember," he says over his shoulder, "Briar and I are going to distract Ben, and Thorne will get Stephen aside."

We both nod.

That plan was mainly Briar's. We sat her down and explained our theory, Rhys produced our shitty list from his glove box, and she laughed at us. Then sobered relatively quick, because the thought of her then-boyfriend doing that to her was not humorous.

Not in the slightest.

"I'm gonna kill him," she muttered.

But unfortunately, this isn't one of those dark romances

people rave about. There's not going to be a murder in the third act. If anything, the asshole is getting arrested.

Hopefully.

When Rhys and I balked at her words, she sighed and shook her head. Then came up with the current plan: distract and separate.

Or rather, wait until they're separated and then distract Ben.

Once we're inside the lacrosse house, the music thumping in my chest, we split up. Rhys trails Briar, a self-appointed bodyguard, and I drift in the opposite direction. I don't want to be parted from her, but there's no way in hell Ben would get into an argument with her in front of me.

My threat of telling Coach about his cheating is still very much active.

"Hey—Thorne, right?"

I tear my attention away from where Briar disappeared and focus on the guy in front of me. Cross Lopez has a split lip and a black eye, and I can't quite say he smiles at me.

"My girl and I are looking forward to your next fight," I tell him.

"Patronage pays the bills," he replies. "Saw your game this weekend. You took a killer hit."

I raise one shoulder. "Part of the game."

"You ever consider fighting?" His dark-brown eyes bore into mine. "Taking hits is half the job. And half the fun."

"Nah." My gaze lifts up and over him. I spot some hockey players, some of my teammates, a lot of girls in tight dresses… no Stephen, though. "Sorry, man, I'm trying to find my friend. I'll see you around."

Cross nods slowly and slips past me. He doesn't seem like the party type, but I put that aside. I spot Stephen heading into the kitchen, where the bar is most likely set up, and follow him.

ME

Now would be great.

BRIAR

On it.

I wait a minute.

RHYS

He's not going anywhere.

He means Ben—which also means that her ex is a sucker. I try not to scowl and instead pursue Stephen. I step up behind him at the keg.

"Hey, McDowell," I say above the music.

He glances back and grins. "Thorne. Want a cup?"

I nod.

He hands me his full one, then pours another for himself. I tip my head toward the sliding doors that lead out onto the back porch, and his eyebrow ticks up for a second. It smooths, though, and he follows me.

The music still reverberates out here, but I can hear myself think. The cold wind blasts through my sweatshirt, though, and Stephen is only in a long-sleeved shirt.

We're not going to last long out here.

I take a sip of the beer.

"What's up, Captain?" Stephen eyes me.

"I wanted to talk to you about something, but it's kind of sensitive."

"Consider me curious."

This could go badly, but… whatever. "I'm worried about Ben."

I wait for his reaction, but he doesn't do anything. He just watches me.

"He's been acting weird around Briar, you know? And I think it's more than him being her ex." *And cheating on her.* "I think it has to do with the fire."

Stephen chuckles. "Like, that he doesn't want to bang a burned chick?"

"Like, maybe he set the fire in the first place."

Silence.

But then, Stephen's expression shifts. He seems to be thinking—or remembering—something.

"I imagine you guys were probably together? Do you remember what he was doing?"

His gaze sharpens. "Yeah. Well, it was horrible. We were close. I remember him telling me that Briar was painting over there. I thought it was kind of a dick move of him to be at the party, and he agreed that he should be with her. Then I heard the sirens a little while after and..." He shivers. "I don't know, man. I didn't think much of it—I guess I just assumed he got to her after the fire started. But do you think someone started it?"

"Yeah, it's looking like it. There's still an open police investigation, but they haven't done much. No leads or something." My stomach twists, and nausea rolls through me. "Thanks."

"Good luck with your search."

He heads back inside, and I text Rhys.

ME

Ben left the party early that night. Before the fire started.

He's got no alibi, Rhys. Meet me on the back porch. This is starting to feel too fucking real.

It's Ben Patterson.

Briar's ex-boyfriend tried to kill her.

CHAPTER 38
BRIAR

IT'S RATHER difficult to remember why I ever dated Ben to begin with.

I stand in front of him and I see his mouth moving, except I don't hear a word he says. I recall the moments we had together as a couple and he seemed normal. Like your typical college guy.

Nothing like Thorne. But still normal.

Why would he try to kill me?

I rack my brain. There weren't even any red flags when it came to him.

Besides, of course, fucking some girl behind my back.

But nothing malicious or even potentially dangerous ever stood out. He grew up fine, too. I've met his parents. They're a lot like mine—middle-class, hardworking, and much kinder than Thorne's.

Ben raises his brows, like he's waiting for me to say something.

"Sorry, I checked out," I say.

Rhys laughs from behind me. "I think that means you're boring."

Ben glares over my shoulder.

"I just want to know why…?" I leave my question open-ended on purpose. I watch him closely to see his reaction.

It isn't what I hoped for. There is no defensiveness or tic of his eye. Only defeat.

"Because I was an ass."

I watch his mannerisms. Instead of acting defensive or worried, he seems…sad.

"After the fire, I didn't know what to do. I didn't know how to handle you or how to make things better. I was a lousy boyfriend and I think cheating on you was my way of self-sabotaging."

He went directly to the cheating. As if starting a fire didn't even cross his mind.

I peer over my shoulder at Rhys, but he's staring at his phone with a scowl.

"I'm sorry, Briar." Ben steps forward, but I immediately back away. He nods, understanding.

Except, I'm not sure he *does* understand.

I'm not stepping away from him because he broke my heart but because he potentially tried to kill me.

"Let's go." Rhys's tone is lethal. He steps forward and snarls at Ben.

Ben rolls his eyes

"Will you fucking calm down, Rhys?" Ben scoffs. "I'm still your teammate, remember?"

Rhys grumbles, and Ben's face twists.

I turn to follow Rhys out of the party because I know the beginning of a fight when I see one. But I don't make it far. Ben's hand wraps around my wrist lightly. I snap my gaze to his and tug my arm back.

He lets go willingly but doesn't step away from me.

"I just wanted to make sure you were okay after the warehouse?"

Confusion silences me.

Ben glances behind me and quickly spits the rest of his sentence out. "I saw you crowded on the floor after the chaos ensued with your hands covering your ears. It made me feel sick to see you scared—"

"Briar?" Rhys calls.

"Coming."

I rush away.

My heart races, and my head reels.

Rhys wraps his arm around my shoulders and walks me toward the back porch.

How *dare* Ben act like he cares about me?

A gust of wind cools my heated skin. The anger doesn't leave, I don't think it ever will, but after locking eyes with Thorne, I feel slightly less chaotic.

He greets me with a tug on my hand. I fall into his chest, and he wraps his arms around my waist.

"Hey, kitten," he whispers. "Did you happen to scratch Ben's eyes out while you were distracting him?"

I think over whether or not to mention that Ben feigned concern about the warehouse incident. I quickly decide it doesn't matter.

He's already on our radar.

I rather not give Thorne more ammunition to feed his anger.

"Should have," Rhys mutters. "I almost did it for you."

A puff of my breath lingers in the chilly air. "Doing any of that will do nothing. He needs to be locked up. Not assaulted by either of us." I pause. "No matter how badly we want to do it."

"She's right." Thorne spins me, and I lean against his chest. His arms wrap around me in safety. "We're going to have to tail him."

I tilt my chin. "You didn't get any info from Stephen?"
Dammit.

Thorne straightens. "Just the opposite, kitten."

It's a swift punch to my stomach.

"Stephen practically paved the way. He confirmed that Ben left early the night of your fire. I think he did it, Briar, and I'm going to fucking nail him."

———

"Your parents sound nice." Rhys crosses his legs, watching me paint from across the room. He stayed in that exact spot as I talked on the phone to my parents, too.

"They are," I reply.

After Thorne and Rhys narrowed down their suspect list with Ben at the very top, I haven't been left alone. It's been several days of them taking turns with me. It's kind of cute. But sort of unnecessary.

Right now, it makes sense.

I'm all by myself in a secluded part of the school, so yeah, I'm happy Rhys is with me.

During class? I don't really need a babysitter.

Or *bodyguard* as Rhys likes to call himself.

"So, what? Are you going to paint every part of the school now?" Rhys throws a lonesome baseball up into the air and catches it. He looks up at me from resting along the net of the batting cages. "The other sports programs got wind of the pretty girl in all black who is an amazing artist? They want a cool painting, too?"

"Hey," I point my paintbrush at him. "Leave my attire out of it."

He grins and goes back to throwing the baseball up in the air.

I finish blending the green and plop the paintbrush back into the paint bucket. "Has he texted back?"

Rhys grabs his phone.

My stomach is uneasy while I wait for him to answer me.

When our gazes meet, my shoulders fall. *No word.*

"I don't like that he's out tailing Ben by himself."

He shrugs. "And we don't like that he tried to kill you when you were all by yourself."

I frown. *Touche.*

The night replays in my head from time to time when I let it. But lately, I've been focusing on everything from *before* the fire. My relationship with Ben wasn't on the rocks, which is why I was confused when he ended up cheating on me. I wasn't in love with him but I was still a good girlfriend. It doesn't make sense.

"Hey." Rhys flips his hat backward and sits forward. "What was the date of the fire again?"

"April twelfth." A date that will forever be burned into my memory.

"And the time? What time did it happen?"

My stomach falls. Rhys is on edge.

"Just after nine."

Rhys jumps to his feet, and I drop the lid to the paint can.

"Why?" I wipe my hands on my black jeans, not caring if they get stained with paint, and get closer to him. "What's wrong?"

Shadows dig into the curves of his furrowed brow from the screen of his phone.

I pull on his arm. "What's wrong, Rhys?"

"He lied," he whispers.

"What?"

"Stephen. He lied!"

"What do you—"

Rhys shoves his phone in my face. I blink and try to make sense of what he's showing me. It's an old social media post with a picture from what I'm assuming is the night of the fire. He pinches the screen and zooms in, right past Ben's face. I recognize the old grandfather clock from the Kappa Sigma house. It was gifted to one of the frat boys the year prior because he got *clocked* by Cross Lopez in the cage.

It still rests in their house to this day.

"I don't understand."

Rhys dials Thorne's number and puts it on speaker. Through the shrill ring, echoing throughout the empty batting cages, he makes sense of it all.

"Stephen told Thorne that Ben left *this* party that night to go find you, but if the fire was shortly after nine, and this clock says—"

Thorne's voicemail cuts through, and we both make a noise of frustration.

He calls again and pulls the photo up so we can inspect it further.

"Okay." My voice shakes. "But… the clock could be broken."

Rhys swipes through the rest of the photos and zooms in on the clock. Ben is there, with a cup in his hand, and the little hand on the clock shifts to the right each time.

Thorne's voicemail cuts through again.

"Fucking hell," Rhys snaps. "You try to call him."

I dig my phone out of my pocket and dial his number. My hands shake.

Rhys scrolls through the photos again before moving onto a different set.

It's from the same party.

"No answer." My chest tightens. I wrap my arms around my stomach. "So if it isn't Ben, then we're back to square one."

Rhys pinches the bridge of his nose. "Fuck. Let's think back to the fire at the warehouse. We practically crossed out half the team because most of them were there. Well, because we saw them when the fire was discovered, and they seemed just as panicked to get out. Like Aaron and Willow. There were a few unknowns, though. Stephen, Ben, and a handful of others—"

I gasp.

Rhys drops his hand and pins me with a look.

"Ben was at the warehouse." I slap my forehead with the heel of my hand.

His brows crowd together. "Wait, he was?"

I nod frantically. "I didn't think anything about it, but when you said warehouse, I remember what he said to me the other night. I was too pissed to mention it to you and Thorne. I didn't want Thorne to get jealous—"

Rhys grabs my shoulders. "Briar, spit it out."

I shake myself mentally. "He said he saw me fall to the floor when the fire started and how he felt awful for how scared I seemed." I take a breath. "If he wasn't there, he wouldn't have known that I fell to the floor. That's too specific."

"Stephen." His gaze shifts to horror. "It's fucking Stephen. He wouldn't have had a reason to lie about Ben otherwise."

Rhys hands me his phone and he pulls me towards his car. "Go through those photos and tell me if Stephen is in any of them."

I swipe while we head towards the parking lot.

With each flick of my wrist, it becomes clear.

"He isn't." I hand his phone back and climb into his passenger seat. I call Thorne and almost cry when he doesn't answer.

"Don't worry," Rhys says. "I have his location."

I nibble on my lip when he brings up Thorne's whereabouts.

"Where is that?" I ask.

Rhys presses on the accelerator, and I fly into the back of the seat, my heart in my throat. *What if something happened to Thorne?* If we're right and Stephen is my arsonist, then he knows we're close to figuring it out. Thorne put a target on his back by questioning Stephen about Ben.

"It's the old boxing gym near the stadium. It's used for storage now."

"Why the hell is he there?" I ask.

Rhys speeds even faster. "I have no idea."

CHAPTER 39
THORNE

I AM BORED out of my mind. I've been following Ben for most of the day, and he's kind of an uninteresting guy. He was in his apartment for a while, then went grocery shopping. Came back, then met up with some guys for dinner.

Now, I follow him toward the outskirts of Shadow Valley. If we continue on this road, we'd eventually end up in Crown Point. Not that it matters—Rhys is with Briar, and as long as I have eyes on Ben, he can't hurt her.

Like any good tailing cop—my lessons learned from watching crime drama, mainly force-fed by Rhys in preparation for this very moment—I stay at least a block behind Ben's car. His headlights glow, and he's a good little driver. He doesn't speed much, he uses his blinker.

It makes it almost *too* easy.

We end up winding our way back to the stadium, and I groan. If he took a roundabout way just to go to the weight room...

But, no. He parks across the street from an old, run-down building. I kill my headlights and stop, too, still a good distance away. The building is vaguely familiar. I think it was a business a few years ago.

A boxing gym, maybe?

But it's empty…

Wait. It's *empty*. That's the point.

I lean forward, squinting through the darkness. Ben parked just before the streetlight, and it silhouettes him as he gets out of the car and jogs across the street. He pauses at the front door, then yanks open the doors and enters.

Holy *shit*. It's happening. I grab my phone and dial 9-1-1, my finger hovering over the green call button. As soon as I see signs of flames or smoke, I'll dial. He'll be caught red-handed.

A giddiness overtakes me, and I can't stop my wide smile.

He's a fucking idiot, and he's gonna go to prison for this.

A car turns onto the street farther down, coming toward me. It pulls in behind Ben's car, though, and a second later, someone gets out. The guy has broad shoulders, but the rest of his figure is obscured in an oversized coat. He hurries across the street and fiddles with the door, then steps away. He goes around, disappearing down a side alley.

That's weird.

I watch for a long moment with my brows furrowed. The not knowing what's going on is kind of killing me.

What am I supposed to do? Call the cops and say… someone broke into an abandoned building and then another guy joined him?

Yeah, right.

I shut off my car and close the door quietly. Not that anyone would notice a slamming door. Maybe. Either way, I use my stealth skills and stick to the shadows, crossing the street and approaching the weathered building. There's an empty parking lot on one side, and an alley separating it from another building.

Since the alley is closest to me, I pause at the opening and scan for movement.

Nothing.

I go down and pause under a window. It's partially boarded up, but I can reach it by climbing onto the dumpster. The metal bows—and makes a rather loud noise—under my weight, but it holds long enough for me to peek inside.

It *is* an old boxing gym. The lights are on. The raised ring in the center is missing a few ropes, and it seems like time just stopped for the place.

In the ring, though, is Ben.

I put my hands on the pane, my eyes wide. He lies on his side, curled slightly into himself, and I wait, but he doesn't so much as twitch.

There's no sign of the other person.

Helping Ben Patterson wasn't on my agenda, but I can't just walk away. It could've been a mugging gone bad, a crime of opportunity…

Either way, leaving him feels wrong.

I hop down from the dumpster and start for the front door, but movement flashes out of the corner of my eye.

Then blinding pain ricochets through my head—and darkness descends.

———

"You with us, Thorne?"

Something sharp stings my cheek. Then the other one.

I force my eyes open, my head lifting.

Stephen crouches in front of me. His gaze burns. "There you are. Thought you were going to sleep forever."

My mouth is dry. I try to rub my face, but my arms are stuck.

Stephen tsks, but he doesn't say anything else. He just watches me figure out that I'm tied to one of the corner posts of the ring. Rope chafes against my wrists, locked around the post behind my back. My legs are stretched out in front of me, my ankles also wrapped with rope.

Beyond Stephen, Ben's legs are visible.

"What's going on?" I force out.

Stephen chuckles. "What's going *on*, Thorne, is that you interrupted my plan. You already suspected Ben of setting that fire, didn't you? I was just going to make it easier to accept. And, perhaps, even ease your girl's conscience. Ben would no longer be around to make things difficult for her."

I yank my arms, but the ropes hold fast. The effort sends a wave of pain through my skull. *He hit me.* Knocked me out. Now, though, I feel it.

"You were going to make it easier to accept, how?"

Stephen rises and spreads his arm. "Look at this place. It's the perfect building. It would just be poor Ben's inexperience with setting fires that trapped him in one he set."

A chill sweeps down my spine.

"Is that fear?" He suddenly comes right back to me, kneeling at my side and grabbing my hair. He yanks my head back. "I know why. You see the end of this, don't you?"

I swallow hard. "You wouldn't tell me all of this if I was going to walk out of here."

His laugh echoes in my brain. He's not sad about it—not turned off in the slightest at the idea of killing another person. One was already in the cards, what's one more?

My stomach twists. Fear takes hold, just like he already saw in my expression, and coldness radiates through me.

I'm going to die here.

My mouth waters like it does before I puke—which generally happens on conditioning days at practice—and Stephen barely has time to get out of the way before I lean over and throw up on his shoes.

"Fucking asshole." Stephen paces away from me, then comes back on the other side.

He kicks my thigh. Pain, then numbness, sweeps down my leg, deadening it for a moment. Then two.

He shakes his head and hops over the remaining low rope,

jumping to the floor. I track him across the gym, to the red gas canisters against the wall.

"An easy accelerant," he explains. "*Ben* bought these for me over the past few weeks. My car's been in the shop, and he didn't mind running over to get the fuel for my dirt bike. Didn't even question it."

"But the police will find record of it." I spit out the bitter taste on my tongue. "You're going to set the fire and leave?"

"And watch it burn," he finishes. "Just like I watched that old building burn months ago. I'm sorry to have missed Briar's fall. I'm sure it was quite spectacular."

"You're not going to get away with this." I struggle harder. My attention swings to Ben. "Ben! Wake up."

He's not tied, but he is bleeding from his temple. His form is limp.

"Stephen," I call. "You don't have to do this."

"No?" He laughs.

The sound scrapes in my brain, and my vision swims. My stomach rolls again, but this time due to the smell of gasoline. He splashes the canister against the base of the ring, and I gag. I glance down. My phone was in my pocket. 9-1-1 was already dialed, ready to be called...

I shift to the side and try to reach my back pocket with my tied hands. The angle is awkward, but my thumb brushes my jeans.

"If you're searching for your phone, I left it outside. So someone knows how to identify your cremated corpse." Stephen pauses on the opposite side of the ring, seeming to consider. "Well, your bones. I don't think this fire will burn hot enough to completely destroy you."

He continues what he was doing, humming as he creates a trail of gasoline to the front doors, then along the wall. He doesn't say anything else to me, and I struggle with the ropes. I twist my wrists, but my vision goes spotty again.

I cannot fucking die in here.

"Stephen, you can't do this." I shift, my mind whirling. "You're not going to get away with this."

He throws the canister and picks up another, stalking over to me. "That's the thing, Thorne. Fire is cleansing. It's all power. One tiny spark will catch, and this whole place will go up like a tinderbox."

"I don't—" My voice breaks. "Please don't."

He sighs. "That's the thing about fire. It doesn't pick and choose."

"*You* are—"

"When I was twelve, my childhood home caught fire. I was outside playing in the yard with my dog and little sister, and we didn't notice until the upstairs windows broke. The smoke that poured out was thick and gray, and it was beautiful. I'd never seen anything like it." He tilts his head. "Then the flames came through. It was a private show just for me."

I stare at him.

"My parents made it out just fine. But the house itself? By the time the fire department left, there was almost nothing left of it. Just the bones." He pats his chest. "No organs, no blood, no *life*. Nothing salvageable."

"That's horrific."

"It was *beautiful*." He shakes his head. "We've lost the meaning of *awesome*. It means to be full of awe. And I was that day. For years, I've wanted to feel that again, and the only time I manage it is when I recreate it."

He's insane.

"You lost your house as a twelve-year-old and you enjoyed it." I raise my eyebrows. "Then burn the building, Stephen. But don't kill us."

"You don't get it." He hops the ropes and gets in my face. Gasoline sloshes out of the canister, soaking my pant leg. "You walk out of here, and I'll never be allowed to touch a fucking matchbox again."

To be fair, he shouldn't even be allowed near a gas stove.

"No." He rises. "This is the only way."

He checks on Ben, pausing with his hand on his best friend's shoulder. When Ben still doesn't wake, he moves away. Out of the ring, toward the back door.

"Enjoy the view, Thorne," he calls over his shoulder. "You've got a front-row seat to the greatest show on earth."

I twist around to keep my gaze on him.

He sets down the final canister by a door and lights a match. It's such a tiny little flame, but the minute he tosses it, the gasoline catches. It spreads fast, racing across the old, worn hardwood floors. It chases the path he set, wrapping around the ring, and too fast to even comprehend, the heat of the flames lick at my skin.

I face forward again, struggling hard. It's no use. The knots only seem to tighten.

Ben lies unresponsive.

We're going to die.

And I never told Briar that I love her.

CHAPTER 40
BRIAR

I SQUINT from the brightness of the fire. My hand blocks the growing orange and red flames. I swear, I feel the heat from the fire even while being in Rhys's car.

"Fuck." He slams on the brakes, and we both fly forward. His arm comes out and braces me before I hit the dash. "Call 9-1-1. Stay in the car."

I follow his instructions, dialing fast, but I open my door and step onto the pavement. I quickly rattle off the address to the operator. She tells me that a fire truck is on the way and warns me not to get close in case burning debris falls.

Little does she know, I know my way around a fire.

My chest tightens, and my feet tingle. Goosebumps blanket my arms, and hot, sticky heat follows.

I walk closer to where Rhys ran off but quickly back away when a gust of fire fans toward me. The heat of it is too much. My vision is hazy. I'm stunned with panic, my feet unmoving but my head screaming at me to do something.

Anything.

I put my back to the fire and try to breathe.

My breaths grow even shakier when I spot Ben's car directly across from the burning gym. I glance around and finally see Thorne's. He parked on the next block, but his car is empty and silent, too.

They're both inside the gym.

I can feel it in my bones.

"Shit!" I slap my hand against my thigh and think.

Rhys's heavy footsteps catch my attention. I spin, and he's never looked more serious. Sweat droplets slip down his face as he grabs my arms.

"Get in my car. Stay there. I'm going in."

"Are you insane?" I shout. "Take it from someone who has been in a fire, Rhys. It's dangerous and it spreads quickly!"

He ignores my pleas and drags me over the gravel to his car. "Thorne and Ben are both inside, Briar. I'm going in. I can at least get them away from the fire. The door has been blocked, but I'm going to go through the window." He yanks open the car door, shoving me into the passenger's seat. "If he makes it out alive, he'll kill me if something happens to you. Get in, lock the door. Don't come out until help shows up."

"The front door has been blocked?"

My panic creeps to an all-time high. The fear from that night is at the center of my thoughts. I can't keep my limbs from shaking.

"Stay. Inside."

Rhys throws the keys on my lap.

"Be careful!" I shout.

The door slams in my face, and I lock it as ordered.

The door has been blocked. I scan the parking lot, searching for any sign of the arsonist—*Stephen*. Not Ben.

I move my attention back toward the fire. Rhys has climbed up on a dumpster in the alley, and he gets level with a window that's been halfway boarded over. The flames haven't made it there yet, by the looks of it. He breaks the glass with his elbow, and I wince.

He disappears inside a moment later.

Nausea pulls me under. I clench my eyes and press on my stomach.

Just breathe, Briar.

If anything happens to Thorne, because of me, I'll never be able to climb out of this dark hole that I've been in since my accident.

He's the only one who's been able to drag me out, and now I'm about to have to drag *him* out.

Rhys and Ben, too.

I open my door and wince at the heat.

The popping, creaking, and wood splinting noises echo all around. The fire roars louder the closer I get. I rush to the entrance of the old building and curse.

Fire has started to eat away at the door, but the wood slab that was wedged under the door handle is obvious.

Stephen. You motherfucker.

I spin and narrow my gaze.

He's here somewhere.

There are many reasons an arsonist seeks fires. After my accident, I did a deep dive on the minds behind arsonists—their reasons, triggers, feelings.

One thing that remained constant was their excitement.

Most like to watch.

I jog over to the wooded area across the street. On the other side of it is the football stadium, the visitors' entrance lit up and just barely visible through the trees.

The heat of the fire swipes up my back, and sweat drips down my spine. I cringe from the reminder but ignore it as I scan in between the trees. Shadows cling to them, making it almost impossible to discern if I'm alone. Impossible with my naked eye anyway.

I grab my phone and press the record button. I give the area the once-over again. The faint sound of siren's catches my ear, and my knees buckle with relief.

I glance back to the fire, and the relief disappears.

Like a monster, the fire grows, destroying anything in its path. Flames flicker through the columns of thick black smoke that pour out of the upper windows.

They need to get out. Now.

The sounds of sirens grow clear, but something snapping in the distance catches my attention.

My jaw snaps shut. I glare with a fierce vengeance. All the anger I've held since that night explodes like the roaring fire behind me when Stephen sees me. One pan of him on the video is all I need and I know I have it.

Our eyes snag.

He's caught and he knows it.

I move with a purpose, but to my surprise, it isn't toward him.

Adrenaline hides the ache in my knee, and I run toward the window that Rhys climbed through. I don't climb as easily as he did but I make it up there in record time.

"Rhys!"

He's dragging an unconscious Ben toward Thorne's still body on the floor. Behind them is a raised platform, which might have once been an old boxing ring. It's completely covered in flames.

No.

Through a raspy cough, he shouts at me, "Get the fuck back in the car!"

He coughs again. The smoke billows around their bodies. I act fast.

"Stay there! Do not move."

"Bri—" I hop down and curse the pain radiating up my leg. I make it to his car in seconds, though it feels like hours. I jump into the driver's seat and twist the key in the ignition.

It comes to life, and I hurriedly put my seat belt on.

I refuse to let anyone live the nightmare that I did. Their football dreams will be ruined if they get hurt. Never mind the fact that they could die.

I fight the panic and past trauma as I reverse, twisting the wheel until the nose of Rhys' car lines up with building's entrance.

They need a way out, and I'm going to give it to them.

The sirens are getting closer, but the firefighters aren't going to make it in time.

Either the flames or the smoke will kill them before they can escape.

I send the video of Stephen hiding like a coward in the forest to everyone I know.

Using voice text, I send Thorne a message, too—hopeful that if I don't make it out alive, he will.

My voice shakes. "I love you, Cassius."

I wrap my fingers around the steering wheel, take a deep breath, and put the pedal to the metal.

CHAPTER 41
THORNE

EVERYTHING HURTS. My heart pounds so loud, it's the only thing I can hear. Then, faintly, *crying*. Like a bubble popping, sound rushes back in, and I force my eyes open.

Hospital. It's easily identifiable from the smell alone, but the quiet beeping of a distant monitor and the hum of machines confirms it. Plus the fluorescent overhead lighting, currently off. Sunlight comes in through a window to my left.

"Oh my God," a familiar voice cries. "He could've *died*."

I blink. My thoughts are sluggish, and it takes a moment to register who's gripping my hand so tightly. My skin crawls, and I yank away.

Instinct.

"Baby," she sobs. "You're okay. You're going to be fine. Your parents are on their way and they asked me to keep you company."

Her face is familiar, but I can't for the life of me remember her name. I stare at her. The blonde hair, the pert, ski-slope nose, the obvious lip filler. It's so unlike the one person I want to see.

"Where's Briar?" My voice is hoarse and rasping, and it

hurts. Pain like never before radiates through my throat. Did I swallow glass?

"Shh." She reaches for my hand again.

I bump the remote in an effort to avoid her and fumble for it, hitting the big red *call* button. My gaze goes to the ceiling, and I try to swallow.

More pain.

My eyes water.

"It'll be okay," the girl repeats.

Her name doesn't fucking matter. She's not Briar.

Eventually, a nurse comes in. She asks the girl to move back and steps in close, checking my vitals. She hits a button on the bed and slowly raises me into a more inclined position.

"Briar?" I whisper.

The nurse shakes her head and grabs a cup of water. She puts the straw to my lips, and the cold water simultaneously hurts and soothes.

"How—"

"I cannot release information about another patient unless you're related." Her gaze softens. "I'm sorry. How are you feeling?"

"Like I was run over by a truck."

"You're due for another dose of pain meds. The doctor will be in shortly. And this is your significant other?" She motions to the girl. "She said you were engaged."

My heart stops, and I shake my head hard. A wave of dizziness crashes over me.

"She's definitely not. I don't even know her name."

The nurse pauses. "Do you know where you are?"

"Hospital. Assuming in Shadow Valley still."

She dips her chin. "Name?"

"Cassius Remington Thorne. The Third."

"And the date?"

I tell her.

"You were intubated for two days. It's now Friday. But,

yes, you're correct on everything else." She faces the crying girl. "Miss, I'm sorry, but you're not authorized to be here. Please come with me."

She shepherds her out, ignoring her pleas and cries. My gaze floats to the ceiling, and I focus on my breathing for a long few minutes.

The last thing I remember is the fire. The *heat*. It hurt to breathe, it was like the very air was on fire. And the fear of dying alone with Ben fucking Patterson.

But then Rhys was there, shaking me awake. He cut me loose and half carried, half dragged me away from the burning ring, to a patch of floor that hadn't been soaked in gas.

Then he went back for Ben.

Rhys better be okay.

And Briar—

A tear slips down my cheek. Why wouldn't Briar be here? She would've kicked out that girl, easy. No questions asked. She would've been holding my hand if she was okay, and I would've felt *relief*.

That seems far away now. My chest tightens, and it gets more difficult to inhale. It's like a mountain has landed on me, the pressure intensifying. There's a distant beeping, and my hearing goes out with a *whoosh*.

Then everything else fades, too.

———

"...it's the immune system's response. Inflammation is severe, yes, but it's also expected. The intubation tube keeps his airway open..."

My chest rises and falls at a steady pace, the power of inhaling and exhaling no longer belonging to me. Helplessness and worry twist through me, and I panic.

Something cool spreads through my arm, and the darkness in my mind reaches up and pulls me back into its depths.

———

"Cassius."

I reach out blindly.

"I'm right here. I'm not going anywhere."

———

My mind is fuzzy. I open my eyes and focus on the ceiling tiles, blinking a few times until my vision clears. My head doesn't hurt like it did before. Everything kind of feels a bit removed, but it's familiar.

I felt this way on pain meds after my knee…

A shudder rolls up my spine. That didn't happen this time, right? I look down at my body. There's a light on behind my head, and it casts strange shadows across the bed. But my body seems to be intact. There's no extra padding or bandages on my legs, just blankets.

I wiggle my toes to prove that I can.

Someone takes a breath, and my attention moves toward the darkened window. Then lower, to the couch under it.

Briar is asleep, her arm folded under her head, a blanket draped over her legs.

My heart squeezes.

She's okay.

She wouldn't be on a shitty hospital room couch if she wasn't.

I gaze at her silently, absorbing her hair piled in a messy bun, strands loose and sticking out at all angles. She's in one of my sweatshirts, the black material swamping her frame. My throat dries when I find the butterfly bandage on her head, over her right eyebrow.

How did she get hurt?

"Bri—" My voice scratches. I clear my throat and try again. "Kitten."

Her eyes flutter open, and she slowly sits up.

I'm rewarded with a brilliant smile, the likes of which I haven't seen in a while. I could bottle that smile and drink it on my darkest days, knowing it would make everything better.

"You're awake." She shifts to the edge of the couch, her fingers digging into her thighs. "How do you feel?"

I don't reply—not verbally anyway. I just hold my hand out to her.

She hesitates, then gets up and crosses the room. When her palm slides against mine, a knot in my chest loosens. I exhale, long and slow.

"Better now," I finally say.

"You had me worried."

"I'm okay." I hope. I don't actually know if that's true. "Come here."

Shifting to the side reveals just how sore my body is, but I try to mask it. I create a space for her and lift the blankets, and she just stares at me for a long moment.

"Kitten, get in this bed."

She shakes her head, a smile pulling at the corners of her lips, and kicks off her shoes. She climbs in and helps me fix the blankets over both of us. On her side, curled into me, she shares my pillow and watches the side of my face.

"I've never been so scared," she admits in a low voice.

My throat works. "Me neither."

"I'm so glad you're alive."

I choke on a laugh. "Same."

I shift again so I can put my arm around her. She wiggles closer, her cheek now on my chest. I absently stroke her arm, her side. Anything I can reach. Her body heat is very real, and I use it to anchor me in the present.

We're safe.

———

The nurses do their best to not wake Briar when they take my vitals at the crack of dawn. One whispers that Briar has been worried sick, and this is the first time she's truly slept. Judging by the dark circles under my girl's eyes, I believe it.

I, on the other hand, didn't sleep much. I relished the feel of her against me, but every time I closed my eyes, flames licked at my skin.

"How long have I been out?" I ask quietly.

"They had you sedated for two days, then put you back under for another four."

Six days. In the blink of an eye.

"Is Rhys Anderson still a patient?"

She slowly shakes her head. *No.* "He was discharged a few days ago. But you didn't hear that from me, you understand?"

"Of course. Thank you."

I hope he wasn't hurt. And I spare a thought for Ben, who Stephen framed, except I don't have that in me right now. I hope he's okay—and that's the end of it.

I'll ask Briar about it when she wakes up, but she looks peaceful. Her palm is splayed across my chest, right over my heart, like she was trying to make sure it was still beating.

"The doctor will be in shortly."

She heads out, and I sigh. Six days—no wonder Briar was so worried. I try to zone back out, but I keep replaying the moments with Ben and Stephen. The dread and certainty of knowing I was going to die still lingers.

The next person to come in through the door, however, isn't the doctor.

It's my mother. My father follows close behind, but Mom's face is a mask of worry. She stops short when she registers that Briar is sleeping in my bed, and her nose wrinkles. It's an expression that would never be let loose in public.

"I was expecting Cynthia to be keeping you company," she says.

Cynthia. Right. The crying girl.

"Why?"

Briar stirs at my sharp tone, and I wince. I rub her arm, but the action is also meant to keep her from scrambling away from me.

"Because she—"

"She's not the one I'm going to marry, Mother." I stare at her. "And she told the nurse we were engaged. That's not true. I'm dating *Briar.*"

"Of course you are, honey." She steps up and pats my foot through the blanket. "And you're playing football. But neither of those things are going to last forever. Cynthia comes from a lovely family. You know this. She said you two really hit it off on your date, so we've been making arrangements."

Dread sucks the air from my lungs.

With sudden, vicious clarity, I realize that everything I've done to bend over backward for my parents has gone unappreciated. It hasn't been viewed as a sacrifice—it's been *expected*. The dates, me joining the family company…

But now it's not just dates.

They're trying to arrange my marriage, too.

Forget *dating* these women my parents handpick. They just want to choose one and set me at the front of the altar for the wedding of this girl's dreams. The duty of it stabs at me, hot as embers.

Briar shifts and sits up slightly, touching the bandage on her head. She looks from me to my parents, taking stock of the situation, and tries to escape.

"Stay," I tell her. I focus on my parents again. "I am not going to marry Cynthia. I'm not going on any more dates. I would've died in that building, and the only reason I'm still here—"

My throat closes.

I know it's because of Briar. I don't remember getting out, but I do remember Rhys's panicked face in front of me, his voice hoarse as he explained that he didn't think he could get me and Ben up through the window. There was nothing to climb up on from the inside. The front door wouldn't open.

Panic crawls along my throat, the smell of smoke in my nose.

"Cassius," Briar whispers. "You're okay, baby. Look at me."

Her hand on my cheek directs my face toward hers. Her gaze crashes into mine, and she puts my hand on her chest.

"Breathe like me."

I mimic her until it's not as forced.

My father clears his throat. "We're going to transfer you to a private hospital. They wouldn't do it while you were intubated."

There is no private hospital in Shadow Valley.

"Where?"

"Back home, of course," Mom says. She circles around, opposite Briar, and reaches out. She smooths my hair back from my forehead.

I hold still. Pulling away always offends her, and I don't want that to be just another thing. Briar, however, glares at her for me.

Then her words register.

"Home?" I echo.

"You can finish out the school year online. We already talked to the school. Everything is settled." She smiles, still *touching* my hair. "We'll give you two some time to say good-bye. The helicopter is going to be here soon."

She finally draws away, and they exit.

Shock radiates through me.

"Helicopter?" Briar scoffs. "You've got to be kidding me."

I grimace, then sit up. I fiddle with the railing and get it lowered, then swing my legs over the edge of the bed.

"Where are you going?" Alarm colors Briar's tone. She gets up and races around, grabbing my arm just as I stand. With her there, I wobble but don't land on my ass.

I'm in a gown that gapes open at the back, which is not my best look.

"I don't suppose you can hunt down some clothes for me, kitten?"

She pauses and stares at me. "Why do you need clothes?"

"Because I'm sure as fuck not transferring. I'm not leaving Shadow Valley. And I'm not leaving you." I catch her chin in my fingers. "I should've told you this a while ago. Our fake relationship became so fucking real for me. And I fell in love with you hard."

"You…"

"I'm so in love with you, you were my first thought when I woke up. And you're always my last thought before I fall asleep." I reel her in closer. "I'd give up everything. My trust fund. My relationship with my parents. The cushy job waiting for me." *Pause.* "Football, even."

Her lips pop open.

"Don't say anything." I shake my head and rub the back of my neck. "I, uh, haven't admitted love to anyone before and I don't think I can stomach a rejection right now. Let's just focus on getting out of here."

She seems dazed, then visibly snaps out of it. "Right. Okay. Clothes and escape route. Coming right up." She hurries to the door, then immediately doubles back. "Just so you know? I love the shit out of you, Cassius."

CHAPTER 42
BRIAR

I SIT across from the dean as calm as ever. Thorne and his coach sit in the other two chairs, awaiting their fate like Dean Winters is the Devil and Thorne's parents are his demons.

"They did call me, yes," Dean Winters confirms, bouncing his attention back and forth between Thorne and his coach.

Thorne scoffs and crosses his arms angrily. "Let me guess? They offered you some fancy building in exchange to transfer me out of school."

Despite Thorne telling his parents—very colorfully, might I add—that he was through being their little puppet, they continue to try and control his life. Their phone calls are daily at this point, and the last argument they had ended with a threat to call the dean from Thorne's father.

Thorne's leg begins hopping up and down with his nerves, so I reach out and place my hand on his thigh. The bouncing stops immediately.

I pat the denim of his jeans and clear my throat.

Dean Winters briefly glances at me before turning away.

It's like he thinks if he makes eye contact with me, he'll burst into flames or something. Or maybe he's afraid I'll start yelling at him like my mother did when he questioned me after I divulged what had happened the *first* time I was caught in a fire.

This time was my fault entirely.

I purposely put myself in a direct path of the raging flames, but it was to save Thorne, Ben, and Rhys.

The dean would have an ever bigger problem on his hands if I didn't ram Rhys's car into school property. There would be three dead football players and a whole lot of questions.

Right now, the only questions he has to answer are from the police and to the parents of those involved. The fire was on the news, and all over social media, but since the investigation is still ongoing, we haven't been public about it.

Stephen *is* behind bars, though the only ones who have noticed are the players on the football team. Apparently, no one other than his family likes him enough to miss him. Once the investigation is over and it goes to trial, people may learn what Stephen did, but for now, things are being swept under the rug. Though, Rhys has a plan in the works to celebrate Stephen's *departure* which will likely cause some attention. Ben, whose injuries were similar to Thorne's and Rhys's, ended up taking the rest of the semester off. Despite the horror of what happened, we're all okay.

Thorne's football coach leans forward in his seat. His elbows dig into his knees. "You're just going to accept their bribe? Rob me of one of the best players I've ever had? He is destined for the pros."

Thorne's leg bounces again, and the rising testosterone in the room is giving me a headache.

I clear my throat, and this time, everyone gives me the attention I'm silently demanding.

"Do you have something to say, Ms. Hart?" Dean Winters is unquestionably assertive and commands the room with his gruff voice.

I don't let it deter me for one second.

"Actually, I do."

His eyebrows rise.

Thorne quietly chuckles.

And his poor coach is hanging on by a thread.

"Do you recall last spring when I was nearly killed?" I don't give him even a second to respond. "Remember when you questioned my report to the police and the retelling of all the details from that night? You scoffed when I said that someone had trapped me in that burning building?"

Thorne's head snaps over to me in my peripheral vision. His coach mutters something.

Dean Winters exhales deeply, however, he doesn't deny it.

I cross my leg—the one that will likely never be the same —over the other. His gaze falls right to it.

"Then, when the police confirmed that it was suspected arson, you looked me right in the eye and practically *begged* me to keep it a secret. You didn't want any of the students to freak out." I use air quotes to really drive my point. "Which really just translated to you not wanting any media coverage over the fact that one of your students was a potential arsonist who was still on the run." I smile softly at him. "You most definitely didn't want any of the parents to know, because most would be fearful and beg their children to transfer to a safer school."

The office fills with silence.

Thorne's coach rubs his hand down his face with stress. The scratchiness of his palm against hair breaks the tension.

Dean Winters nods slowly. "Your point?"

I glance at Thorne, and he's smirking at me. I keep his attention when the next words flow from my mouth with ease. "You tell Thorne's parents to take their money else-where. You allow him to finish out the year and the next, if he chooses to complete his degree before furthering his football career." I turn and pin the dean with a glare. "Or I'll leak the police records and make sure every news station from here to

Crown Point knows what happened to me last spring, and that it's connected to what happened last week."

"There's my grumpy cat," Thorne whispers in awe.

I smile. I'll be damned if someone takes away his ability to play football like someone took away my ability to play hockey.

The football coach leans past Thorne and has the expression of a child on Christmas morning. I smile triumphantly in his direction before the dean steals our attention with his acceptance.

"Oh, thank God." The football coach jumps to his feet and grips Thorne's shoulder. "You're out for one more game, but then, you're back on the field."

Thorne nods. I feel the weight lift off his shoulders.

"You better keep this one," his coach adds, dipping his head in my direction.

Then he walks out of the office, leaving Thorne and I alone with the dean.

Dean Winters sighs and grips his phone, dialing Thorne's father's number. We sit in silence as he works his magic, sugar-coating a fabricated excuse as to why he cannot take any funds and force Thorne to transfer schools.

Once he hangs up, I mentally dust my hands off and move to leave.

Thorne stops me. He grips my knee and gently pushes on it. I sit hesitantly and trace the tight edge of his jaw.

What is wrong with him?

"Apologize."

My eyebrows furrow. He's staring directly at Dean Winters, and there is no mistaking his irritation.

"Excuse me?" I don't have to glance at the dean to know he's appalled.

Thorne slowly turns to make eye contact with me.

My heart slips, and my breath hitches. *God, I love him.*

"I said," he reiterates, "*apologize.*"

He winks at me before glancing back toward the dean.

"To whom?" the dean asks.

"To my girlfriend." Thorne's voice is even and poised, but I know he's burning up on the inside. I open my mouth to tell him that this isn't necessary but to my surprise, the dean shifts and stares me dead in the face.

"I apologize, Ms. Hart." He glances away, unable to meet my eye, but an apology is an apology.

"Thank you," I say.

Thorne stands and holds his hand out for me.

I grab on to it, and he pulls me up to my feet gently.

The dean stops me before we leave his office. I glance at him over my shoulder.

If he takes back his apology…

"You're an art major, are you not?"

I raise an eyebrow. He knows I am.

"You should consider being a lawyer, Ms. Hart."

I can't help it. I smile wider.

When we're out of the dean's earshot, Thorne leans in close and whispers, "Do you think he'd know it was you if a mural of his face with a nice set of devil horns on top of his head appeared somewhere on school grounds?"

I laugh, and Thorne catches the tail end of it with his mouth.

My back presses into the wall with gentle force. He takes both of my hands in one of his and traps them above my head while his tongue sweeps inside.

I'm breathless by the end. When our lips part, Thorne stares into my eyes, and it feels like our hearts are beating as one instead of two.

What started out as us working together as a team has ended the same.

He has my back, and I have his.

"I like seeing you happy," I whisper. "I wasn't going to let your parents, nor the dean, take away your happiness."

Thorne's brow furrows. "The only thing that could take away my happiness is you, kitten." He shakes his head. "You know that, right?"

A genuine smile slips onto my lips. "Mm-hm," I press my mouth to his briefly before I pause. "But I kind of like being a jersey chaser."

Thorne laughs against my mouth. "You know being a jersey chaser means you have to wear my jersey to all my games, right?"

"The horror."

"You know the best part about wearing my jersey?"

I think for a second, nipping at his mouth. "What?"

Thorne's free hand roams over my body before falling to the small of my back. He brings me flush against him. "That I get to peel it off you after every game."

A hot thrill rushes through me. "Maybe we should practice that. Aren't you the one who said practice makes perfect?"

Thorne's warm, golden eyes darken. "We can never have too much practice, kitten." He picks me up and swings me over his shoulder. "I've got several jerseys you can borrow."

My laughter follows us all the way to his bedroom where we stay for the rest of the night.

BRIAR
THREE YEARS LATER

THE PLANE LANDS WITH A WHOOSH. I stretch my stiff leg and roll my ankle a few times. My phone comes to life, and I smile with the text messages that come through.

CASSIUS

It's half-time. We're up by 3.

I can't wait to hear all about your trip. I hope you make it in time. If not, I'll see you at home.

I love you, kitten.

DAD

Wow, that man of yours can really throw a spiral.

I laugh quietly when I read the last text. My dad says the same thing every single time he watches a game. Thorne is the son he never had, and my dad is the father who Thorne never had.

My parents have loved Thorne from the moment they met him. They weren't happy three years ago when they found out that he was training me to play hockey again, but they quickly got over it once we graduated and moved on to other things.

Like Thorne being successful as a quarterback in the NFL, and me, a commissioned painter for businesses all over the world.

I've been in countless magazines, and my travels are becoming more frequent.

I hate missing Thorne's games—something I never thought I'd hear myself say—but it's good for the soul to have something that's my own.

After rushing off the plane and through the airport, I spot Marley's car.

Lydia climbs out of the passenger seat and wraps me in a hug.

"Lydia!" I fold my arms around her waist. "What are you doing here?"

She lives three states away and has a baby on the way.

"I came to surprise you! Plus, Jack got front-row tickets thanks to Thorne, so he was very much willing to accompany me."

I laugh and throw my things in the trunk. I make her sit in the front and slip into the back.

"Hey, babe." Marley smiles at me in the rearview.

She navigates traffic as I tell my two best friends all about my time in New York to complete my most recent mural.

We get to the stadium with six minutes left on the clock in the fourth quarter.

I change into one of Thorne's jerseys, something that makes him entirely too happy, and we find Larry—the security guard who knows me well enough to let us through without question.

Lydia waddles over to Jack and gives him a kiss. He leans

forward and raises his eyebrows at me. "Thorne was good in college, but this is next level."

He redirects his attention to the field.

Lydia rolls her eyes playfully. "You've had too much to drink."

"Baby, I'm drinking for both of us."

Marley and I both laugh, but I'm quickly swept up in the excitement of the game.

When Thorne heads off the field to let special teams take over, hopefully getting the field goal to secure their win, I shout his name.

"Cassius!"

Rhys, who scored a hefty contract to play alongside his best friend, hears me and pivots with a ready smile. He waves and then nudges Thorne.

It doesn't take long for him to find me in my rightful spot. He quickly scans the sideline, gaze landing on his coach, and then takes off toward me.

The crowd is roaring from the field goal when Thorne jumps toward the front row. His hands grip the metal barrier, and he hoists himself closer to me.

"You made it."

I wink and plop a kiss to his lips. "Go before you get in trouble."

This is exactly the position we were in when I accepted his proposition. When I showed up to his practice all those years ago... My cheeks heat. If not for that moment, *this* moment wouldn't exist.

He scoffs. "I've played a good game, I'm not getting in trouble."

I flatten my lips. "Remember last time?"

He grins. "That was totally worth it. But fine, meet me on the field after the game."

"Always."

Jack slaps Thorne's shoulder pad. "You're so fucking good, man."

Thorne smirks and glances at me before hopping down and running back to the field.

The game ends without any other excitement.

I head down to the field and realize that Marley, Lydia, and Jeff are all following me.

"You coming for the craziness?" I ask, joking.

They typically head off and try to miss the traffic.

They share a look that I can't quite decipher.

I don't get a chance to either, because Thorne's arms slip around my waist and I'm hauled backward into his chest.

"Kitten," he murmurs.

He spins around so fast, it dizzies me. The cameras are on us, I can feel it, but I don't care.

"Cassius," I say. "Good game."

"Better because you're here." He kisses me. "I missed you."

I smile against his mouth. "I missed you, too. Now hurry up and go do your interview so we can go home."

"Is your leg okay?" he asks.

Always so concerned.

I smile. "I'm fine."

Something flashes across his face, and then I'm slowly sliding down the front of his body and being placed on the ground.

"What's going on—?"

My words die on the end of my lips.

Thorne slips down to one knee. He holds his palm out. One of his teammates appears with a little black box and hands it to him.

The camera is mere feet from us, but everything disappears when Thorne opens the box and a diamond ring is gleaming under the stadium lights.

"Briar Hart," he whispers. "Marry me."

My heart stops.

I stare at the golden flakes in Thorne's eyes, and peace floods through me. This is it.

My lips slowly curl into a smile, and I nod.

He slips the ring onto my finger, and like in a movie, everything else comes rushing back in.

There are cheers and claps from his teammates, our friends, everyone. A reporter comments on Thorne's proposal.

None of that steals the moment, though.

I throw myself into my fiancé's arms. He rises, lifting me with him, and I wrap my legs around his waist. Despite him being a sweaty mess, I press my lips to his. "I love you, Cassius."

He pulls back slightly, stares up at me, and has never looked more serious. "I love you, too, kitten." His mouth comes close to my ear. "Now let me go home and strip that jersey from your body and fuck you with nothing but that ring on your finger."

THE END
What's next?
The series continues with Cross Lopez. Pre-order here:
https://mybook.to/svu3

Early readers were super interested in Rhys… and we're happy to confirm he's getting a spicy holiday romance, *The Christmas Playbook*, in 2025! https://mybook.to/thechristmasplaybook

ABOUT THE AUTHORS

S. Massery is a dark romance author who loves injecting a good dose of suspense into her stories. She lives in Western Massachusetts with her dog, Alice.

Before adventuring into the world of writing, she went to college in Boston and held a wide variety of jobs—including working on a dude ranch in Wyoming (a personal highlight). She has a love affair with coffee and chocolate. When S. Massery isn't writing, she can be found devouring books, playing outside with her dog, or trying to make people smile.

Join her newsletter to stay up to date on new releases: http://smassery.com/newsletter

S.J. Sylvis is an Amazon top 50 and USA Today bestselling author who is best known for her angsty new adult romances. She currently resides in Arizona with her husband, two small kiddos, dog, and cat. She is obsessed with coffee, becomes easily attached to fictional characters, and spends most of her evenings buried in a book!

Join her newsletter to stay up to date on new releases: https://www.sjsylvis.com/newsletter-signup

ALSO BY S. MASSERY

More at http://smassery.com

ALSO BY S.J. SYLVIS

ACKNOWLEDGMENTS

Thank you *so* much to everyone who has helped and/or encouraged us to continuing co-writing together! We truly have so much fun and having one another to lean on in this career is the best perk!

Thank you to Studio ENP and Booktastic Blonde for polishing Thorne and Briar! Thank you so much to our beta readers who not only encourages us and makes us laugh, but catches pesky plot holes too. And thank you to our cover designer who made our vision come to life!

Thank you to each of our PAs, and Valentine PR for helping spread the word about Heart of Thorne— and to all the amazing readers who have read/reviewed/shared! We appreciate you so much, and we promise not to make you wait forever book 3!

S. Massery & S.J. Sylvis

Made in United States
Troutdale, OR
01/03/2025

27531353R00217